Upon his retirement, Edward Hewitt at last saw the opportunity to realise the ambition of a lifetime.

His first novel, 'Where Waters Meet', was published in 1997, and was greeted with great acclaim.

EMMA

This is a story of jealousy and envy between two very different sisters, Rose and Charlotte, the daughters of the miller of Watersmeet. Also, tragic consequences of the First World War, and an extremely callous, premeditated murder . . . Through all the years of hate and mayhem, the love of a beautiful woman for Charles Cartwright never waned. Yet, it was because of a wonderful, inspirational idea by Emma, the love child of Charlotte, that the shipyard of Earnshaw & Cartwright was able to survive and flourish for the rest of the century.

Books by Edward Hewitt
Published by The House of Ulverscroft:

EDWARD HEWITT

EMMA

The Cartwright Saga
Volume Four

Complete and Unabridged

ULVERSCROFT
Leicester

First published in Great Britain in 1998

First Large Print Edition
published 2000

British Library CIP Data

Hewitt, Edward
   Emma.—Large print ed.—
   (The Cartwright saga; v. 4)
   Ulverscroft large print series: romance
   1. Love stories
   2. Large type books
   I. Title
   823.9′14 [F]

   ISBN 0–07089–4254–7

Published by
F. A. Thorpe (Publishing)
Anstey, Leicestershire
Set by Words & Graphics Ltd.
Anstey, Leicestershire
Printed and bound in Great Britain by
T. J. International Ltd., Padstow, Cornwall

This book is printed on acid-free paper

Prologue

Christmas At 'Mount Pleasant' 1916

The Great War, ground inexorably on. Two years ago, the men of these Islands, had joined the services and marched confidently off to war, brimfull of an optimistic patriotic fervour, mistakenly bestowed upon them by certain shallow minded politicians, who forecast 'it would all be over by Christmas'!

Now however, this was Christmas nineteen sixteen, and it looked like being a very bleak mid-winter indeed for the men deployed in the trenches. For the two armies appeared to have reached a deplorable stalemate, virtually bogged down in the indescribable mud at Verdun, and the great British offensive at the Somme.

The Flower of English manhood was lost for ever in these hopeless battles, where hundreds of thousands of men from both sides were used as cannon fodder, being mown down in waves, and for months neither side moved more than a mile, then quickly lost the blood soaked ground they had gained.

1

Rose had invited Charlotte to come and stay at 'Mount Pleasant' for Christmas, and they were preparing to have as good a Christmas as was possible, for of course many luxury items which were normally associated with the seasonal festivities. were unobtainable, because of the wartime rationing.

However, people who were fortunate enough to live in the country, always seemed to fare better than townsfolk in times of shortage. For in the village nearly everyone kept their own pig, and a few chickens, consequently there was always sufficient meat and eggs available.

For the whole of that day prior to Christmas, Rose had been trying to contact her husband, but to no avail, until finally she had to send a maid into Hull to purchase one or two last minute items, she had previously forgotten.

At approximately four-o-clock in the afternoon of that cold clear Christmas Eve, Rose happened to glance out of the window, and in the gathering dusk, saw her husband's car coming down the drive. she quickly turned away, and continued wrapping the last of the Christmas presents, prior to placing them beneath the beautifully decorated Christmas tree, standing in a corner of the room. For since the outbreak of war, Miles had discontinued the tradition of a Christmas party in the main hall, for all the servants, not only because of the rationing, but chiefly because of the fact that there were very few servants remaining at 'Mount Pleasant', that was a part of life which had gone for ever.

1

When Charles entered the room a few moments later, Rose didn't even bother to look up, pretending to be annoyed, because she couldn't contact him earlier.

'Hello darling,' he greeted her genially.

'Don't you darling me, you big — !' she stopped dead in mid-sentence. 'Father!' she almost screamed.

For standing beside Charles was Edward. Her husband had been to Watersmeet to bring his father-in-law back to 'Mount Pleasant' for Christmas.

Rose flung her parcel and wrapping paper on to the table, and was nearly in tears, as she rushed across the room and hugged and kissed her father. 'Oh! Charles, what a wonderful surprise. This is the best Christmas present ever.'

He kissed her. 'Were you about to say something when we came in darling?' he asked, with a twinkle in his eye.

'Yes, you know perfectly well what I was going to say. However, it doesn't matter now I know where you were all day.' Then, turning from Charles. 'What about

5

the livestock father, who is going to attend to everything?'

The miller emitted a deep throated chuckle. 'Now don't you worry your pretty head about them my dear, everything is taken care of. With this being Sunday, your husband was able to find a couple of men at home in the village, and he brought them to 'Mill House', where we showed them what to do. More than that, he even paid them in advance for three days work.'

'Three days!' echoed Rose. 'How long do you intend staying with us father?'

'Well, tonight. And being as it's Christmas Eve, I thought I might as well hang my stocking up, just in case 'He' comes, then tomorrow Christmas Day, and also Tuesday, Boxing Day. Anyway I killed a couple of cockerels and brought them along, and a few choice eating apples from our apple chamber.'

'Father you shouldn't have brought all that,' she admonished him gently. 'There really wasn't any need to. It will be lovely having you here, all through Christmas, though I do think I should ask Charles' mother if it will be alright.'

A soft feminine voice came from the direction of the doorway. 'No need to my dear. This was entirely my own idea.'

Rose turned quickly. 'Oh! Mother, I had no idea you had sent Charles to Watersmeet.' It was only recently she had began addressing Ruth as 'mother', and as it had sounded so natural, and no-one seemed to mind, she had continued to do so.

Rose moved to meet the older woman as she came into the room, gave her a hug and kissed her. 'Thank you mother,' was all she could manage to say.

At that moment the strident tone of the telephone in the hall, interrupted any further conversation.

Charles went to answer it. 'Hello,' he said.

'Hello Charles,' said a voice he instantly recognised. 'Richard Brackley here. Terribly sorry to bother you Charles old boy, especially on Christmas Eve and all that, but this is rather important. Can you please tell me where Charlotte is? I know it seems like a devilish cheek old chap, but I really would like very much to see her.'

'Yes Richard, she's here, I'll get her for you.' He placed the receiver on the small telephone table, and went to fetch his sister-in-law.

'Hello,' said Charlotte rather tentatively, still not quite sure about this new fangled thing called the telephone.

7

'Hello Charlotte. What the devil are you doing there? I'm home on Christmas leave from France. I called at your house this morning, expecting a hero's and a lover's welcome, only to find the place empty and everything locked up, so I surmised you may have gone to your sister's house for Christmas. Darling, how long are you staying? I only have a few days leave.'

There was a moments silence. 'Charlotte. Are you there?'

'Yes. Yes. Sorry Richard, I was thinking. You being home has come as quite a surprise. You see I never expected you, otherwise of course I wouldn't be here. Our Rose took pity on me, thinking I would be all on my own for Christmas, and invited me to come and stay at 'Mount Pleasant' with our baby. I'm supposed to stay for the whole week, but I imagine it will be possible for me to return home, after lunch on Boxing Day. Will that suit you?'

'Yes. Darling. Great, I have to spend tomorrow with my dreary family anyway, so that will suit me fine. Can't wait to see you and little Richard. Love you darling. Bye.'

There was a click, and the line went dead. Charlotte carefully replaced the receiver upon it's hook. She sat for a few moments, alone in that vast hall, staring vacantly at the now silent inanimate instrument, and she experienced a modicum of surprise at the unprecedented spate of euphoria which had surged through her entire body, at the impact of Richard Brackley's voice upon her senses, and she marvelled once again at the modern technological miracle of the telephone.

Finally, mentally shaking herself back to reality, Charlotte rose from her chair, and with a light step, returned to the drawing room.

'Who was that Charlotte?' asked Rose curiously, wondering who on earth could possibly wish to contact her sister at this address, and what could have brought such a high colour to her complexion.

'Just Richard,' Charlotte replied nonchalantly, obviously inferring that was the end of that particular conversation.

However, Rose ignored the inference, and persevered. 'Whatever did he want, and on Christmas Eve too? I thought he was supposed to be fighting in France, and anyway how did he know you were here?'

With a sigh, Charlotte resigned herself to the inevitable. 'He didn't know I was here. He just thought this was the obvious place to look first. Yes he is supposed to be fighting in France, but he happens to have been granted a few days Christmas leave. Oh, and he telephoned because he would like to come and see me at my house, during the afternoon of Boxing Day. Does that answer all your questions big sister, and put your mind at ease?' she asked, with heavy sarcasm.

'All but one. Are you going?' replied Rose with a smile, completely ignoring the sarcasm.

'Yes of course. I can't knit socks or mittens, but at least I can provide some small comfort for the troops. It's what I'm good at, and what I call helping the war effort,' she ended with a throaty chuckle.

'Our Charlotte!' cried Rose in simulated disgust. 'Whatever will you say next? Will you be staying when you return home, or will you come back here for the rest of the week?'

'Oh no Rose, I shall stay in Hull. You see, Richard wants to spend as much of his leave with me as he can.'

'I should have thought he would want to spend his Christmas leave with his family,' remarked Miles, rather coldly.

Charlotte gave him one of her dazzling smiles. 'Oh! No, Richard isn't a bit like that, he's not at all selfish. You see, he really does believe in sharing the best things in life!'

'Really Charlotte, you're completely

10

incorrigible. You shouldn't say things like that in front of Charles' parents.'

'That's quite alright Rose,' interposed Ruth with a gracious smile. 'Both Miles and I were young once you know.'

In the ensuing tension, which had resulted because of Richard's telephone call, everyone seemed to have forgotten the presence of the girl's father. However, they were quickly reminded, when he suddenly spoke. 'Who is this Richard chap, our Charlotte? And why does he want to spend part of his leave in some other house with you?'

A monastic silence greeted his remarks, while inevitably Charlotte looked appealingly at Rose.

Finally, Rose turned to the miller. 'Well father, Richard is a very good friend of Charles, and Charlotte met him at our wedding. He is an officer in the British Army, and is at home on leave for a few days from France, and he would like to see her again, that's all.'

'Why. Why should this chap want to see our Charlotte, if as Miles says, he should be at home with his family, particularly at Christmas?'

Charlotte pushed her sister aside. 'It's quite simple really father,' she said in her sweetest, good daughter tone. 'Dear Richard discovered I had been made a widow through this ghastly horrible war, and immediately took pity, and wished to comfort me in my terrible loss. I'm sure Halle wouldn't mind me seeing him,' she added rather plaintively.

To the relief of everyone, the miller smiled. 'No lass, I'm sure he wouldn't. If this chap thinks so much about you, then you go and meet him, and tell him he'll have me to answer to, if anything happens to you.'

To say her captive audience were dumbfounded, as they watched this precocious wayward daughter, fling her arms around her father's neck and hug him, whilst showering him with kisses, would be an understatement. 'Oh! Father thank you, I think you're marvellous,' she gushed. 'It really is wonderful having you here for Christmas, so we can all be together. This is going to be the best Christmas ever.'

And so it was, well nearly!

At precisely ten-o-clock on Boxing Day morning, the old butler came to the dining room, where the family were just finishing breakfast, to announce 'The Honourable Richard Brackley!'

However, Richard had followed the man, and apart from a 'Good morning everyone,' he stated the purpose of his surprise visit, without any further preamble. 'Please pack your things Charlotte, I'm taking you to London, for the rest of my leave!'

Charlotte immediately leapt to her feet. 'Oh! Richard, how wonderful,' then turning to her sister. 'Will you look after young Richard for me, please Rose. This is the chance of a lifetime, and I would hate to miss it.'

Rose, as usual agreed to her younger sister's whim, and her extravagant request. 'Yes of course. Now you run along dear, and pack your suit case.'

Richard and Charlotte, walked separately into Paragon Station, bought their tickets separately, and boarded the same carriage, but at opposite ends.

The happy co-conspiritors, changed trains at Doncaster, where they boarded the train for Kings Cross, travelling first class. The upholstery was so sumptuous, and Charlotte was so full of herself, and the luxury of her surroundings, all complemented of course, by the presence of this very handsome young aristocrat, she never complained when Richard closed the curtains, locked the compartment door, and proceeded to undress her.

A taxi dropped them off at the Savoy Hotel, and Charlotte literally floated through the foyer, in and out of the lift, and through the door of their suite, into a complete new world. She ripped off her clothes, and ran naked into the most luxurious bathroom she had ever seen, laughing all the time like a child.

Her mood was infectious, Richard caught it, removed his own clothes, and quickly followed her, and together they enjoyed a most exhilarating bath.

Later that evening, they went down for dinner, Charlotte very thankful she had called at her house, to enable her to collect her best suits and dresses. The two lovers enjoyed a marvellous meal, considering the war, and how rationing seemed to affect them at home, complemented with two bottles of very good, rather heady wine.

As they were leaving the dining room, someone called Richard's name, and looking round he spotted two of his fellow Guards officers leaning against the bar. 'You run along to our suite darling, and warm the bed for me, I'll join you later,' he kissed her, and turned away to join his friends.

Enjoying the effects of the wine, and singing happily to herself, Charlotte opened the door to their room, closed it softly behind her, undressed and climbed into the lovely soft bed. She lay there and waited, and waited — .

She must have eventually drifted off to sleep, for suddenly she was rudely awakened by someone trying to tear off her nightdress!

The tablelamp beside the bed was still switched on, and now she was wide awake. 'What the devil do you think you're doing Richard?' she asked coldly.

The intonation in her voice should have been sufficient to warn him, but he was far too drunk, both with alcohol and lust, to notice any such subtleties.

It was then the real Charlotte surfaced. She fought him, she clawed his back and his face with her long finger nails, and suddenly he hit her.

'You little whore,' he shouted. 'You dare to scratch me. I'll make you suffer for that,' again he drew back his fist to hit her, but it never landed.

His breath reeked of beer and spirits, and Charlotte fought like a wildcat, scratching and clawing, hitting him with everything she had, never emitting a sound, when suddenly she savagely brought up her knee, hard in his groin.

The Honourable Richard Brackley, Captain in the Grenadier Guards, gave one stifled gasp, clutched his nether regions and passed out, having no more interest in the proceedings.

Charlotte squeezed herself out from under his inert body, dressed, quickly packed her case, took her return train ticket from his wallet, had one last look at him, and softly closed the door behind her.

When she reached the foyer, she walked to the desk and handed the man standing there, a couple of sovereigns, then said nonchalantly, 'Please give me one hour, then go up to our room, and check to see if the person lying on the bed is still alive!'

At eleven-o-clock the following morning, Charlotte opened her own front door, and with a heart felt sigh of relief, went to put the kettle on.

At approximately the same time, Richard Brackley was in the bathroom of his hotel suite, trying to remove all the bloodstains from his face and body. Eventually he was satisfied, though still very conscious of his appearance, for he looked as if he he'd been dragged naked through a thorn bush.

Going over to the phone, and putting it gingerly to his ear, he asked for Charlotte's number. 'Hello,' he said when she answered. 'How are you this morning?'

'Oh hello. Fine thank you. How are you? Do you have a headache?'

16

'Yes, and not only my head, thanks to you.'

'I see. Well you know I'm your's any time you want me, but I will not allow you to rape me, especially when you're drunk! Are you coming back here?'

'No. I'm staying in London until Saturday, then going over to France. I think I'd rather face the bloody Germans than you, at the moment.'

'Why thank you darling. That's a lovely remark for a lover to make to the mother of his child. Enjoy your war!' came the repost, and the line went dead.

2

One fresh sunny morning during the early spring of nineteen hundred and seventeen, America entered the war, and the British, Canadian, and Australian troops opened up a new Spring Offensive, against the Germans manning the Hindenburg Line, opposite Arras.

Many miles, and a world away from the opposing armies, Charlotte had decided to take her baby out for a walk in the park. Alice had asked for a few days off, and now Richard was no longer a tiny baby, Charlotte had discovered she was able to handle him more easily. She could see in the distance, a young woman sitting on the park bench, with a little boy beside her.

As Charlotte approached, the young woman rose to her feet. 'Good morning Al — . Oh! I'm awfully sorry. I thought you were Alice. We often meet here in the park, and seeing this pram, well I naturally thought — ,' she floundered to a stop, for Charlotte wasn't listening, she was staring intently at the golden haired little boy sitting so calmly on the seat.

Suddenly she realised the young lady had stopped speaking. 'Sorry, did you say Alice? Well she has gone home for a short holiday, so I have brought Richard out this morning.'

'Oh I see, strange she never mentioned a holiday. Begging your pardon, but you must be Richard's mother?'

Charlotte smiled at the sudden awe in the woman's voice, and vaguely wondered what Alice had told her during their strolls in the park. 'Yes, you're quite right, but who are you?' she asked quietly, trying not to appear too inquisitive, for she was convinced she had seen this child somewhere before. with his blonde curly hair. Or maybe it was a photograph? Charlotte stood very still, a frisson of unprecedented excitement coursing through her veins, for she had just remembered. Yes, she must be right!

There was a photograph of this boy, or his identical twin, on the sideboard at 'Mount Pleasant'. Charlotte sat down upon the seat.

'Are you all right madam?' asked the woman apprehensively.

Charlotte's thoughts were almost racing out of control. She had loved and desired Charles Cartwright, from the first moment she had seen him, and with her evil predatory mind, had thought of all kinds of ways to steal him from her sister, all to no avail. Now however, she was certain she had found the perfect solution to her long felt want.

For the photograph of the golden haired little boy, on the sideboard at 'Mount Pleasant', was of none other than Charles Cartwright!

Trying to hide her euphoria, and choosing her words very carefully, Charlotte turned to her companion, and displaying her best charismatic style. 'Please call me Charlotte. Tell me, are you married?' She could see immediately she had struck a nerve, for the young woman blushed to the roots of her hair.

She appeared to hesitate, but only momentarily, then removed her glove. 'I wear a wedding ring to show to the world, but no, I am not married. There is no point in lying to you, for I'm sure you would have found out sooner or later, if not from Alice, then from someone else.'

To relieve the tension of the moment, Charlotte turned desperately to the little boy, for she was nearly bursting out of her skin with excitement and curiosity.

'Paul, say hello to your auntie Charlotte,' said the boy's mother.

'Paul. Now that's a lovely name. What is your second name Paul?'

The boy just smiled shyly, then looked appealingly at his mother.

'Hunt,' his mother said quietly. 'And I'm Dorothy Hunt.'

Charlotte turned back to the boy's mother. During the previous few minutes, she had decided exactly how to execute her plan, and now calm, cool and very collected, she locked her beautiful green hypnotic eyes, upon those of her new friend. 'I know we have only recently met Dorothy, but will you consider walking home with me, and staying for a cup of tea? Then you will know where I live, and perhaps wish to call again,' she said sweetly, showing no hint of guile or hidden malice.

'Oh thank you very much. Yes, we would love to come, wouldn't we Paul?' replied Dorothy, standing up and taking Paul by the hand.

To Charlotte's surprise, she thoroughly enjoyed the company of Dorothy and her boy Paul, on that memorable spring morning, so much so in fact, that she invited them to stay for lunch, and it was quite late in the afternoon when they left, but not before Charlotte had extracted a promise from Dorothy, that she would call again, and of course bring her son Paul along too.

Three weeks later, when the days were becoming longer and warmer and the evenings lighter, Charlotte had decided to invite Charles and Rose to tea. Unbeknown to either of them, she had also invited Dorothy and her son Paul, for she had made a point of meeting them several times recently in the park, explaining to Alice, that she needed the exercise to regain her svelte figure.

Of course Alice had acquiesced immediately, for she was quite content to take Richard out in the afternoons, and had no suspicion whatever, of any ulterior motive in this charade, being carried out by her mistress.

During these strolls in the park with her new friend Dorothy, Charlotte had learned much more about her, and had managed to bring Paul out of his shell. Consequently, the little boy was always pleased to see his 'Auntie Charlotte', and would run to hug and kiss her, whenever they met.

After each encounter, Charlotte became more convinced she was on the right track, and now after the last three weeks, she had decided to take the plunge on this particular Sunday evening.

Alice and Paul had been in the house about half-an-hour, and Charlotte was beginning to feel the strain of waiting, when suddenly she leapt to her feet, as someone knocked on the front door, and though she rushed to answer it, the door was opened before she reached it, and Rose came in, followed by Charles.

Charlotte intently scrutinised the faces of Dorothy and Charles, as he and his wife advanced further into the room, watching and waiting with suppressed excitement, and maniacal hatred of her sister, for the slightest hint of recognition, between her sister's husband, and her new friend, for she was utterly convinced that the child Paul, was the bastard offspring of Charles Cartwright!

However, even in her wildest dreams, Charlotte could never have envisaged the sequence of events which followed, and which completely obliterated any hopes she may have harboured, of ever persuading her brother-in-law into her bed through blackmail!

Charlotte's face was a picture of incredulity, and undisguised frustrated anger, as Rose moved forward, shook Dorothy by the hand, and kissed her on the cheek. 'Hello my dear,' she said. 'How are you and young Paul?'

'Very well thank you Rose. I didn't know you knew Charlotte, my new friend? We met one morning in the park, a few weeks ago, when I was out walking with Paul.'

Rose laughed aloud. 'Did you hear that Charles? Dorothy didn't know I knew Charlotte. Oh yes dear, I know Charlotte.

She just happens to be my beloved sister, don't you dear?'

Charlotte, who was now almost bereft of speech and any logical thought, turned her green hypnotic orbs upon her sister, and struggling to speak. 'Do you mean to say you knew all about this, this kid, our Rose?' she said in a high pitched tone.

Again Rose laughed, which only served to further infuriate her sister. 'Yes, you silly girl, of course I knew. Charles told me all about Dorothy and Paul, before we were married,' she lied nonchalantly.

Actually, Rose had only known a couple of days, for on the previous Thursday, Dorothy had called to see Charles at his office, and warned him that she thought Charlotte was hatching a plot of revenge or something, because all of them were to be invited to tea on Sunday.

Knowing of Charlotte's vitriolic nature, of her hatred for her sister, and the fact that he had spurned her advances, and 'That Hell hath no fury like a woman scorned', he had, during that same evening unburdened his soul to Rose, and told her everything.

At first Rose was shocked, but when she realised all this had happened long before she even met Charles, she forgave him for his lamentable youthful indiscretion, and immediately showed her concern for the unfortunate young lady involved, which really, was very typical of her, and served to endear Charles even more closely, to his beautiful wife.

Charlotte realised that all her plans had come to nought, and now, fighting to control the rage rising within her, yet failing miserably, she turned on her three guests and Alice. With her features now contorted almost out of recognition, she hurled abuse at Rose, then Charles, and finally Alice and Dorothy.

Neither Alice or Dorothy, had ever seen or heard anything like the show of hatred or the flow of obscenities which Charlotte manifested that afternoon, and at last Dorothy, unable to take any more of this verbal assault, gathered Paul in her arms, and ran out of the house, followed closely by Charles and Rose.

When they caught up with her, she was leaning against a wall, sobbing into her handkerchief, the little boy looking up at his mother, with a troubled expression in his almost sea blue eyes.

Rose pushed Charles back a little, and moved forward, and he, realising this was woman's work, took the hand of Paul, and led him to the park seat.

Charles thought, how strange life is, and what tricks she plays with the frailties of men, as he sat there with his son, and thought what a handsome young boy he is, and how different things might have been, if he hadn't attended his grandparents funeral, that day at Watersmeet. For Dorothy was still a very attractive young woman! But then he switched his gaze to his wife, inwardly cursed himself for his unprincipled thoughts, and remembered how lucky he was to have found such a treasure, in an out of the way village like Watersmeet.

Suddenly Charles remembered his son was sitting quietly beside him. He turned to the boy. 'Well Paul, how are you?' he asked.

'Very well, thank you sir. Excuse me sir, may I ask you a question please?'

'Yes of course you may,' replied Charles, much to his surprise, finding it very easy to hold a conversation with one so young. 'And if I can possibly give you an answer, I most certainly will.'

The boy turned his serious gaze upon his companion. 'I don't know if this will be correct sir, but may I please call you Uncle Charles,' he asked hesitantly.

Charles placed his arm around the boy's shoulders and hugged him. 'Yes my boy, indeed you may, if that is what you wish.

I shall be proud to be called Uncle, by a fine strapping young man like you, and with such good manners too.'

The boy brought up his hand, and gripped that of Charles. 'Oh! Thank you very much Uncle Charles, I shall remember you in my prayers tonight, and all the nights to come, and I shall love you for ever.'

Charles saw that his wife's words had soothed away Dorothy's tears, and now she was actually smiling. 'Come along young Paul,' he said, helping the boy to his feet. 'The showers seem to be over, and we have sunny blue skies once again.'

Paul, showing a unique intelligence above his years, obviously caught the inference, and chuckled aloud with Charles.

As the two young women were moving away from their seat, Rose turned to her new found friend. 'Dorothy, haven't you ever thought of looking for another man, one who would be willing to take on Paul, and make you both happy?'

Dorothy smiled to herself, a trifle wistfully, Rose thought. Then with a far away look in her eyes, she said. 'Who could possibly follow Charles? Anyway, as they say. 'It is better to have loved and lost, than never to have loved at all.'

When they reached Charles and Paul, Rose

suggested they could give the boy and his mother a ride home.

'Oh No Rose, that will not be necessary, thank you very much. You see we only live just along the road, that is how I came to meet your sister, when she was out with her baby.'

'Why that is marvellous,' Rose replied. 'Please show me which one is your house, then when I come to see Charlotte, perhaps you will allow me to call and visit you, just so that I can keep an eye on Paul, and make sure Charles is fulfilling all his obligations,' she said, as she turned to her husband and smiled.

'Of course you may come and visit,' replied Dorothy, amazed at the request, and struggling to understand such a rare warm quality of forgiveness, in a wife who knew she was speaking to her husband's former lover, and the mother of his five year old son.

'Thank you,' was all Rose said, then they walked towards the car and drove away.

There was very little conversation on the way home, but when they were in the privacy of their own bedroom that night, Rose suddenly asked. 'Why didn't you marry Dorothy?'

Charles was silent for so long, she was

beginning to think he had gone to sleep, when he turned to her, and gazed upon his beautiful wife. 'I really don't know darling, but something stopped me. Perhaps, I could see into the future, and realised that somewhere, somehow, one day I would walk into a cemetery, and meet the girl of my dreams. That may seem a lame kind of an excuse my dear, considering Dorothy was pregnant, but I salved my conscience by making a promise to her, that I would always make absolutely sure both her and the child were well provided for, and that promise I have adhered to implicitly.'

'That was quite a speech my darling,' replied Rose drowsily, secure in the knowledge that Charles would not return to his old love. 'We must do everything we possibly can to help Paul with his education, and treat him almost as though he was one of our own, and also of course make sure his mother is adequately provided for.'

Charles still could not completely assimilate the wondrous nature of his beautiful wife, and with that last thought in his mind, he drifted off into a fitful dreamless sleep.

3

Though several months had passed, since Charlotte retired from the Ambulance Service, she still returned occasionally to the hospital, to see her old friends. For though she would never admit it, those days and weeks she had spent driving the ambulance, were some of the most exciting and memorable times of her young life, chiefly because of the wonderful camaraderie extolled by the drivers, nurses, patients and everyone connected with the hospital.

As she walked along the path leading up to the entrance of the hospital, on a warm autumnal day in late September, she was suddenly jerked out of her ordinary mundane thoughts, by a voice which caused her heart to flutter, one she would remember till the day she died, and which now stopped her dead in her tracks.

Only one word, that voice had uttered. 'Charlotte!'

Turning quickly, she made out the figure of a man sitting in a chair, shaded by the spread of a large elm tree. He was wearing a blue dressing gown and pyjamas, and Charlotte ran towards him, shouting 'Richard! Richard!'

At last she reached his side, and stood waiting for him to leap up and take her in his arms, but he didn't move. 'Richard, how lovely to see you, but I thought you would have had the good grace to stand up and kiss me.'

He looked up at her, and she saw the dark circles beneath his eyes, the pale hollow cheeks, the pain racked emaciated body, and suddenly, shatteringly, she realised for the first time, this was no ordinary chair in which he was sitting. No this was an invalid chair!

For the first time she could ever remember, Charlotte, she who had always boasted of her toughness, of her almost devilish ability to ride roughshod over everyone and everything, suddenly fell to her knees upon the grass, and collapsed sobbing into his lap. 'Oh! My poor darling Richard,' she gasped, through heart rending sobs. 'I had no idea you were sitting in one of these. Please forgive me my dearest. and tell me what I can do to help. Whatever happened to you? Will you be able to walk again?'

He gently stroked the jet black ringlets of her beautiful hair, inwardly amazed at the genuine show of her love for him, and suddenly he realised, here was someone with whom he could share all his secrets, his aches and pains, his occasional wild outbursts of temper, which besieged him when the pain struck and became unbearable. Also, if the necessity arose, someone he could trust with his life, or his death!

'I was hit by shrapnel from a shell, whilst fighting on the outskirts of Ypres. It caught me in the lower back, and completely paralysed me below the waist.'

He was speaking quietly, in a matter of fact voice, as though this was an every day occurance, and the more he spoke, the greater became Charlotte's anguish.

'No, my darling, I shall never be able to walk again!'

It was at that point Charlotte ceased her flow of tears, and lifting her red rimmed eyes, she gazed into his. Then with a show of consummate courage and sheer grit, she actually forced a smile. 'All right my darling, I shall have to look after you, and drive you around, when you finally leave hospital,' she said lightly.

Miraculously, he returned her smile. 'Funny you should say that Charlotte. For some time now, I have been absolutely dreading leaving this place, and having to return home, but now, if you are willing, I have just thought of the perfect solution. I am due to leave hospital in two week's time, so if I insert an advertisement, in the situations vacant column of the evening paper next week, for a full time private nurse and companion, will you please reply?'

She stared at him in disbelief and utter amazement. 'But Richard, I know nothing of being a nurse, of dressing or attending to wounds.'

'Charlotte,' his voice had changed, this was beginning to sound rather like a command, and yet he still continued to smile. 'I have no wounds that require any dressing, all my wounds are completely healed,' he lowered his voice, as though ashamed of what he was going to say next. 'You see my dear, you would have to do everything for me, and I mean everything.'

'Surely Richard, your wife is the correct person to help you in all of this?'

'No!' His voice cracked out like a pistol shot, and scythed through the warm air as would a bullet. Several people dotted about on the grass, patients and visitors, temporarily ceased their conversation, and just stood and stared.

'What the hell are you all gawping at? mind your own business damn it,' he almost screamed at them, and the embarrassed onlookers turned sheepishly away. Then lowering his voice, he again addressed his companion. 'No I couldn't let her touch me, not in those private places. She would never be able to anyway,' he was speaking more softly now. 'No my darling, there is only one person I could ever trust to do what is necessary, and you must agree to answer my request, otherwise I don't think I shall be responsible for my actions!' his voice broke as he finished the sentence, and her heart went out to him.

'Oh my poor darling,' said Charlotte, though his recent outburst, should have given her some inkling of what her life would be like if she accepted this position, she knew in her heart, she could never refuse, and determined not to break down again, she quickly realised, though Richard needed sympathy, he would never appreciate any from a broken reed. She would have to try and be cheerful at all times.

'Very well Richard,' she said lightly, as she put her arm around his shoulders. 'You place your advertisement, and I promise you, I will answer it. Just one other item though my dear. Do I receive any increase in my salary for all these extra services?'

He laughed aloud, like a child, and brought up his hand to grip hers. 'Yes, Charlotte the mother of my child. If you are a good nurse and companion, I will pay you double, and all found. By the way, talking of our child, how is young Richard coming along? Of course you will be able to bring him with you when you move to 'Brackley Hall.'

Charlotte stared at him askance. 'Richard! That would be utterly impossible. How can you ever imagine that your mistress and your child, could possibly live under the same roof as you, your daughter, your outrageously snobbish sister, whom incidentally I detest, and your wife? No my darling, there is only one solution, I shall have to take him back to Rose at 'Mount Pleasant'. I can ask Alice to look after him, there is plenty of room there, and I shall easily have sufficient money to support her and Richard.'

For the first time, he seemed to relax. 'Right Charlotte. May we assume that this matter is settled, and when I place my request in the paper, you will definitely answer it?'

'Yes. Oh yes Richard. Absolutely. You need have no fear on that score. There is just one other small point we haven't mentioned though. How far away from your bedroom, will I be sleeping?'

He laughed. He was certainly in much higher spirits, than when she had first approached him. 'While I was in France my dear, the old man passed away, and being the only son and heir, I inherited the lot. Consequently, you and I have the choice of approximately fifty-six bedrooms. Well I have already decided which they will be. I shall turn mine into a bedsitting room, and you will have the one next to it.'

She caught his mood, and laughed with him. 'But Darling, what about your wife. Where will she sleep, and won't it appear awfully suspicious, if we sleep so close to each other?'

He tried to be patient. 'I'm sorry Charlotte, but you don't seem to understand the enormity of the task you are taking on. You see, sometimes I wake during the night, because I suffer terrible nightmares, and I will need you close at all times. Regarding my wife, please don't worry your pretty head about her, she made her position quite clear when she visited me here, and saw the state I was in. Anyway, we shall be living in the west wing, and she will be in the east, so there is very little chance of your paths ever crossing. Also I don't know which room Daphne will be occupying, but I can assure you, I shall make damn sure she will never bother you. You may now accomplish your first chore. Please light me a cigarette.'

Charlotte fished out his packet of cigarettes, and a lighter from his jacket pocket, put the cigarette in her own mouth, lit it and then passed it to him. He inhaled deeply. 'Thank you darling. Can you now push me back to my ward please?'

As she began to move the wheelchair, Charlotte had a sudden thought. 'Richard, what about my house? I don't want it standing empty for any length of time.'

'No, I quite agree. Perhaps it might be a jolly good idea to try and find a suitable tenant, on say, a yearly basis, and let it, furnished of course.'

'Yes, that's a brilliant idea Richard, that way I should still be able to keep my little house, and also earn a small income from it.'

That night, Charlotte lay wide awake in her bed, turning over in her thoughts, all that had happened to her on that memorable day. And though at the time she was with Richard, and she had almost convinced herself she loved him, she knew deep down, the evil instincts were only just below the surface, and her mean mercenary mind, had been thinking of how much she would be able to make out of this extraordinary turn of events.

The following morning, Charlotte went over to 'Mount Pleasant' and informed Rose of this latest development. Rose wasn't very thrilled at first, at the thought of baby Richard and his nanny, coming to take up semi-permanent residence in her home, until she told her of the amazing salary she had been offered.

Charlotte visited Richard once more while he was in hospital, then one evening a week later, her telephone rang.

'Hello darling. Richard here. I shall be leaving hospital tomorrow afternoon, so will you please be all packed ready to come and join me? The car will call for you at two-o-clock. Alright darling?'

'Yes of course I will be ready Richard. You are not bothering to insert anything in the paper then?'

'No, I couldn't see any point really. You don't mind do you?'

'No of course not. It did seem a bit silly, particularly if I was going to be hired anyway. Still I wish you had given me a little more time for packing, you see I have young Richard to attend to, as well as myself.'

'Sorry, but I have only just been told I can leave tomorrow. Anyway you have Alice to help, and I'm sure Charles will send a car to collect her and the baby. Bye darling, see you tomorrow.'

At precisely two-o-clock the following

afternoon, a large Rolls drew up outside Charlotte's house, and a few minutes later it had gone, carrying Charlotte and her suit case into a completely new world. A fascinating world, yet one which would be fraught with jealousy and intrigue.

The middle-aged, liveried chauffeur was quite amiable towards his passenger. 'I understand you're coming to the Hall miss, to look after his Lordship,' he began in a friendly manner.

'Yes, you understand correctly, er. Look I'm Charlotte, what is your name?' she asked, winning him over immediately with one of her devastating smiles.

'George, just call me George. Charlotte eh, now that's what I call a real name. Have you met Mr. Richard before?'

Charlotte quickly realised the old chap was inherently nosey, yet he didn't seem to be, for he was so easy to talk to, and it soon dawned upon her he was very charismatic, and she was sure he would be able to charm the birds from the trees, if he set his mind to it, for his tongue was his greatest asset.

'Yes George, I have met Richard, on several occasions, he was best man at my sister's wedding actually, over at Watersmeet.'

'Over at Watersmeet eh? I thought your accent wasn't Hull like. If you are from

Watersmeet, why are you living here my dear?'

He asked his questions so kindly, and in such a way, she felt it would have been terribly impolite not to have replied, even if some of her answers were only half truths. 'Well you see George, I married the school master from Watersmeet, and when he joined the army, we came to live in Hull, so I could be near my sister, but he was killed in France, so now I'm a war widow, and perhaps that is the reason Richard Brackley took pity on me, and gave me this job.'

'Your sister married a Hull man then, did she?'

'Yes George, and before you ask, as I'm sure you're going to, his name is Charles Cartwright. I think he has something to do with shipping.'

George sat bolt upright, gave a low whistle, and almost forgot he was driving. 'Charles Cartwright!' he shouted, swerving just in time to miss a brewer's dray. 'You think he has something to do with shipping? My God Charlotte, he's only the heir to the biggest shipbuilders in Hull. I'll tell you one thing, you and your sister certainly know how to pick em,' he ended with a dry chuckle.

Charlotte laughed with him. 'Why thank you George. I'll tell you something though,

I wish I had known you when you were a young man.'

George laughed again. 'That wouldn't have been much good miss Charlotte, you would only have been a baby.' As the big Rolls drew up, outside the main entrance to the hospital, the only sound it made was from the tyres on the gravelled drive.

George jumped out and held open the door for Charlotte, for which she thanked him with her inimitable smile. A hospital porter appeared and indicated they should follow him. They were ushered into a room and told to wait. After a while a nurse came and asked them to step into the hallway, and there was Richard sitting in his wheelchair, waiting for them.

Charlotte thought he suddenly appeared old beyond his years, and correctly assumed it had something to do with the horrible sights and sounds he must have witnessed whilst fighting in France. His spirits however, seemed buoyant enough as he greeted her. 'Hello Charlotte. Thank God you have come to rescue me from this hospital. Not that I have any desire to leave all these wonderfully attractive angels, who spend their time here in the guise of nurses, but I am well ready for home. Will you miss me sister?' he asked a rather buxom lady, whom Charlotte judged to be in her late thirties.

'Oh yes of course we shall miss you sir,' she replied. 'Now take good care of yourself, and do try to stay away from here. Goodbye sir, you have been a lovely patient,' she added, as she kissed him, at the same time brushing away a tear.

Two male nurses took Richard outside to a waiting ambulance, for his chair was too wide to fit into the car, and after they had lifted him in, complete with his chair, Charlotte climbed in and sat beside him. George led the way, with the ambulance following in his wake, and eventually the two vehicles drew up outside the front entrance to 'Brackley Hall'.

The great oak door swung slowly open, and an elderly butler stood there, waiting to welcome his master.

'Good day sir, tis' good to see you,' said the man, as the two ambulance men lowered Richard to the ground, and proceeded to negotiate the wide steps leading into the Hall, with his wheelchair.

'Good afternoon Bains, tis' good to see you too, and to be home, thank you. Now will you two gentlemen please take me straight upstairs to my room?' Then turning to George. 'Thank you George, I don't know what I would do without you. After you have brought Miss Charlotte's suitcase upstairs, you may put the car away.'

Charlotte gazed around her, as she followed the others up the wide, curved staircase, fascinated by the huge portraits of other members of the Brackley family, now buried in the private cemetery, within the grounds. She had noticed no other person had come to welcome Richard home. Not his wife, or his sister the Lady Daphne, and she wondered vaguely what kind of an emotional household, she had so blithely wandered into. She didn't have many hours to wait, before she found out!

Richard occupied a huge room in a corner of the West wing of the Hall, and even though the evening was mild, he had insisted on having a fire in the large fireplace. A pretty young maid had earlier brought them a pot of tea and some biscuits, and Charlotte was on the point of pouring a second cup for each of them, when there was a light knock upon the bedroom door, and a tall middle-aged woman with a head of luxuriant silver hair came in, leading by the hand, the most enchanting child, Charlotte had ever seen.

Charlotte could see immediately, by the woman's bearing and deportment, she was obviously a person of class, and of some importance in the Brackley household, she had to wonder no further, for suddenly Richard answered all her thoughts.

'Nanny!' he shouted gleefully. 'How marvellous to see you again. How are you? And how is my darling Sophia?'

The woman rushed forward, and with tears in her eyes, she embraced and kissed Richard on the cheek. 'Oh! my poor baby. What have they done to you?' she asked, a sob in her voice.

Richard appeared slightly embarrassed. 'There, there nanny, I'm not your baby any longer you know. Please don't distress yourself. This is supposed to be a happy time, I'm home now, and home I'm staying. I don't think they will need me again, over in France,' he ended with a dry chuckle, in an attempt to lighten the conversation. Then he noticed nanny glance in the direction of Charlotte.

'Ah, yes nanny. Sorry I should have introduced you. Please meet Charlotte. She is my companion, my friend, my secretary, my helpmate. In fact everything unfortunately, except my bedmate. Charlotte, meet my wonderful, glorious nanny, who has lived in this house since time began. Since it began for me anyway.'

The two women shook hands, and murmured the appropriate greetings.

'What a beautiful child Richard,' gushed Charlotte, as she dropped to her knees and hugged the little girl. 'And your name is Sophia. Is that correct my dear?' she asked. The child nodded her head vigorously, and they all laughed, which immediately eased any tension that had been building up, during these few hours of Richard Brackley's homecoming.

On that first night, Charlotte really learned what life was all about, living with a man, who was paralysed from the waist down, and she nearly broke down, when she saw the terrible state his body was in, and remembered how he used to be, as they both undressed and made love together, in that small wood, below Watersmeet. It all seemed so long ago.

Charlotte lay awake for hours that night, unable to sleep, her thoughts full of Richard, of how this stupid war had ravaged his body, and of how beautiful he used to be.

Sometime in the early hours, when the house was silent, her reverie was suddenly shattered by the most unholy screams, emanating from Richard's room. She flung back the bed covers, and rushed through the adjoining door, and then stopped dead in her tracks.

Richard Brackley, this young aristocrat,

this handsome looking man, with whom she could so easily have fallen in love if she hadn't already given her heart to another! was cowering back in his bed, his eyes wide and staring, and screaming at the top of his voice 'No. No. Don't shoot! Please don't shoot. Please don't shoot,' his voice then sank to little more than a whimper, and his words became incomprehensible.

Charlotte moved towards the bed, placed her arms around him, and showing great care, she gently eased him down into the bed. He sensed she was there, and putting an arm around her, pulled her into the bed beside him, holding her close.

At that precise moment three women burst into the room. Richard's wife, his sister and one of the maids.

'What the devil is going on in here?' shouted Daphne. 'And what the hell are you doing in my brother's bed? Ha I see who you are now. You're the miller's other daughter, sister of the fast little tart that talked Charles into marrying her. Get out of that bed, and get out of this house, before I set the dogs on you. Now!'

Charlotte looked down at Richard, to make sure he was alright, then slowly she lifted her head, and locked her brilliant, hypnotic green eyes upon those of her antagonist.

'I think you have just made one of the biggest mistakes of your frivolous, useless life Daphne dear,' she said, in a voice so cold, Daphne shivered as she pulled her dressing gown more tightly around her slim figure.

In the same cold tone, Charlotte continued. 'How dare you two come in here and tell me to leave. You, his wife, and you his sister, who could only spare the time from your terribly busy lifestyle, to visit Richard just once, during his six weeks in hospital. God you make me sick!' her words dripped with sarcasm. 'No! It is you who shall leave this room. Leave it now, and don't ever come round here bothering him again. Go on. Get out!' she ended shrilly.

There was a soft chuckle from beside her, and Richard raised himself on one elbow. 'Good for you darling, that told em'. Now I think it would be an excellent idea if you two ladies carried out Charlotte's instructions without further delay. Otherwise, she may have to throw you out, and I can assure you, that is a feat of which she is quite capable!'

The haughty Lady Daphne, had never met anyone quite like Charlotte before, and with a last furious glare in her direction, she turned towards the door. There she stopped and turned again. 'You have not heard the

last of this, you . . . you hateful little whore!'
she screamed.

However, she rushed out of the room, as
Charlotte made a move forward, as though
she was going to throw the three of them
out. She called the maid back. 'Milly, please
come here.'

Milly stopped, and returned to the bedside.
'Yes miss?' she said, complimenting the
words with a small, yet quite distinct curtsy.

'Which room do you sleep in,' asked
Charlotte, in a warm friendly tone, completely
different to the one she had used in her
verbal diatribe with Daphne.

'In a room upstairs miss, up in the roof.'

'I see.' Charlotte appeared to be thinking.

'What is it darling, what's troubling you?'
asked Richard.

She flashed him one of her inimitable
smiles. 'I think it would be a very good
idea, to move Milly down to a room on this
floor Richard, then if something happens that
I can't cope with on my own, I can always go
fetch her.'

Richard didn't miss the sudden look of
happiness which suffused Milly's features,
as she waited for his reply to Charlotte's
suggestion. 'Yes Charlotte, that's a brilliant
idea. Would you like that Milly?'

'Ooh yes, please sir,' then thinking she may

have shown a little too much enthusiasm, she said quietly. 'That is if you think it will be alright with the mistress and the Lady Daphne, sir.'

'Now Milly, listen to me. From now until I tell you differently, Miss Charlotte is your mistress, you will take all your instructions from her, no-one else, you understand? Not my wife, nor my sister. Miss Charlotte is now in complete charge of all the rooms in this wing, and on this floor, and that includes your room Milly.'

'Thank you very much sir. Yes I understand,' then turning to Charlotte. 'Shall I fetch my things down now Miss Charlotte, or shall I wait until the morning?'

'I think perhaps you had better wait Milly, and now I think it's time you returned to your bed.'

'Yes Miss. Goodnight and thank you Miss. Goodnight sir,' just the hint of a curtsy, and she was gone.

Charlotte was just going to bid Richard goodnight, when the bedroom door opened, and once again his wife and sister burst in.

Richard's wife, normally a quiet, demure mousy kind of soul, had suddenly cast aside her lifelong image. For she stood in the middle of the bedroom floor, actually bristling with righteous anger, as Daphne looked on in bemused amazement. 'Now listen to me Richard Brackley! I'm not having you bringing your whore home to sleep in your bed, whilst I'm still married to you!'

Charlotte turned her beautiful eyes on the two women, gave them a withering look, bent down and kissed Richard, then with a 'Goodnight darling. Try and get some sleep,' and completely ignoring his wife's remarks, she slipped through the adjoining door into her own room.

Richard laughed aloud at the look of utter amazement, upon the faces of his wife and sister. 'There you are. It's all in your dirty little minds. You were both so sure Charlotte was sleeping with me.' Then he began to raise his voice. 'Well now you know. What the hell could I do for her anyway?' he was shouting now. 'Go on. Get out! And stay out!'

Charlotte had stayed close to the other side of her door, and had overheard everything. She smiled triumphantly to herself, as she snuggled down into her bed that night.

4

The following morning, Charlotte was rudely awakened from a deep sleep, by Richard banging on the other side of her bedroom wall. with the sharp end of one of his crutches. Her eyes still cobwebbed by sleep, she dashed into his room.

He was still raised up on the three pillows she had stacked behind him, and clutching the lower part of his body. 'For God's sake pass me a bottle, before it's too late, this bloody pain is driving me mad,' he gasped.

Charlotte handed him the bottle, then she noticed the clock. 'Good Heavens Richard! Look at the time. Do you realise it's still only four-o-clock? No wonder I was fast asleep before you started your banging, you must have awakened the whole household.'

'Yes well, serve 'em right if I did. Anyway I can't control these calls of nature you know, and you must realise, this is all part of your job. Here empty this for me,' he said, handing her the partially filled bottle, with no mention of a 'please' or 'thank you'.

Upon her return from the bathroom, Charlotte gave him the now empty bottle.

'What's this for?' he asked in some surprise. 'I've only just filled the damn thing.'

Charlotte smiled sweetly. 'Yes darling I know, and as you so succinctly put it, this may be part of my job, but if you think I'm going to leap out of bed at this unearthly hour in a morning, just to give you a stupid bottle, then you don't know me very well. You can keep it in your bed in future, at least it's warm, so the warmth may help you sleep. Good morning darling, do try and get some sleep,' then she kissed him, and was gone.

Later that same week, Richard remembered he had left his service revolver, complete with holster and leather belt, in the safe back at the hospital, so he sent Charlotte in the car to collect them.

Matron was engaged in her office, consequently Charlotte was sitting out in the hall, because the safe was in Matron's office, when a printed card, pinned to the notice board on the opposite wall, caught her attention.

ACCOMMODATION REQUIRED IN GOOD
RESIDENTIAL DISTRICT FOR DECENT
CLEAN LIVING DOCTOR. PLEASE REPLY TO
DR. PETER SINCLAIR.

On the way to the hospital, Charlotte had been mulling over in her mind, the extraordinary events of the past few days, and though she was reasonably happy with the life she had volunteered to share with Richard, she was well aware it could only be of a transient nature. For she knew that eventually, the tedious abhorrent tasks she had to perform daily, would gradually grind her down. Since her early teens, Charlotte had always been a frivolous, promiscuous, fun loving girl, and now this huge gap in her love life, was becoming decidedly intolerable.

The fact that she spent so much of her time, in such close proximity, to the near naked body of the man with whom she had once shared an extremely torrid love affair, did little to allay her longing, and the stark fact that he could do nothing for her, only served to exacerbate the problem.

Therefore, with these thoughts still fresh in her mind when she read the notice, Charlotte suddenly saw a small window of opportunity beginning to open for her, and jumping up from her chair, she crossed the hall, and quickly removed the card from the notice board.

As she turned, Matron's office door opened, and a nurse stepped out, but before she could close it, Charlotte had

53

knocked upon the open door, and walked into the office.

Matron looked up. 'Good afternoon, er' let me think a moment. Ah yes, Miss Charlotte isn't it? Companion to Sir Richard Brackley. How can I help you my dear?'

As Matron indicated a chair, Charlotte accepted it and sat down. She was astounded at the woman's memory, for they had only met on two previous occasions, and then very briefly. 'Good afternoon Matron. Yes you are quite right, I am Charlotte, though how you remember, considering the number of different people you see in a week, baffles me.'

Matron smiled, and looked at her beautiful visitor approvingly. 'My dear Miss Charlotte, I don't remember everyone, not by name anyway. However, you are rather special, and are somewhat inclined to stand out from the usual throng of visitors who pass through my office.'

Charlotte received the compliment, and thanked Matron with her wondrous smile. 'Yes I think perhaps you may be able to help me,' she produced the printed card. 'I saw this pinned to the notice board, can you please tell me where I can locate Dr. Sinclair? You see, since I moved to Brackley Hall, my own house is unoccupied, and I thought perhaps the doctor may be interested.'

'Why of course Miss Charlotte, what a kind thought, how very generous of you.' Matron pressed a small button on her desk, and almost immediately the door to an adjoining room opened, and a smartly dressed young woman came into the office.

'You rang Matron?' she asked.

'Yes Joan. Please take this young lady to Dr. Sinclair's office.'

Charlotte thanked Matron, and followed Joan out of the office and down the corridor. After passing several doors, her guide finally stopped outside the last door but one, and the sign on this particular door stated in bold capital letters; DR. PETER SINCLAIR.

Joan knocked and waited. A male voice bade them enter, and she walked in and held the door open for her companion, then followed her into the office. 'Miss Charlotte wishes to speak with you doctor.'

'Very well. Thank you Joan.'

Charlotte's escort walked out, and closed the door, the doctor was busily engaged writing something on a pad, and still hadn't lifted his head. Finally, he put down his pen and looked up. The shock to his system was far greater than anything he had diagnosed in his medical career, or had ever experienced in his life.

For the young lady sitting so nonchalantly on the other side of his desk, was the most beautiful creature he had ever seen. Beautiful? No! That wasn't good enough. She was ravishingly magnificent! He sat for a moment, utterly bereft of speech.

However, it was Charlotte who finally broke the silence. 'Good afternoon doctor. Please forgive me for coming to see you, without previously making an appointment, and I'm well aware you are a very busy man, but I think I may be able to help you with this,' she produced the small printed card.

Peter Sinclair didn't look at it, he was still staring in blatant admiration at his gorgeous visitor, who had seemed to light up his dingy office, like a ray of sunshine. Suddenly he realised she had stopped speaking, and mentally jerking himself back to reality. 'Sorry, you were saying?'

Charlotte smiled secretly to herself. Obviously Dr. Sinclair hadn't heard a single word she had said, and she knew the reason why. She was well aware of the impact she had upon most men, and for a brief moment she allowed her vivid imagination to run riot, as she studied the slim tapering fingers of the doctor, sitting behind his desk, and fantasised about his 'in' bedside manner!

Charlotte had been pleasantly surprised

when she entered Peter Sinclair's office, for she had never expected the doctor to be so handsome or so young. She correctly assumed him to be in his late thirties, [actually he was thirty nine]. He spoke again, breaking her line of thought.

'Sorry, what did Joan say your name is?'

'Charlotte. Miss Charlotte.'

'Very well, now how can I help you Miss Charlotte?'

His voice had a deep haunting quality, which seemed to ricochet off the back of his throat, and which Charlotte found quite fascinating. She allowed her beautiful green eyes to wash over him, then bestowed upon him her dazzling smile, and seeing the change in his expression, and the unguarded desire in his eyes, as they locked on to her's, Charlotte knew she could have him anytime she wished!

'It's not so much how you can help me doctor, it's how I may be able to help you. I removed this card from a notice board in the corridor, because I think I may have the answer to your housing problem.'

He laughed. 'It will be a miracle if you have my dear. That card has been on show for the last six months, and no-one has ever found me any suitable accommodation yet.'

Again Charlotte ravished him with her

smile, and her hypnotic green eyes. 'Well perhaps this is a miracle doc — please may I call you Peter?'

He replied in the affirmative, thinking at the time, that he would find it very difficult to refuse this particular young lady anything.

Charlotte pressed on. 'For you see, I have a small house overlooking the park, and at the moment it is standing empty, and I would very much prefer it to be occupied. If you can spare an hour this afternoon, I will drive you there now.'

He looked surprised. 'You drive?' he asked.

This time it was Charlotte's turn to laugh. 'Oh yes. I was driving ambulances for several months, during the heaviest casualties of the war, until the endless trains crowded with dying and wounded men, became too much for me, and I had to get out.'

He looked upon his elegant, beautiful visitor, with a new light of respect sharing the admiration in his eyes. Standing up, he removed his white coat, and replaced it with a very smart tunic, bearing the insignia of a major.

Somewhat to Charlotte's surprise, he was only two or three inches taller than herself, but quite broad, and she didn't mind his lack of height anyway, for it certainly did nothing to detract from his appeal, and she couldn't bear the thought of being seen in public with another 'bean pole'!

They walked out of the hospital together, and she stopped when they reached the Rolls.

He looked on in amazement, when Charlotte opened the car door. 'My God Charlotte! You can't take this. It belongs to Sir Richard Brackley. His family crest is on the door.'

Her black silken lashes fluttered, and she smiled at him. 'Please go round to the other side of the car Peter, open the door and get in. Yes I know this car belongs to Richard, and I can take it, for you see, I work for him.'

He stared at her. 'You work for Richard Brackley?' he stood there, apparently bereft of speech or further movement.

'Peter. Please get in the car.'

As though in a daze, he walked round the front of the car, and climbed in, he seemed incapable of any conversation, consequently Charlotte just concentrated on her driving.

Peter Sinclair had experienced a savage kaleidoscopic flashback, to eighteen years ago, when he was only twenty-one, and still at medical college. He had been courting Elaine for nearly three years, they were very much in love, and had become secretly engaged. It was Christmas, and they had both been invited to a ball at Brackley Hall. During the evening, he had suddenly missed Elaine, and had left the ballroom to search for her. Eventually, he had entered Richard Brackley's bedroom, and found the two of them in bed. A tremendous fight ensued, during which Elaine fled from the room, and finally Peter knocked out The Honourable Richard Brackley, leaving him sprawled unconscious across the blood spattered sheets, upon the bed where only moments before, he had been enjoying his latest conquest.

Two months later, Peter and Elaine were married, and he had accepted full responsibility for the handsome baby boy she had duly presented him with. He had taken his wife and son, and moved down south, but on the outbreak of war had joined the army, being sent over to France, and wounded during the early days of the war. After a while in hospital, and then convalescence, he had been promoted to Major, and posted to this hospital in Hull. He had never seen Richard Brackley since that fateful night, so long ago, and now here he was, riding in a car which belonged to the man he hated above all others, and sitting next to, who? Who the devil is she? She can't be Lady

Brackley, but if not, who? His mistress? His chauffeur?

The car had stopped, and Charlotte interrupted his line of thought. 'Here we are Peter. This is my house.'

She was about to open the car door, when he placed a restraining hand upon her arm. 'Please, just a moment Charlotte. Who are you? and why are you driving Richard Brackley's car?'

Charlotte looked at her passenger, and wondered if he knew Richard, and why he seemed so interested. 'As I told you earlier, I used to drive an ambulance, and one day whilst at the hospital, Richard asked me if I would go and live at Brackley Hall, to act as his companion. Well I agreed, and that is the reason my house is empty, and also why I'm driving his motorcar.'

Peter Sinclair emitted a short harsh laugh, though he wasn't smiling. 'Yes, when he saw you, I'll bet he invited you to his Brackley Hall. Companion 'eh, that's a new word for it, if ever I heard one.'

Slowly Charlotte turned her head, and locked those twin, brilliant hypnotic orbs upon his, and Peter knew instinctively, he had made a mistake.

'Sir Richard Brackley spends his life confined to a wheelchair,' she said coldly.

'And might I suggest, in future you keep all your dirty thoughts to yourself doctor!'

Charlotte was convinced, she had seen a macabre flash of joy, sweep across the countenance of Peter Sinclair, when she had mentioned the wheelchair. However, it had gone in an instant, to be replaced by a look of sympathy.

'Poor fellow,' said Peter. 'Didn't mean to upset you my dear. What happened?'

'He was an officer in the Guards, and was badly wounded in France. Unfortunately he will never walk again. Do you know him?'

'Did,' came the short reply.

'Whatever do you mean. Did? I was always under the impression that if you knew someone, then you knew them forever, or at least until you become senile.'

He smiled, bitterly, she thought. 'I knew him once, many years ago, in another life. One day, when I know you better, I will tell you the whole sordid story. However, please under no circumstance, reveal to Richard my name, or even that you have met me, and if I take your kind offer of accommodation, you must never tell him who your new tenant is. Will you promise?'

He placed his hand over her's, and looked pleadingly into her eyes, and immediately Charlotte melted. 'I promise,' she murmured, as she turned on that smile, which until now, only one man had ever been able to resist, and he was married to her sister! As Charlotte watched Peter's expression change, and that blatant look of naked desire cloud his eyes, the look with which she was so familiar in so many others, she knew her insatiable desire for close male contact, and endless lovemaking, would once again be satisfied.

Suddenly, quite spontaneously, he leaned across the car and kissed her full on the lips, and was instantly apologetic. 'Very sorry my dear, please believe me I am not in the habit of doing that kind of thing, but really you are so damned attractive.' He struggled to open the car door. 'How the hell do you open this thing?'

Charlotte realised he was obviously embarrassed, and decided to intervene, before he began to regret his impulsive gesture. She placed a comforting hand upon his arm. 'Peter, please calm down, there's no harm done, I wanted you to kiss me, and anyway I thoroughly enjoyed it.'

He ceased his frantic tugging at the door handle, and turned towards her, his expression an amalgam of disbelief, coupled with relief, and she detected an undercurrent of excitement in his voice when he spoke.

'You did? You really wanted me to kiss you, and you actually enjoyed it? My dear Charlotte, I don't give a damn what your house is like, if it was a tent I'd take it, if only to see you once a week when you come for the rent!' he abruptly stopped speaking, for he had blurted out those words at great speed, and was now almost gasping for breath.

Charlotte laughed. 'Oh! Peter, do please slow down a little. Are you married?'

The question came suddenly, yet she had spoken quietly. Even so, a sadness shadowed his face. 'Was. My wife died six years ago. Please forgive me if I seem a little disorientated, but you see I have had no contact with any woman, since Elaine's death.'

Charlotte felt her toes beginning to curl inside her shoes, and fought back an almost overwhelming desire to strip off her clothes right there in the car, and seduce this lovely man! Six years he had said. Hallelujah! Damn! shouldn't use Halle's name, not at a time like this. Miraculously, she spoke normally as she placed her hand over his. 'I'm terribly sorry about your wife's death Peter,' and she actually appeared to be, for as Charles had discovered, when Rose had introduced them, Charlotte was a consummate actress.

'It must be fate that brought us together this afternoon Peter, for you see, I too am alone in the world. My husband was reported missing, believed killed in France, during the early days of the war, that is the reason I joined the Ambulance Service, to try and help a little with the war effort, after he was so cruelly taken.'

She had tears in her beautiful eyes, and a break in her voice, and he was touched, as she fully intended he should be.

In an effort to break the emotion of the moment, he coughed slightly. 'Shall we have a look at your house now, please Charlotte?'

She understood what he was trying to do, and thanked him with her eyes.

They were in the living room, and he picked up a photograph from several standing on the sideboard. 'Who are these Charlotte?' Her name came easily to his lips, as if they were old friends.

'That is my sister Rose, her husband Charles Cartwright, me and our babies.'

His interest heightened. 'You have a child?'

'Yes, a boy, he lives with Rose and Charles at 'Mount Pleasant', the Cartwright family home in the country.'

'I thought I recognized that man!' David gesticulated. 'I have been out there to shooting parties a couple of times. Sister to the wife of Charles Cartwright 'eh? and companion to Sir Richard Brackley? My word Charlotte, you certainly move in the higher echelons of society.'

She smiled. 'Now please follow me Peter,' she said, as she climbed the stairs.

He did so with alacrity, studying her ankles, what little he could see of them. She had shown him two of the bedrooms, and now they were standing in the main bedroom, when he picked up a photograph of Richard Brackley, from a bedside table. 'Is that who I think it is?' he asked harshly

Charlotte, inwardly cursed herself for leaving a photograph of Richard, where anyone could see it, as she realised this latest catch was on the point of slipping the net, before she'd even had time to make a conquest! She was so long in replying, Peter spoke again.

'You expect me to believe that you only drive that bastard's car, and push him around in a wheelchair, when you have his photograph standing beside your bed?'

So desperate was Charlotte for the affection of a whole and fit man, with a supreme effort of will, she quelled the sudden surge of fury, and held at bay, the devil within, which would normally have erupted in a situation such as this. Instead of flaying him with her vitriolic tongue, she turned on her devastating smile, and in a voice which could only be associated with a soft summer breeze, she murmured softly. 'I'm terribly sorry you have taken this attitude, dearest Peter, for I can assure you everything I have told you about Richard and myself, is perfectly true. You see he is a very close friend of Charles Cartwright, actually he was best man at my sister's wedding, and when Charles heard how terribly Richard was wounded, and that he needed a live-in companion, he suggested me, because I had suffered so much trauma losing my husband, and then meeting all those wounded soldiers at the station every day, he thought a job would help me forget. There is no more to our relationship than that.'

'If that is so, then why for Heaven's sake, do you keep his photograph beside your bed?'

Charlotte, for all her gritting of teeth and biting of tongue, was now beginning to lose what little patience she possessed. She lifted her head, and her green hypnotic eyes bored into his. 'You may not have noticed, but I don't happen to live here anymore, and anyway, what the hell has it to do with you, whose photograph I have beside my bed? Now look here, do you want this bloody house or not?'

His expression changed, as he realised how riled she was. 'I'm dreadfully sorry Charlotte. You are quite right, of course it has nothing to do with me. I just couldn't bear the thought of a lovely young woman like you, being caught in the ghastly tentacles of a philandering pariah like Richard Brackley! Please forgive me. Yes of course I will take this house, I would be a fool to refuse it. How often will you require the rent? Monthly, or quarterly?'

Charlotte had been gazing out of the bedroom window. Slowly she turned, and once again allowed her beautiful eyes to lock onto his. 'Weekly,' she replied softly.

'Weekly?' he echoed. 'Do you have any specific reason for calling here, and collecting the rent every week? apart of course from the fact, that I may suddenly decide to leave the country.'

He was smiling when he asked the question, though the ever watchful Charlotte detected a definite undercurrent of excitement and expectancy in his whole demeanour. 'Yes I do,' she replied quietly. 'I have no wish to appear forward doctor, but I need you to thoroughly examine me, every week. And make love to me at the same time!' she added nonchalantly.

His brain in a turmoil, Peter stared in disbelief at this ravishing, very desirable young woman, who had sashayed into his office, and his life, less than a couple of hours ago. He suddenly remembered who she was. The paid companion, or whore, of Richard Brackley, the man to whom he bore a burning simmering hatred, the like of which, he could not begin to describe even to himself. He began to sweat, as he realised the wild possibilities of long awaited, sweet revenge, being offered to him so blatantly, by the devil's handmaiden, in the guise of this lovely creature, who had snared him so adroitly.

Suddenly he laughed. 'You. Forward? How could I ever think such a thing? Come here you little minx!' he said, as he crushed her to him, and they both fell, very conveniently, onto the bed!

So began a tempestuous, passionate relationship, which was doomed from the start, one which would rock the local aristocracy to it's very foundations, and which could ultimately, only end in disaster!

★ ★ ★

After that never to be forgotten afternoon of such wonderful emotions, in the arms of her new lover, Charlotte drove Peter back to the hospital. They kissed goodbye in the car, and as he was opening the car door, he turned to her. 'Now please don't forget my darling, you must never, under any circumstance, mention my name to Richard Brackley. Will you promise?'

She was warm and content now, and her beautiful green eyes were glowing with happiness. 'Yes my love, I promise,' she replied softly.

At the mention of Richard's name, Charlotte suddenly remembered the reason she had come to the hospital earlier that afternoon. 'Good Lord! I completely forgot. I came here today to collect Richard's service revolver, his holster and his belt. There you see, that's how you affect me.'

Peter chuckled, and walked round the car to hold the door open for her, then went into the hospital and stayed with her until she had retrieved her employer's possessions, then kissed her again, before she moved off.

As she drove home to 'Brackley Hall' during the late afternoon, Charlotte pondered the events of that day, and she experienced a frisson of pleasure, as she recalled the passionate lovemaking, with this new man in her life, and she actually began to tremble with excitement and anticipation, at the thought of the long halcyon days ahead.

Quite abruptly her mood changed, for she remembered the promise Peter had exhorted from her, and now she trembled, not with excitement, but with apprehension about the future, as she wondered what the deep secret was, which could cause such dire enmity, and stir up so much hatred between two grown men, both of whom had been her lovers!

5

In the autumn of that year, Rose presented Charles with a beautiful baby daughter, and on his way back to the yard, after registering the child's birth, he met Dr. Peter Sinclair.

The two men just stood and stared at each other for a few seconds, then almost simultaneously, recognition dawned on their faces.

Charles was the first to speak. 'Hello Peter,' he exclaimed. 'Sorry I didn't recognise you at first, it must be the uniform.'

'Probably,' agreed Peter, as the two friends shook hands. 'I say Charles, it must be nearly twenty years since we last met. How have you managed to stay at home? or are you on leave?'

Charles smiled grimly. 'No Peter, I am not on leave. I volunteered for the army, but the powers that be turned me down. They said I should do much more for the war effort, helping to build ships, here in Hull, than I could ever do over in France. Anyway Peter, look it's almost time for lunch, and I know of a good restaurant quite near, will you join me?'

Peter Sinclair agreed, and the two friends walked into the establishment, only to find, much to their disgust, that rationing was beginning to bite in the U.K. for meat was off the menu for two days a week, and of course this just happened to be one of those days. However, they were reasonably satisfied with a large helping of egg and chips.

After they had ordered, Peter turned to his companion. 'You know Charles, it was quite a coincidence bumping into you today, for you see I happen to be living in a house owned by your sister-in-law Charlotte.'

Charles was quite naturally surprised by this snippet of information. 'Why? Don't you have a house of your own? I seem to remember you were at medical college, and then you married. What happened Peter, did you become a doctor?'

'Oh yes, I'm a doctor Charles. At the moment I'm a major in the Medical Corps, stationed at one of the hospitals in Hull. I was serving in France, but received a wound which apparently was bad enough for me to be returned to England. I did get married Charles, but unfortunately my wife died. However, I have a son Michael, who at the moment is studying law at Cambridge. There, enough about me, what have you been doing these last few years?'

Charles told his friend, how he had attended the funeral of his grandparents at Watersmeet, of how he had caught a fleeting glimpse of this lovely girl in the cemetery, and had eventually persuaded her to become his wife, and of how he was now the proud father of two lovely children, first a son, and now a daughter.

The two friends became so involved in their conversation, and catching up on old times, they completely forgot about the time, until Peter suddenly looked at his watch. 'Good Heavens Charles, it's nearly two-o-clock, I have an appointment in fifteen minutes.'

So, they parted company, but not before Charles had extracted a promise from his companion, that he would call and meet his family at 'Mount Pleasant'.

★ ★ ★

Charlotte's life moved steadily on, but seemingly, never forward. She saw herself, as stuck in a rut of interminable drudgery, and disgusting unenviable, everyday tasks, lightened only by the occasional afternoon romp in her bed, with Dr. Peter Sinclair! Until the afternoon of Christmas Eve nineteen seventeen.

74

During the morning of that fateful day, Charles had called upon his old friend Richard at Brackley Hall. Charlotte was just as pleased as her employer to see him, for she had been trying to think of an excuse to get away and visit the hospital, to take a few small Christmas presents for some of the more seriously wounded patients.

However, she was delayed by a few of the more vociferous among them, each wanting to thank her personally, and to bestow upon her a good will Christmas kiss. Consequently, lunch was over by the time she returned, and Richard was fuming.

'Where the hell have you been until now,' he shouted, immediately she appeared in the doorway

Charlotte stopped and stared uncomprehendingly, amazed at the ferocity of his verbal onslaught, and quite naturally, though wrongly, suspected he must be suffering a particularly bad spasm of intolerable pain. She smiled reassuringly. 'Sorry darling, I was unavoidably delayed at the hospital, though I did think you would have waited for me, before you had your lunch.'

'Wait for you!' he exploded, the colour rushing to his cheeks, and his whole demeanour showing the pain he was now suffering, though Charlotte could see it was largely self induced.

'Wait for you!' he shouted furiously. 'Why the hell should I? You two timing, conniving bitch! I want you out of this house, and out of my life forever, within the hour!'

Very slowly, Charlotte lifted her head and stared at her employer, and though her brilliant hypnotic green eyes were boring into his, her face remained a mask. At last, through a red slit of a mouth, and lips which hardly seemed to move, she asked, in little more than a sibilant whisper; 'Richard, will you please tell me what I have done, to warrant such vile treatment as this?'

He emitted a short laugh, though no smile accompanied the sound, or wrought any change in the hard lines of his cruel aristocratic mouth. 'Don't try and play the innocent with me miss. Tell you? Yes I'll bloody tell you. I have been given to understand you have been having afternoon orgies with that bastard, Peter Sinclair!' He was becoming more agitated now, and was quickly losing what little self control he had, as he began to shout at her again, his language interspersed with many vile epithets. 'My God Charlotte! To think you were carrying on with that — that — and in my house!'

It was then that Sir Richard Brackley saw the real Charlotte. The glimpse he had seen of her in his room at that London hotel, was as nothing compared to the snarling she devil, who turned on him now. Her glittering eyes seemed to be glowing with a green luminosity from within, and as though in some kind of trance, he sat mesmerised, as a rabbit before a snake, unable to move or speak, while she verbally tore him apart.

'You poor stupid pathetic fool,' she hissed through her slit of a mouth. 'You knew perfectly well what I was like, before you ever offered me this bloody awful stinking job, and if you think I'm going to spend the rest of my life attending to the needs and every whim of a totally useless, selfish moron like you, then all I can say is, you're a bigger damn fool than even I thought. Damn it all Richard, I'm still young, and to some men, apparently very desirable, and if one of those men wishes to take me to bed occasionally, then so be it, for what I do in my spare time has absolutely nothing to do with you. Incidentally, that is not your house, it is mine. You put the deeds in my name, remember? Anyway, why all this enmity between you and Peter? For I can assure you, he is equally as full of hate for you, as you are for him. Now I'll go pack, while you try and find some other poor stupid idiot to look after you, and clean up your filthy mess!'

She turned to go, but when she had almost reached the door, he called her name. 'Charlotte!'

She stopped, and slowly turned to face him. He was white with rage, no-one had ever previously spoken to him like that, and now as his lip curled in an ugly sneer, his voice was no more than a snarl. 'So, obviously your lover has not told you the reason for his all consuming hatred of me. Please allow me to enlighten you, my dear Charlotte,' each word was a barb, tipped with venom.

'One Christmas Eve, some twenty years ago, we had a Ball here at Brackley Hall. Well your current lover, Peter Sinclair, and the girl to whom he was engaged, were invited. I have no wish to boast, but the ghastly young thing couldn't leave me alone, and consequently we finished up in my bed. Unfortunately, Peter walked into the room and caught us 'at it', you might say. There was the most unholy row, which resulted in him receiving the thrashing of his miserable life, and me throwing him out. I have never seen him since that night.'

Without so much as a second glance or a 'good bye', Charlotte turned on her heel, and strode out of the room. She packed her cases, and then, amid much wailing from Milly, she finally persuaded the girl to go and find George.

There was very little conversation on the journey to her house, and it was a very sad faced George indeed, who brought the car to a halt, in exactly the same place he had parked, when he'd been sent to collect Charlotte, only those few short months ago.

Charlotte turned in her seat, gripped his hand and kissed him on the cheek. 'Thank you George, for being my friend,' she said huskily. 'If ever you happen to pass this way again sometime in the future, please call and see me.'

George forced a smile. 'Thank you Miss Charlotte, I might just do that. Now I don't know why you're leaving, and I'm not asking, but I do know, his Lordship will never find another one to match you, and I'll bet in less than three months, he'll be round here, wanting you back again. Go let yourself in lass, and I'll bring the cases.'

Charlotte thanked him with her wondrous smile, and alighted from the car. She walked down the short path towards her front door, the key in her hand, yet when she tried it, she discovered the key wouldn't fit! In a sudden blind panic, she wondered if Peter had changed the lock, then even worse. Maybe Richard had changed it! Then quite suddenly the door opened, and Charlotte received one of the greatest shocks of her young life.

For standing there, holding the door open was a very handsome young man! However, this was no ordinary young man, for he was the exact replica of the beautiful young man, with whom she had laid naked in a small wood, on the hillside just below Watersmeet, and with whom she had made such wonderful, exquisite, unforgettable love!

She stumbled forward and would have fallen, but for the strong arms of the young stranger. For a moment he held her tight, and enjoyed the fragrant closeness of her, before leading her to a chair beside a good fire in the front room, and gently lowering her on to the seat.

Charlotte's mind was in a turmoil. She had just left Richard Brackley, no more than a pathetic shell of his former self, and now, standing beside her after helping her across the room, was a younger perfect clone of the Richard she had once known three years ago! Then through her clouded chaotic mind, came some of the last words he had said to her, before throwing her out less than an hour ago. 'She couldn't leave me alone, and we finished up in my bed!'.

Hardened as she was to life's vicissitudes, Charlotte paled beneath her make-up, as she gripped the arms of her chair.

'Can I get you anything,' asked her companion apprehensively.

With a trembling finger, Charlotte pointed to the sideboard. 'Brandy. Left hand cupboard,' she blurted out

Quickly he found the bottle, and poured out a good measure. Silently he passed her the glass, and watched intently as she gulped down the contents. Miraculously, almost within seconds, her colour and her composure had returned, as the fiery liquid burnt it's way down.

At that moment, there was a light knock on the door, and George stepped into the room. 'Begging your pardon Miss. Your cases are in the hall, I'd best be on my way now, before his Lordship sends out a search party. It's been good knowing you, look after yourself, and best of luck Miss.'

George turned to go, but Charlotte, now fully recovered, jumped to her feet, and called him back. 'Here George, I have something for you, and thank you once again for all you have done for me,' she brought a gold sovereign from her purse and thrust it into the hand of an embarrassed George.

Though he protested vehemently, Charlotte was adamant, and made him accept her offering, then she slipped her arm through his, and walked with him to the car. As she silently watched him drive away, she was surprised by the tears pricking behind her eyelids, and angrily wiped her eyes with a minuscule piece of almost transparent lace, which apparently went under the name of a handkerchief.

When Charlotte returned to the room, the handsome young stranger was standing with his back to the fire, waiting for her.

'Sorry about that slight interruption,' she said lightly, forcing a smile. 'Now let's see, where were we?' she asked, as she removed her coat, and laid it nonchalantly over the back of a chair. 'Ha yes. I remember. You opened the door for me, and scared me half to death. By the way, I hope you don't mind me asking, but who are you?'

The young man frowned slightly, and waited for her to sit down. Then seating himself, he looked at this vision of beauty who had suddenly invaded his privacy. 'Don't you think it is I, who should be asking who you are? I mean you come wandering in here, have your man dump your cases in the hall, with never so much as a please or thank you. Incidentally, how did you know the brandy was in that particular cupboard?'

While he was speaking, Charlotte had been staring into the fire, now however, she slowly turned her head, and allowed her beautiful hypnotic eyes to wash over him, and for the first time, the young man caught the full impact of those wondrous green orbs, and he knew instantly, he was lost, and that whoever she was, he would worship this beautiful woman for the rest of his life!

She smiled, that alluring captivating smile, which only one man had ever been able to resist. 'I knew the brandy was in that cupboard my dear, because I put it there. You see, I own this house, and I lived here until Dr. Sinclair moved in.'

Her youthful companion's countenance was an amalgam of disbelief, incredulity and embarrassment. At last he spoke. 'So, you must be Miss Charlotte,' he stammered. 'I say, I'm awfully sorry, I had no idea. Fancy my father finding someone as beautiful, and as young as you, for his landlady.'

Realising what he had blurted out, the young man blushed to the roots of his hair. 'Oh! Terribly sorry Miss Charlotte, forgive me. Please may we start again?'

The youth held out his hand, and suddenly smiled. 'Pleased to meet you Miss Charlotte. I'm Michael, Michael Sinclair! As you may have already deduced, my father is Dr. Peter Sinclair. He asked me to come and stay with him for the Christmas period, you see I'm on holiday from college for a couple of weeks.'

Charlotte enjoyed the bloom of youth emanating from her new friend, and noted the firm grip, as she accepted the proffered palm, and as usual, she held on just that moment longer than was really necessary.

All manner of wildly differing plans and schemes, for the future of Michael Sinclair, were darting around in Charlotte's ever fertile mercenary brain. Also, when she looked at Michael, she found it impossible to forget her wonderful ex-lover, Richard Brackley!

Still with that thought in mind, she said quietly. 'How wonderful for you, being able to spend Christmas with your father.' She then walked into the hall. 'Please Michael,' she called over her shoulder.

In a few quick strides, he was by her side. 'Yes Miss Charlotte?' he replied expectantly.

'Michael. Please drop the miss bit, and just call me Charlotte. After all, we are almost the same age,' she added seductively. 'Now if you will carry my cases upstairs for me, to the main bedroom at the front, I shall be forever in your debt.'

'Yes M — . Charlotte, of course,' he replied, picking up the two heavy cases, and staggering upstairs with them, doing his best to make them appear light and of no consequence.

Charlotte followed, smiling quietly to herself, yet admiring his youthful, handsome physique, and knowing exactly how she was going to seduce this perfect copy of her previous lover!

Michael preceded her into the bedroom, where he hoisted the two cases up onto the bed, then wiped his brow with a clean white handkerchief.

'No Michael, not on the bed please. They may be a nuisance later,' she remonstrated.

After he had removed the offending cases, Charlotte turned her back on him. 'Michael, please be a dear and unbutton my dress down the back!'

With trembling fingers he did as she asked.

That afternoon Michael Sinclair was transported to realms of ecstasy, dizzy heights he could never have imagined existed, only in books, and certainly not in any law books he had read at college!

Later, the two lovers were dressed, and sitting before a lovely fire in the front room, enjoying a cup of tea, and Charlotte was mentally hugging herself with glee. For she had hit upon a plan so devastatingly wild in its concept, and yet though fraught with danger and risk to herself, so brilliant in it's execution if she were to succeed, that her future and that of her son, would be assured forever! She became so excited with her idea, she almost cried out aloud in jubilation.

Fortunately, her and Michael were sitting in separate chairs, for at that moment, with no warning, Peter Sinclair entered the room.

His face lit up when he saw Charlotte. 'Hello my dear, I see you have already met my son. What are you doing here at this time of day? Has that moron Brackley given you a holiday for Christmas?' he asked jokingly, as he bent down before the fire to warm his hands.

'No Peter,' said Charlotte quietly, yet with a look which told him to be careful what he said. 'He's given me the sack!'

He stared at her incredulously. 'Given you the sack!' he repeated. 'What the hell for? Anyway I have been granted a few days leave for Christmas, so we'll have a wonderful time, all three of us.'

Michael stepped forward. 'I have put Charlotte's cases in the bedroom you were in father, so you will have to move into the other one.'

Charlotte was saved any embarrassment,

for at that precise moment, just as Peter opened his mouth to protest, there was a knock on the front door, then they heard it open, and stood waiting expectantly.

A moment later Rose came into the room.

Charlotte rushed to meet her. 'Oh! Rose, how pleased I am to see you,' she greeted her fervently. 'Allow me to present Dr. Peter Sinclair and his son Michael,' she turned to the two men. 'My sister Rose.'

When the introductions had been duly completed, Charlotte turned once again to her sister. 'Are you staying for tea?'

With some difficulty, Rose tried not to appear too surprised by this very unusual, cordial welcome extended by her sister. 'No my dear. Actually, I have come to take you home to 'Mount Pleasant', to stay with us for Christmas. You see I telephoned you at Brackley Hall, but Richard said you had left, so I naturally thought you might be here. Will you come with me?'

Charlotte thought quickly. If she went with Rose, and stayed for the Christmas holiday, then that would save Peter any embarrassment through his son being at home. On the other hand however, she definitely didn't want to lose touch with Michael, particularly when he was only staying for a short while. Suddenly, she came to a snap decision. 'Why thank you Rose,' she beamed. 'Yes of course I will come with you, and stay over for Christmas, providing you will bring me back the day after Boxing Day. One thing, you won't have to wait for me to pack. Michael, be a dear and please bring my cases downstairs again.'

Rose flung her arms around her sister and hugged her. 'Oh! Charlotte, of course I will bring you back,' she said happily. Then in the wonderful generous way she had, she turned to Peter. 'Would you and your son, care to spend Christmas Day with us tomorrow Peter?'

Peter Sinclair looked at this beautiful woman, and thought how lucky his friend Charles Cartwright was. 'Yes, indeed. We shall be very pleased and honoured to spend the day with you and Charles.'

6

As they emerged from the trees, in the gathering gloom of that Christmas Eve, Charlotte could see the welcoming glow of flickering firelight, through two of the downstairs windows at the front of 'Mount Pleasant', yet it was with a strange feeling of foreboding, that she entered the house.

Miles and Ruth met her in the hall, and Ruth greeted her with an affectionate hug and kiss, then Charles stepped forward, and she experienced mixed feelings of ardent love for him, and passionate hatred of her sister, as he bent and kissed her on the cheek. Even so, Charlotte had great difficulty in fighting back an overwhelming desire to crush her lips upon his!

However, she was quite unexpectedly saved, from what could so easily have become a very embarrassing bizarre situation, by the sudden appearance of her father.

Apparently, Charles had been over to Watersmeet, to bring Edward back for the celebrations again this year. Charlotte immediately released Charles, and moved quickly forward to greet her father.

'Hello father,' she gushed. 'What a lovely surprise, I had no idea you were here, Rose never told me.'

'I know lass, I asked her not to. You see I wanted to surprise you,' replied her father, as he embraced her affectionately. 'By, you look well our Charlotte, motherhood must suit you.'

'Yes I believe it does father,' she replied gaily, never giving a thought to the fact, that she hadn't been near her son for at least four months! 'Have you seen Richard yet?'

'Yes lass, I have that, and he's the image of his father, poor Halle, may God rest his soul.'

Charlotte stared at him, open mouthed. 'What do you mean? Like his father?' she asked, in little more than a whisper.

Edward looked at his wayward daughter, a puzzled frown upon his brow. 'Why, exactly what I say lass. Your baby is the absolute image of his poor dead father!' Edward turned to his other daughter. 'Isn't that right, our Rose?'

Rose was smiling. For some strange reason she was actually enjoying her sister's obvious discomfort. 'Yes father, indeed it is, as you say Richard is the absolute image of his father Halle.'

'All right our Rose, there's no need to

appear so damned happy about it,' Charlotte flung at her. 'Where is he, I want to see him?'

Rose led her sister upstairs to the nursery, where the two boys were playing happily on the floor with Alice.

Alice jumped to her feet when her employer entered the room. 'Hello Miss Charlotte. How lovely to see you. Are you staying for Christmas?'

'Yes Alice. Now which one is Richard?'

Both Rose and Alice looked at her askance. Rose was the first to find her voice. 'Really, our Charlotte! Do you mean to say, you have no idea which one is your own son?'

Charlotte whirled on her. 'No I haven't, anyway what's so important about that? You know perfectly well, I haven't seen him for some time, and all kids at this age look alike to me.'

'Alice, please just show her which one is Richard,' said Rose quietly.

Alice picked up the little boy and brought him to Charlotte. 'Here you are Richard. This is your mummy,' she murmured.

Charlotte took the child in her arms, then turned him around, and gazed intently at his face. 'My God Rose!' she exclaimed, the colour suddenly drained from her countenance. 'You are right, he is the

91

image of Halle! How can I ever explain this to Richard Brackley.'

'Why should you have to explain anything to him?' said a quiet voice from the doorway.

The three women turned as one, to find Edward standing there. Apparently he had come upstairs unheard and unseen, and they had no idea how much of their conversation he had overheard, though he had certainly listened to the last part.

For once in her short, yet chequered career, Charlotte was completely at a loss for words. She turned automatically to her sister for help, but this time there was none forthcoming, and she just stood, staring almost pleadingly at her father.

'I see,' said Edward. 'Apparently, you either have no explanation for your remarks, or you have no wish to give me one. Well, let's see what you have to say, if I tell you what mine is. I believe that you thought, Richard Brackley was the father of your child, and that would explain the reason you are living in his house, instead of all that other rubbish, you told me the last time I was here. I'm pleased I was here to see this day. It's high time you were brought down a peg or two our Charlotte. So, what will you do if your fancy man wants his house back, when he discovers the boy isn't his?'

Charlotte stood perfectly still, she was thinking furiously, when suddenly she remembered her exploits in the bedroom of her house, earlier that afternoon, and the plan she had begun to formulate, and which now manifested itself so clearly in her assiduous mind. She shocked her companions, with a sudden loud horrible laugh, though it was more like a cackle. 'So, you all think I'm done for, do you?' she shrieked. Then turning her glittering eyes directly upon Edward. 'Don't you worry about your little Charlotte, father. I shall be all right. I have a plan which will bring me out right on top of the heap, without any help from this baby, or anyone else. Here take him Alice, and thank you for looking after him so well.'

Edward snorted. 'So, you have a plan do you? I shall never know how I ever came to spawn a whore such as you!'

Everyone was saved any further embarrassment, or verbal insults, by the faint jarring ring of the telephone, down in that cavern of a hall, and immediately after it stopped, Charles shouting from the bottom of the stairs for Charlotte.

She leaned over the landing. 'Who is it Charles?' she asked.

'Richard, asking for you.'

'I'm sorry Charles, I don't know any

Richard,' she replied glibly.

'Is that what you wish me to tell him?'

'Yes,' came the short reply.

She could hear faint muttering from below, then Charles came to the foot of the stairs again, and looked up, she was still leaning over the bannister.

'He says, if you don't come to the phone Charlotte, he will ring continuously, all through the night if necessary, until you do.'

With a tiny triumphant quirk of a smile, just touching the corners of her sensuous mouth, Charlotte descended the stairs, and relieved Charles of the instrument.

'Hello,' she said, sounding as offhand, and as cold as she possibly could.

'Charlotte,' came the faint pleading voice from the other end of the line. 'Please, my darling Charlotte. Please come home. I'm terribly sorry for what I said. I can't live without you Charlotte. If you don't come, I shall kill myself! I mean it. I will give you anything, everything, I don't care anymore. Please say you forgive me, and you will come back to me,' his voice faded, and his words became almost incoherent, towards the end of the sentence.

Charlotte smiled to herself. 'Very well Richard, I will return to your home, but

I'm afraid I shall have some rather stringent conditions for you to accept, before I do. Also, I won't be able to come, until the afternoon of the day after Boxing Day. Do you understand?'

'Yes, I understand,' he broke off as a spasm of coughing racked his frail and wasted body. At last the spasm was over, and Charlotte waited.

'Sorry about that. Yes I understand. I will abide by any conditions you care to set, no matter how harsh they may be, only for God's sake come to me Charlotte! Charlotte, are you there?' he sounded panic stricken.

'Yes, yes, of course I'm here Richard. Now don't you worry anymore, I'll see you after Christmas, and Richard, do have a Happy Christmas!' she just couldn't help but smile to herself at the irony of her last remark.

Charlotte had seen her sister come downstairs, so she rejoined the rest of the family in the drawing room, instead of going up to see her son.

'Was that Richard Brackley,' asked her father abruptly.

'Yes father, it was. And before you ask, he wants me to go and look after him again, after Christmas.'

Edward snorted. 'And of course you said

95

yes,' he said, with heavy sarcasm.

Charlotte smiled wickedly. 'However did you guess father? Yes, I shall be going on Thursday, the day after Boxing Day.'

The conversation was slightly muted, that Christmas Eve at 'Mount Pleasant'. However, Christmas Day dawned bright and clear, with a good sharp frost, and a short spell of a winter's sun. All the family went to church, which of course, was a must, on Christmas morning, and they had just returned, when Peter Sinclair and his son Michael, came down the drive.

The family were gathered before a blazing log fire in the large drawing room, when the visitors were shown in. Charles moved quickly forward. 'Peter, how good to see you,' he greeted his friend. 'And I suppose this fine looking young man, is your son, am I correct?'

'Yes Charles, indeed you are. Michael, meet an old friend of mine. Charles Cartwright,' the two shook hands, and then father and son were introduced to the remainder of the family.

Peter Sinclair and his son Michael, enjoyed themselves immensely, that Christmas Day at 'Mount Pleasant'. The goose complete with all the trimmings, then Christmas pudding with brandy sauce, was absolutely scrumptious, and it was with regret, that the two had to leave, and return to their quiet house, overlooking the park in Hull. Not, however, before Michael had the opportunity to have a few words with Charlotte.

He had walked into the library alone, and was examining the fine array of books lining the many shelves, when the door opened and she joined him.

Immediately Charlotte saw her new lover, she quickly closed the door, ran across the intervening space between them, and literally threw herself into his eager arms. 'Oh! Michael,' she purred. 'It was dreadful having to sit opposite you at the dining table, and not be able to say to you, all the things I so much wanted to say.'

He crushed her to him, and held her close, almost losing his self-control, as the glorious scent of her luxurious hair, assailed his nostrils, and he felt the heat of her sensuous body, through his clothes. 'No! darling. Not here, it's far too dangerous. Charles or my father could walk in at any moment,' he gasped, wiping the perspiration off his brow, as he felt the sweat weld his shirt to his back.

Realising the wisdom of his words, Charlotte slowly, reluctantly, and very regretfully eased her burning vibrant, slender young body, very gently away from his, and with a heartfelt cry of passionate resignation. 'Oh! Dammit Michael, why must we always have to conform to these old fuddy duddy's rules? Why don't we make some of our own? I do love you so. When can we meet again?'

He was still holding her, though not quite so tightly, and he had now regained his normal composure. He kissed her lightly. 'Anytime you say darling. I'm on my own all day long, while father is at the hospital, and I'm home for another two weeks. So you see, it is entirely up to you,' he kissed her again.

'Alright, stay by the telephone, I will call you at the first opportunity.'

She allowed him to indulge in one more passionate lover's kiss, then gently but firmly pushed him away, and moved towards the door. 'Goodbye my darling. I'll see you later in the week. By the way. Under no circumstance breathe a word of our relationship to your father,' and she was gone, leaving him to ponder over the meaning of her last remark.

When Charles and Rose were alone together later that night, he turned to her. 'Rose,' he said quietly.

She was almost asleep. 'Yes darling,' she replied drowsily.

'Who did Michael Sinclair remind you of?'

Rose was silent for so long, he thought she must have dozed off, and was on the point of giving her a nudge, when she suddenly spoke.

'I know what you are going to say Charles, and really it doesn't bear thinking about. Dr. Sinclair must also be aware of the resemblance his son has to Richard. I presume it is he, we are discussing.'

'Yes Rose, it is Richard we are discussing. How old would you think Michael is?'

'I really don't know. He's a fine well built young man. He could be anywhere between eighteen and twenty three. What do you think?'

Charles was thinking hard, delving deep in his memories of times long gone. He was thinking of a rather special night, many years ago, when he had escorted a young lady to a certain Ball, held at Brackley Hall, and of how the night had ended in a complete fiasco, when Peter Sinclair had found Richard Brackley in bed with his fiancee. Of how this had resulted in a terrible fight, and of how he, Charles had been called upon to rescue his friend, otherwise Peter would have very probably killed him!

'I asked, how old do you think Michael is?'

said Rose, wondering if Charles was losing interest in the matter.

'Yes, so you did my dear, and now I think I know. I would say he will be twenty years old next September.'

'How on earth can you possibly know that Charles?' she asked curiously.

He told her the whole sorry story, and when he had finished, the only comment Rose made was. 'How sad. Poor Peter, and he seems such a nice man.'

When Charlotte left her sister's house, during the morning of the day after Boxing Day, instead of going straight to Brackley Hall, she called in at her own house, and as she hoped he would be, Michael was there.

He saw her walk down the short path, and by the time she reached the door, he was holding it open for her. 'Hello my dear Charlotte, what a lovely surprise, I never expected to see you this morning,' he greeted her, as he took her in his arms, and hungrily sought her lips with his own.

Charlotte immediately reciprocated, and within minutes, they were upstairs on her bed, as though the world would end before they had time to continue, where they had left off during the afternoon of Christmas Eve.

Afterwards, they just lay quietly in each

other's arms, as naked as the day they were born. At last Michael raised himself on one elbow, and allowed his gaze to trawl the length of her glorious body, finally looking into those beautiful green hypnotic eyes, he found so fascinating, and which he had found impossible to resist.

'Michael, will you always love me like this?' she murmured happily, as she snuggled closer.

He kissed her. 'Yes my darling. You know I will. I really think we should be getting dressed now my dear, it must be lunch time. I don't know about you, but personally, I'm ravenous.'

After lunch, Charlotte telephoned Brackley Hall, and asked to speak to Richard. 'Hello Richard, will you please send George along to my house to collect me and my luggage?'

There was a moment's hesitation at the other end of the line, finally he spoke. 'Your house? I hope you are not sleeping with that moron Sinclair! I thought you were staying with your sister,' his voice sounded decidedly unfriendly.

Charlotte fought to hold her temper in check. 'I'm sorry Richard, I was under the impression you needed me to come back to you,' she replied, a touch of sarcasm in her voice.

'Of course I do. You know perfectly well how I feel about you, and I just can't carry on living without you.'

He sounded desperate, and she smiled to herself. 'Very well then, if that is the case, you really must change your attitude towards me Richard, because if you continue to think and talk in this vein, about every man with whom I associate, then your peaceful olive branch is already broken, and it will be much better for us both, if I stay as far away from you as possible.'

'Charlotte! No! No, please don't say such things. I promise I will not interfere in any aspect of your life, ever again, if only you will come to me.'

Charlotte experienced no sense of pity, for the gibbering wreck of a man on the other end of the line, only a feeling of nausea, at the thought of some of the gruesome tasks which lay ahead, if she returned to Brackley Hall. Yet return she must, if she wished to carry her plan through to a successful conclusion.

She took a firm grip upon herself and her voice. 'Very well Richard. Terribly sorry if I sounded just a little harsh, but you see, from this distance darling, it is very difficult for me to visualise how ill you really are. Please send George for me my dearest, and I will come to you immediately.'

As Charlotte replaced the receiver upon it's hook, she turned around to find a distressed looking Michael standing in the doorway, leading to the kitchen. Not knowing how much of her side of the conversation he had overheard, she moved quickly to his side, and putting her arms around him, she held him close.

'Dear Michael. Please take no notice of anything you may have just heard. Believe me, I was only acting, and everything I said, was in the best interests of both of us.'

He stared at her. 'Do you mean you and I?'

'That is exactly what I mean Michael, and one day, soon I hope, I shall be able to reveal to you all the marvellous details of my wonderful plan.'

Michael looked deep into those beautiful eyes, and though he felt she was lying, he couldn't help but believe her!

As George staggered into her bedroom with the second suit case, and hoisted it up onto the bed, Charlotte kissed him affectionately upon his cheek. 'Thank you George. The best part of being back here, is seeing you again.'

Had he been a younger man, George may have taken advantage of such an extravagant compliment, however, he was well aware of his limitations, and smiling broadly, 'Thank you Miss Charlotte. That kiss, made carrying them cases up here a real pleasure,' he replied, wiping the perspiration from his brow.

After George had gone, Charlotte was in the process of removing the contents from one of her cases, when there was a light knock upon her bedroom door, and Milly came in.

'Oh! Miss. It's grand to see you back here again,' she enthused, as she began to help Charlotte hang her clothes in the wardrobe. 'I couldn't have stayed much longer. It's been awful since you left us. He's been ranting and raving, nobody could do anything right, and sometimes his language was terrible. Please Miss Charlotte, don't ever leave us again,' the girl pleaded tearfully.

Charlotte was about to reply, when Richard blasted the quiet of the afternoon, from the next room. 'Milly! Milly!' he roared. 'Where the hell are you?'

Milly turned a shade paler. 'Oh! Miss. You go please. I can't stand much more.'

Charlotte could see the girl was nearly scared out of her wits, and tried to calm her. 'There there dear, don't worry, I know how to handle his Lordship. You stay here, and continue putting my things away, while I go and surprise him.'

Once again the silence was shattered. 'Milly! Are you there?'

Charlotte quietly opened the adjoining door, and slipped into his room. He was sitting in his wheel chair, gazing out the window. She crept up behind him, and placed both her hands over his eyes.

He jumped. 'Who the hell is that?' he snorted. 'Don't play silly bloody games with me Miss, or I'll sack you!'

She removed her hands, and turned his chair round. 'Please don't sack me yet kind sir. I've only started today.'

'Charlotte!' he shouted ecstatically. 'Thank God you have come at last. I'm going mad living with these morons. Don't ever leave me again, if you do, I shall kill myself. I have very little to live for anyway, but without you I should be far better off dead!'

'Now Richard, that is no way to talk,' she replied sternly, for she was sure he meant what he said, and he would definitely be of no use to her, if he carried out his stupid suicidal threat!

'Anyway Richard, you will never speak like that again, when you have heard my news.' Charlotte had previously thought out her plan very carefully, and had not intended to broach the matter for a few days, but his morale seemed so low, she was afraid he may try to harm himself.

'Why. What news could you possibly bring, that would make me feel any better?' he asked disconsolately, for the joy he had manifested upon her return, had quickly evaporated.

'Well my darling,' she began, dropping to her knees in front of him, and holding his hand, while looking up into his face with her beautiful, green hypnotic eyes. 'I have some very good news, and some very bad news for you. First of all, I will give you the bad news. I saw our baby whilst at 'Mount Pleasant' over Christmas, and I hate having to tell you this Richard, but I'm afraid he isn't our baby!'

He gripped her hand so hard, she cried out, and he was instantly apologetic. 'Sorry Charlotte, didn't intend to hurt you. What the hell do you mean, he isn't our baby?'

'Exactly what I say. He is the image of Halle, his dead father, everyone has noticed the likeness, and talked of little else, all the time I was there. I didn't know how to tell you, after all you have done for us, opening a bank account for young Richard, and putting that house in my name, so we had somewhere to live. Oh! Dear Richard, I'm so terribly sorry, I don't know what to do. Of course I shall have to give you back my lovely house. I cannot possibly keep it now, or the money you have given me,' her eyes had filled with tears, and Charlotte was quite pleased with the act she was putting on!

'There, there Charlotte. Please don't cry, here,' he said quietly, handing her a clean white handkerchief. 'Now wipe away your tears, remember you're supposed to be here to cheer me up, and before we have anymore silly talk about you giving up your home, tell me the good news.'

She accepted the proffered handkerchief, released her grip upon his hand, and stood up. Wiping her eyes, she looked down at him and produced a wan little smile. 'Oh! Richard, you're so good to me, what a fool I was to leave you. However, some good may have come out of my short stay away from you. I know you hate the mention of his name, but I discovered one or two interesting snippets of information about your friend Peter Sinclair.'

Instantly his whole attitude changed. 'What the hell do you mean?' he shouted. 'You know very well, he's no friend of mine, and I don't want you associating with him, is that clear?'

'Perfectly, my Lord,' she answered coldly.

'And I'm telling you now, don't ever shout at me again.'

He realised she was hurt. 'I'm terribly sorry Charlotte, please forgive me, don't let's go down that road again, I don't want to lose you a second time, but you know I can't bear to hear that man's name mentioned.'

She flashed him a brilliant smile. 'Yes I know my darling, only I think you may change your mind a little, when you have heard what I have to say. When I left here on Christmas Eve, I had George take me home. Well the front door wasn't locked, and a handsome young man opened it for me. I was so shocked, I had to go in and sit down, and it was quite a few minutes before I recovered.'

'Why, had someone broken in?' he asked, a worried frown creasing his brow.

She smiled. 'No, he wasn't a burglar. What so devastated me, was the fact, that I had just left you, and yet, here you were holding the door open for me!'

He stared at her. 'What do you mean, how the devil could it be me?'

'That is just what I thought, then when I looked more closely at this young man, I could see he was obviously too young to be you, but he was the exact image of what you must have been, when you were a younger man. Well bearing in mind what you had told me, about your fornicating with a certain gentleman's fiancee, and after asking Charles, one or two surreptitious questions over Christmas, I came up with the distinct conviction, that the handsome young man, living in my house, is none other, than the only, albeit illegitimate, son and heir, of one Sir Richard Brackley, to put it simply. You my darling!'

Richard just sat and stared at his lovely companion, momentarily bereft of speech, whilst she was quite content to wait, and allow his brain to assimilate this momentous piece of news.

At length he spoke. 'Charlotte, are you telling me, that after all these years, I really have a grown up son?' he asked, a restrained eagerness in his voice, which he completely failed to hide.

'Yes Richard, that is what I'm telling you, and you can believe me. You know I would never joke about anything as serious as this.'

'No of course not. I must see him. Can you arrange for him to come and visit me? What does he do? Hell! just imagine my son being brought up to think that moron is his father!'

'I will try and arrange for him to meet

109

you, though you must appreciate it will be very difficult, and under no circumstance can you give the slightest hint of your relationship towards the young man, not at this stage anyway. He is studying law at college, and is only home for another week, incidentally, his name is Michael.'

'I see,' he paused a moment, as if in deep thought. 'Michael. Well that sounds quite a reasonable name for a son of mine. What about his mother. Where is she?'

'She died two years ago. Now remember, Michael is only here for another week. I think it will be a very good idea if I call round to see him tomorrow, and providing I can persuade him, to bring him back here for the afternoon.'

'Yes. Yes indeed. That is a marvellous suggestion Charlotte. I always knew you were good for me. You see I'm a different man, now you have returned. Better take the Rolls tomorrow, it may help to create a good impression,' he chuckled, obviously much taken with the thought of discovering a new son and heir.

Charlotte had great difficulty in finding any relaxation in sleep that night, for her mercenary mind was too full of ideas, on how to turn this situation to her own advantage. At last however, she hit upon the perfect solution, and almost immediately, dozed off into a dreamless sleep.

The following morning, she was up early, feeling refreshed, and eagerly looking forward to the day, which she hoped, and firmly believed, would become a landmark in her life.

By ten-o-clock she had parked the car outside her house, and was walking down the path, when once again the door was opened, and Michael was standing there, waiting for her.

He closed the door behind her, then took her in his arms, and before either of them had spoken a word, they hungrily sought each other's lips, continuing to exchange searing lover's kisses, all the way up the stairs, until finally they were in the bedroom.

As they lay naked on the bed, and she stroked his heaving body, after they had satisfied their mutual voracious sexual appetites, she turned to him, and for the first time since she had entered the house that morning, she spoke. 'Good morning Michael,' she said laughingly. 'Lovely morning, do you love me?'

He sat up, and allowed his gaze to trawl the length of her nakedness, then in no more than a whisper. 'Of course I love you. I worship you. There is nothing in this world,

I wouldn't do for you.' He lay down again, and crushed her to him.

Charlotte was silent for a while, wondering if this would be a good time, to broach the subject which was uppermost in her mind. Finally, she decided there could never be a better time than this. Turning towards him, she kissed him gently, yet lingeringly, and then eased herself very slightly away from his eager embrace.

'Michael,' she said quietly. 'I have something very important to tell you.'

He laughed, pulled her to him and kissed her again. 'Oh! My darling, you do sound serious. This is no time to look like that. Just make love to me again.'

She flashed him a brilliant smile, yet gently pushed him away. 'No darling, not now, later perhaps. First of all, I must ask you something.'

'Ask away, my dear, I can't wait forever,' he chuckled.

She began again, in the same quiet serious tone. 'Michael, suppose — just suppose, that the man you live with, and have always looked upon as your father, turned out to be someone else.'

He sat up now, and looked down at her, his eyes wide with an amalgam of apprehension and astonishment. 'Whatever do you mean Charlotte? Turned out to be someone else? Of course he is my father, I have known him since I was a baby. Anyway, what reason do you have to make such a monumental statement?'

She looked up at him, and then stirred herself. 'Come along darling, let's get dressed, go downstairs and then I will tell you the whole sorry story, over a cup of tea. We can both do with some refreshment after our exertions this morning,' she finished on a lighter note.

When they were dressed, and seated before a good log fire, with their cups of tea and buttered toast, Charlotte decided to take the plunge. 'Some years ago, your mother and the man whom you call father, were invited to a Christmas Eve Ball. Unfortunately, the son of the house took an instant liking to your mother, and being fully aware of his undoubted charms, and the effect he had upon members of the opposite sex, he enticed her upstairs to his bedroom, and successfully seduced her. Well, Peter who was looking for his fiancee, inadvertently, stumbled into the room, and caught them in bed. Of course there was the most fearful row, and a terrible fight, in fact if Charles Cartwright hadn't intervened and stopped them, Peter would very probably have killed the other man!' Charlotte paused, and took a sip of her tea.

Michael appeared pale and distraught. 'That is a terrible story Charlotte, and if I didn't know you so well, and love you so much, I should throw you out of this house, without the slightest hesitation. However, even if all you have told me is true, what causes you to assume, that I am the son of this, this philanderer?'

She reached across and gently took his hand in her's, then she looked directly into his eyes, so that he received the full impact of her own brilliant green hypnotic orbs, their brilliance accentuated, by the flickering firelight.

'I do not assume Michael, I know. You remember when I first met you on Christmas Eve, and how I almost fainted, and you poured me a glass of brandy? Well, the reason was, that I had just left this certain person, and when you opened the door, I thought it was him again. For you see Michael, you are the absolute image of your real father, when he was a young man, and this afternoon, I'm taking you to meet him!'

He sat, as though in a trance, his gaze locked onto those beautiful eyes, and knew he must obey. He had the strange feeling, that Charlotte had taken complete control of his mind and body, and he sat perfectly still, apparently awaiting his next instruction.

She knew exactly what she was doing, for she had previously placed other young men under her hypnotic spell, and she revelled in this power she had over men. 'You will agree to come, won't you darling?' she asked softly.

He blinked, and mentally shook himself back to reality. He had lost his vacant look. 'Yes Charlotte, of course I will come with you, I will follow you to the ends of the earth. As I told you before my darling, I will do anything for you.'

Charlotte smiled upon her latest conquest, inwardly seething with childish excitement. 'Anything? did you say kind sir? Very well darling,' she said gaily, springing up and moving towards the door. 'You may come with me into the kitchen, and help prepare lunch.'

He pulled a face at her, yet acquiesced immediately.

After a cold light lunch, for they had both eaten far too much over Christmas, Charlotte allowed him to make love to her one more time, before going out to the car, and heading towards Brackley Hall.

As Charlotte turned into the huge gateway,

at the entrance to the drive leading up to the Hall, Michael sat up and suddenly began to take a very keen interest in his surroundings. He gazed in astonishment at the long tree lined drive, and gasped with amazement, when she finally stopped at the foot of the broad steps, leading up to that great front door.

'My God! Charlotte. Who on earth lives here? This is no place for me. What are you trying to do? Make a fool out of me?'

She reached over and held his hand. 'No Michael, I would never do that. Just trust me, that is all I ask. Now when you meet your real father, you may receive quite a shock. You see, he was wounded in France, and only recently returned home from hospital. Please treat him gently Michael, he's been through an awful lot, also he has no idea who you are! However, I believe that when he discovers your true identity, it will be the finest tonic he could possibly have. Of course, you must not say anything, just tell him your name,' she flashed him her wondrous smile, and squeezed his hand, before he opened the car door, and set foot upon Brackley land, for the first, but not the last time, in his life!

She led him up the magnificently carved oak staircase, and he gazed wonderingly at the various huge portraits of Richard's ancestors, decorating the walls. At length Charlotte stopped before a door, about a third of the way along this very long landing. She silently turned to Michael, patted his hand, reached up and kissed him on the cheek, and then knocked softly upon the door, before opening it and walking into the room, hand in hand with her young companion.

Richard Brackley was sitting by the window in his wheelchair. He turned and looked up as they entered, and gave an audible gasp of astonishment, as a frisson of excitement shook his frail body. 'My God Charlotte, you said he was like me, but you never warned me of such a likeness as this. Come closer young man, so I may have a better look at you.'

Michael, slightly embarrassed, moved nearer to this emaciated, old looking man sitting in his invalid chair, and he, as Richard had, immediately saw the uncanny resemblance.

Richard gazed intently at the youth, and saw himself, as he was nearly twenty years ago! For a moment, Sir Richard Brackley, this Captain of the Guards, this Aristocrat, this Leader of men, this self confessed fornicator of women, was too overcome to speak.

Suddenly, without warning, some long dead paternal instinct, caused Richard to hold out his hands towards the youth, and Michael, as though in a trance, moved forward and reciprocated, falling to his knees, at the feet of this stranger in the wheelchair, and gripping both the proffered hands!

Charlotte, strangely moved by this exhibition of love and instant recognition on the part of both father and son, though inwardly terribly excited by the way her plan was unfolding before her eyes, uncharacteristically remained quietly in the background, and allowed the two men to become better acquainted.

At last Richard found his voice, though still a little thin and strained. 'So, my boy. What is your name?'

'Michael, sir. Michael Sinclair. My father is a doctor sir. I believe you once knew him. Sorry sir. I er — I didn't mean to say my father,' the youth stammered.

'That's perfectly understandable,' smiled Richard. 'Though I would perfer it, if you could stop calling me sir, and find it in your heart, to call me father occasionally.'

Michael looked troubled. 'Yes perhaps I will be able to call you father eventually, but you must realise I have lived with Peter Sinclair, and looked upon him as my father, for nearly twenty years. He has always treated me as his own son, and been very good to me. Charlotte has told me of how he found you in bed with my mother, yet in all those years, I can not recall one single instance, when he upbraided her, for her indiscretion, so you can understand, I am worried about the effect all this will have upon him.'

Richard admired the honesty and obvious integrity of the youth, and had to grudgingly admit to himself, that apparently, Peter Sinclair had done a first rate job of raising his son. 'Yes Michael, I can understand your worries, but believe me, they are completely without foundation. I shall treat Peter Sinclair as gently as possible.' He lied glibly, and only Charlotte could read the truth behind his words.

'Are you following in Sinclair's footsteps Michael? Do you also wish to become a doctor?'

The young man appeared to think deeply, before replying. 'Not really. No,' he seemed to hesitate, then continued. 'You see, I only studied law, because he expected me to. Actually, I wanted to become a painter, you know, an artist. I know that is my true vocation, and I think, to become a good, lawyer one has to be dedicated, and that I most definitely am not!'

Richard didn't speak for a full two minutes. 'How much longer do you have to attend college Michael,' he asked abruptly.

'To become a fully qualified lawyer, at least another three years, but I don't think I can stand it,' he replied, his feelings mirrored in the way he spoke.

Richard chuckled. 'Good, I'm glad to hear it. Now look here, cheer up my boy. I have great plans for you, and the first thing is to get you away from that college. You see I need you living here with me, so I can teach you how to supervise the running of this vast estate, which incidentally, will all be your's one day!'

Michael sat rooted to his chair, bereft of speech or movement by this staggering announcement, until Charlotte stepped forward and standing behind him, placed both her hands upon his shoulders. 'Please say something Michael,' she murmured softly.

He visibly shook himself, and standing up, began to pace the floor, yet never taking his eyes off Richard Brackley. 'Do you really mean that sir?' he asked, a new throb of excitement apparent in his voice.

'Yes my boy. Of course I mean it, every word. You could have any one of the many bedrooms there are on this floor, live in the Hall, and be treated as my son and heir!'

Michael suddenly ceased his monotonous pacing of the room, and flopping down into the nearest chair, he turned in desperation to his new love. 'My God Charlotte. What can I do? What do you suggest?'

Charlotte was having great difficulty in suppressing her own euphoria, she could never have envisaged, even in her wildest dreams, that everything she had hoped and planned for, would have happened so quickly. Taking a firm grip upon herself, she tried to sound calm. 'You must accept Richard's wonderful offer Michael,' she replied nonchalantly. 'You must realise this is a marvellous opportunity, and one which can never be repeated. If you are worried about what Peter will say, about you leaving the law profession, and coming to live here with Richard, please don't be. I will have a word on your behalf. Anyway there is nothing he can do to prevent you, for after all, Richard is your real father!'

Once more Michael rose to his feet, and moving forward, held out his hand to his prospective benefactor. 'Thank you sir for everything you are offering me. I cannot bring myself to call you father at the moment, but I have no doubt that will come in time.'

An elated Richard accepted the proffered palm, and gripped it as hard as his failing strength would allow. 'Thank you my boy. That is all I ask. After all this excitement, I am feeling a little tired, and would like to rest for a while, so if you wish, Charlotte will show you a small part of the Hall on your way out. Goodbye my son, I shall look forward to welcoming you home, as soon as possible.'

The two lovers walked hand in hand along the landing, and Charlotte stopped at her bedroom door, opened it and led Michael in. Pausing only to quietly close the door, she turned towards him. They kissed passionately, then with complete abandon, began to rip off their clothes.

Later that afternoon, Charlotte returned to Richard, and told him she was going to take Michael back to her house, and would probably wait for Peter Sinclair to come home from the hospital, so she could inform him of this latest development.

Michael Sinclair was completely infatuated with this beautiful young woman, he had met on his doorstep on the afternoon of Christmas Eve, and even though he had known her less than a week, she had taught him so much about making love. As they snuggled close together on the sofa, in front of a blazing log fire, with lamps lit and curtains drawn, he turned to her. 'Charlotte,' he loved to speak her name. 'Charlotte, if everything works out for me, as we planned this afternoon, and Richard Brackley actually accepts me as his son and heir. Please will you marry me?'

Charlotte lay back, resting her head upon his shoulder, eyes tightly closed, while she mentally pinched herself, to make sure she wasn't dreaming.

Finally, she opened her eyes, and he caught his breath, as the reflected firelight accentuated their green brilliance. She turned her slender sensuous body, pulling his head towards her, and their lips met in a searing lover's kiss.

'What the hell do you think you're doing?'

The harsh voice scythed across the semi-darkened room, as the two lovers sprang apart. Apparently, they had been so engrossed in each other, they had completely failed to hear the approach of Peter Sinclair!

Charlotte casually smoothed her crumpled dress, and looking up, smiled engagingly at Peter. 'What's the trouble Peter, had a bad day?'

'Don't try anymore of that sugary sweet talk on me, you little whore!' he snapped.

Instantly, Michael leapt to his feet, his countenance flushed with anger. 'If I ever hear you refer to my fiancee in that vein again Doctor Sinclair, I won't be responsible for my actions!'

Peter stared at his son. 'Fiancee? Doctor

Sinclair? Michael, what the hell's going on?'

Charlotte moved forward, she was seething at the name he had called her in front of Michael. 'Please allow me to inform you Peter,' she said coldly. 'Since you have apparently deprived your so called son of his birth right, for nearly twenty years, I think you should be the first to know, what the hell's going on, as you so succinctly put it. This afternoon, Michael visited his natural father, Sir Richard Brackley! As we are aware he is no great friend of your's. We didn't intend informing you of this visit, not for a while yet. However, when you come barging into people's rooms without even bothering to knock, and then start calling me names, and accuse me of being a whore, simply because you find me in the arms of this lovely young man, then I have no sympathy for you. In fact, I think it will be better if you are told everything right away.'

That had been quite a long speech for Charlotte, and as she paused for breath, a distinctly shaken Peter, all the colour drained from his face, gripped the back of a chair, and without speaking, worked his way round to the front, then almost collapsed upon the seat.

'I also think it will be much better if you are made aware of the situation right away,' said Michael, feeling a little left out of this conversation. 'As Charlotte has stated, we went to see Sir Richard this afternoon, and he suggests that I give up college, and go live at Brackley Hall.'

'Give up law? Go live at Brackley Hall, with that philandering conniving bastard?' his voice was weak, little more than a whisper, though the vitriol behind his words, came through clear enough.

Michael whirled round on the older man. 'I think you should choose your words more carefully doctor,' he said, the colour high upon his cheeks. 'If you care to remember, I'm the only one born out of wedlock in this particular situation, and if only you had paid more attention to my mother, on that fateful night of the Ball, even I may have been legitimate!'

Peter slumped in his chair, and looked as if he had been dealt a severe blow with a hammer, or some other similar weapon. Suddenly he stirred himself, and drawing deep upon unplumbed depths of sheer grit and will power, he looked Michael straight in the eye. 'I did my best that night,' the fury rising within, at the way this harlot had seduced, and then ruined the future career of Michael, the son whom he had loved and cherished all these years, even knowing he was not of his own blood, was giving him strength, and as it returned, his voice became stronger.

He turned on Charlotte. 'All of this is your doing, you two timing bitch!' he roared. 'Not content with the father, you had to have the son. My God! I wish I'd never set eyes on you.'

Michael stared in horror at the man he used to call father. 'What the devil do you mean. Not content with the father?' he asked tremulously.

Charlotte opened her mouth to say something, but Peter forestalled her. 'I mean exactly that. Ever since I came to live here, your wonderful fiancee, if that's what you call her, has been coming here, two or three afternoons a week, just for one reason only, and that was to spend a couple of hours in bed with me! Go on, ask her.'

Michael stared at Peter in disbelief, then whirled round on Charlotte. 'Is this accusation true?' he asked, his voice strained, his colour pale and unnatural.

Charlotte, using all the power of her brilliant, green hypnotic eyes, locked her gaze upon those of her new love, and determined not to lose him, she spoke softly, seductively. 'No my darling, of course not. How do you think I could ever, even think of going to bed with an old man like Peter Sinclair.'

'You lying whore,' shouted Peter. 'Is there nothing you won't do, to gain your own ends. If you want her Michael, you take her, it will be your own undoing, but at least I shall be well rid, and if you are determined to go and live with that pariah at Brackley Hall, well there isn't a great deal I can do to stop you, even though you're being a bloody fool!'

Raising himself to his full height, Michael stepped forward and stood over the older man. 'I think the time has come for you to leave this house Dr. Sinclair,' he said coldly. 'I'm sure Charlotte and I have heard enough of your pathetic lies, and hurtful insults for one day.'

However, Charlotte had other ideas. 'No Michael,' she remarked softly. 'I have a more sensible suggestion. I believe it will be much better, if you move out now, and allow me to drive you home to Brackley Hall, to take up your rightful place under the same roof as your natural father!'

He turned to her, incredulity written across his features. 'Do you really mean that darling?' he cried. 'Will it really be possible for me to return with you, and move in to live permanently at Brackley Hall?'

She flashed him one of her brilliant smiles,

enjoying immensely, his youthful enthusiastic exuberance, at the same time, gloating over the foul looks she kept receiving from the man who had dared to call her a whore! 'Of course it is possible. My dear Michael, your father told us both, that he needed you to live with him as soon as possible. Don't you remember?'

'Yes I do now. Oh! Charlotte, it's going to be wonderful, actually living in the same house as you and my new father. I can't wait to get out of here.'

Peter Sinclair turned away in disgust, then as an afterthought, he stopped. 'What about the rent Madam, shall I post it to Brackley Hall?'

Charlotte replied with a devastating smile, as though the verbal battle of a few moments ago, had never happened. 'No of course not Peter darling, if you did that, I should have no excuse to call here to see you, and that would never do,' she murmured softly.

The two men gazed at her in astonishment, though Michael was the first to find his voice. 'Charlotte, whatever are you thinking of? You called him darling!'

She fixed her eyes upon the youth. 'Did I?' she asked demurely. 'Well I shouldn't worry too much about it darling. There you see, I call everyone darling.'

128

It was a simple explanation, yet Michael wasn't quite satisfied, for a niggling doubt persisted, that perhaps Peter Sinclair had been telling the truth, about sharing his bed with Charlotte.

Michael dismissed the horrible thought, almost before it occurred, how could he ever contemplate such a bizarre situation? Having finally convinced himself he was utterly and completely, in love with this beautiful creature, he turned to her. 'Yes, of course you do dear, it is due to your generous sunny nature, and I love you all the more because of it.'

It was late when they eventually arrived at Brackley Hall, even so, George was on hand to help with Michael's luggage, and to garage the car.

Charlotte had installed her new love, in a room two doors further along the landing than her own, and after he had been introduced to Milly, and the three of them had emptied his suit cases, and put away his clothes, she turned to the young housemaid. 'Have you given Richard a sedative, to help him sleep Milly?'

'Yes Miss Charlotte, about an hour ago. I imagine he will be fast on by now.'

'Good. Now listen Milly. I want you to air Michael's bed tomorrow, with hot bricks

129

and those bed warming pan things, that you use.'

'Yes Miss, but what about tonight? he can't possibly sleep in that bed.'

Charlotte smiled wickedly. 'Don't you worry your pretty head about Michael my dear. I shall take care of him. If, as you say, Richard is fast asleep, then Michael will share my bed. Of course you know better than to tell anyone, don't you Milly?' she added silkily.

The maid coloured slightly, and Charlotte wondered if it was because of the sleeping arrangement, or because she had voiced her doubts on the subject of Milly's loyalty.

'Yes of course I do Miss, nobody will ever hear a single thing against you, not from my lips they won't,' she replied sharply.

So Milly left them, and hand in hand, the two lovers tip-toed along the landing to Charlotte's room. Immediately they were inside, Charlotte moved quickly, yet silently to the adjoining door, which opened into Richard's room. Very carefully easing it open just sufficient, to enable her to verify that Richard was fast asleep, she closed it equally as softly, then turned and flung herself into the eager, waiting arms of Michael Sinclair, very soon to be Michael Sinclair-Brackley!

7

Safe within the confines of these English shores, far removed from the sights and sounds of battle, Rose sometimes found it difficult to comprehend all the atrocities, deaths and ghastly carnage, of which she read daily, generally in screaming headlines across the front page of her morning paper.

Until, one morning during the third week of February, nineteen hundred and eighteen, she was suddenly made all too aware of the terrible tragedy of this war, and of the horrific price humanity was having to pay for freedom. She was in the nursery playing with the children, when from the hall below, the faint jarring note of the telephone, assailed her ears. Obviously, someone had answered it, for the ringing abruptly ceased. A moment later, one of the maids entered the room. 'Beg pardon, Mrs. Alan Cartwright is on the telephone, and wishes to speak with you.'

Never for a moment contemplating the horrendous news, she was about to hear, Rose gaily tripped downstairs, and picked up the instrument. 'Hello Joan darling,' she trilled. 'How are you, on this lovely cold February morn?'

For a full ten seconds, there was no reply, then a single heart breaking sob, came over the wire.

Instantly Rose, realising something was dreadfully wrong, became a changed person. 'Sorry I answered the phone in that silly manner. Please tell me what has happened Joan,' she said softly.

Another pause, then the sound of sobbing, interspersed with almost incoherent words. 'Oh! Rose. — I don't know what I'm going to do. — It's Alan — he's dead Rose — gone down with his submarine!' she choked on the last words, and could say no more.

Immediately, the unflappable Rose knew exactly what to do. 'That's terrible news Joan,' her voice was purposely strong, with a resonance of authority behind it, for she knew that soft words of sympathy would bring no solace to her sister-in-law during this terrible time, and that she would need a strong arm to lean on, not a bending reed. 'Go and keep warm dear, I'll be there as soon as possible.'

There was no car available, for Charles and his father had taken the Bentley to work, and Ruth had taken the smaller car, to do her work for the Red Cross in City

Hall. Consequently, Rose had to summon the old groom to prepare the ancient pony and trap for her. The groom was old because all the young men had gone to war, and the pony was ancient, because the army had commandeered all the best horses.

However, she managed to inspire a modicum of speed into the old chap's movements, and was soon on the road. The pony turned out to be a more difficult problem, for he would only just plod along, and resolutely refused to be hurried. Because of this, Rose was becoming desperate by the time 'The Gables' hove into view. She left the pony and trap out on the drive, 'I don't think there's much chance of you running away,' she muttered aloud, as she jumped down from her seat.

Dashing up the steps, she went straight in and called Joan's name. A faint voice answered her, through a door just to her left. Rose opened it, and strode quickly across the darkened room to the window, where she flung back the curtains. She gasped when she turned and saw the terrible state of her sister-in-law. Joan's normally shining, silken fair hair, which fell to her shoulders, was lank and matted. Her face was tear stained and grubby, and there were large dark circles beneath her red rimmed eyes.

Rose gently placed her arm around the grieving woman's shoulders, and tried to quieten her, for with her arrival, Joan had begun sobbing again, great heaving sobs which seemed to shake her whole body, and for the first time in her life, Rose was at a loss, not really knowing how to treat this terrible show of utter despair.

Suddenly, the crying ceased as abruptly as it had begun, and a savage angry intensity seemed to be filling Joan's mind and body. She lifted her head and looked at Rose. 'Do you know how my Alan was killed?' she screamed. 'Not in action! Oh no! Not by the enemy! No, in collision with Royal Navy ships and another submarine! On some bloody stupid, night time navel exercise in the Firth of Forth, on January thirty first. One hundred and three sailors died, and two submarines were lost. Can you imagine the utter waste, and the stupidity of such an exercise? My Alan had survived three long years of depth charges, bombs and shells, in one of those damned sardine tins, throughout the oceans of the world, and now he has been killed in friendly waters, by his own side!' it was then she broke down again.

Some two hours had elapsed, before Rose had finally managed to settle Joan's incessant sobbing, and that was only after a visit by the doctor, and she had persuaded her to take a sedative to help her sleep.

After satisfying herself that her sister-in-law was at last in a deep sleep, Rose left the room, closing the door quietly behind her, and went downstairs. It was then she remembered, neither of Alan's parents had been informed of this tragic family loss. Not wishing to break the dreadful news to his mother by telephone, she rang Charles at the yard. A man's voice answered, 'Hello, Miles Cartwright speaking.'

Rose took a firm grip upon herself, and tried to sound natural.

'Oh hello, Rose here, may I speak with Charles please?'

'Hello Rose, what are you doing, ringing at this time of day?' he asked jocularly. 'I'm sorry, Charles is in a rather important meeting, is this something urgent?'

Rose hesitated, but only for a moment. 'Yes, I think you had both better come here immediately, I'm at 'The Gables'.'

'Why? Whatever are you doing there? What's happened Rose?' the voice on the other end of the line, had suddenly become serious and agitated.

'I'm sorry, I can't tell you over the telephone. Please come quickly!' her voice broke, as she replaced the receiver.

Half-an-hour later, the big car skidded to a halt on the gravelled drive, outside the house, which, many years ago, had been the home of Lucy, Ruth's mother.

Father and son, leapt out of the car almost before it had stopped, and raced up the steps, pushing open the wide front door and rushing straight in. Charles was just in front of his father. 'Where are you Rose?' he shouted.

Suddenly she was in his arms, sobbing uncontrollably. He led her into the front room, sat her down, and holding her closely, asked Miles to ring for the maid.

'Bring some tea please my dear, and plenty of sugar,' he told the astonished elderly woman.

Rose became calmer as he gentled her, but not knowing what was wrong, he had no idea what to say.

Then, at last she was able to speak coherently. 'I asked you both to come here, because I couldn't possibly tell Alan's mother over the telephone,' she stammered.

'Tell her what? For God's sake Rose, what has happened?' asked an agitated Miles.

Rose took a deep breath. 'Joan was informed this morning, that Alan has been killed, gone down with his submarine!'

She spoke barely above a whisper, yet the

awful words had shocked her two listeners into a stunned silence.

In the meantime, the woman returned with a pot of tea, and the necessary tea things on a tray, and chiefly to occupy herself, Rose commenced to pour out a cup for each of them, putting an extra spoonful of sugar in her own.

Charles was the first to speak. 'But how could this happen? I only received a letter from Alan two weeks ago, and then he was in Home waters,' he said quietly.

Rose told them the details, as Joan had given them to her. It was then that Miles interrupted violently.

'Do you mean to tell me, that my son was killed on some stupid bloody, nightly exercise, orchestrated by his own side?' he shouted aggressively.

Charles moved swiftly to his wife's side. 'Now steady on father. There's nothing to be gained by blaming Rose for the stupidity of the Royal Navy. Remember, she dropped everything and came over here, immediately she heard the dreadful news, in order to be with Joan, and to try and comfort her, in her hour of need. Incidentally Rose, where is Joan?' he asked gently.

'On her bed, sleeping I hope,' she replied, handing each of them a cup of tea. 'Now drink this, and please try to be brave for Joan's sake, and for Alan's mother.'

'Dear God, how can I tell Ruth this terrible news? It will finish her,' muttered Miles brokenly.

Charles placed his hand upon the older man's arm. 'No father, I think you will be surprised how tough mother can be in a situation like this.'

Miles turned on him. 'How the devil can you say a thing like that? Your mother has never been faced with a situation such as this. None of us have.'

'I know father, but mother has seen, been with, and comforted, dozens of other families who have suffered terrible losses in this war, and I know she has prayed for the strength to meet any similar tragedy, should it befall us.' Those quiet words spoken by his son, seemed to have a soothing effect upon Miles, for after that he ceased his cursing and wailing, and sat quietly drinking his tea.

On the following Sunday, a memorial service to the memory of Alan Cartwright, was held in the same church his grandparents, Thomas Cartwright and his beautiful elegant bride, Kate Earnshaw had been married, many years ago. It was a poignant occasion for Miles. For he could not seem to erase from his memory, that scene, when as a little boy, he had left Maria by the churchyard wall, and stumbling over graves, rushed towards his father as he left the church.

Suddenly, he turned startled, as a hand was placed upon his arm, breaking his train of thought, and bringing him out of this nostalgic reverie, and a voice murmured, 'Come along father, the hymn is finished, and the service is over.'

The voice was that of his youngest son Charles, and even on this sad terrible occasion, Miles raised his eyes to Heaven, in a silent prayer of thanks, for the fact that at least he had two sons still alive, even though Brian was at this moment, fighting with his regiment somewhere in France, and had been unable to obtain compassionate leave, in order to attend his brother's memorial service.

As they were leaving the church, Miles felt a hand upon his shoulder, and turning quickly, was pleasantly surprised to see his old friend, Billy Hind and his wife Ivy.

'Very sorry to hear about Alan,' said Billy, as they warmly shook hands. 'It's a real shame we only meet on occasions such as this.'

'Yes I know, somehow we never seem to have any time for visiting these days. However, I will try and keep in touch. I'm sorry, but I shall have to go now, Ruth is waiting,' and Miles moved away.

Charles was proved quite correct, in his assessment of the way Ruth would stand up to the awful loss of her eldest son, and Miles was both amazed and justifiably proud, of the quiet dignified way, in which his wife bore the trauma and interminable stress, of meeting sympathetic friends and relatives, whom, even though she knew they meant well, she wished with all her heart, they would leave her to grieve in peace.

However, Ruth's main concern was for Joan and her four children. For though they were still at school, she knew life would be very different for them from now on, and also very difficult for Joan. Yet she was also well aware, that Miles would never see them wanting for the chief necessities of life. She did wonder though, over the coming weeks, if Joan would be able to afford to continue living at 'The Gables.'

Just when the Cartwright family were beginning to come to terms with the horrific death of Alan, they were plunged once again into terrifying depths of utter bitterness and despair.

Because the Eastern Front was now inactive, this had enabled the Germans to bring in massive reinforcements on a forty mile front in the Arras sector, where three million German troops were deployed. They dealt a shattering blow to the Allied lines, taking as many as eighty thousand prisoners, the obvious intention being, to roll back the British to the Channel, before any American troops had time to arrive!

It was on a beautiful summer's day in late May, when the jarring tone of the telephone, shattered the peace and tranquillity at 'Mount Pleasant', during the afternoon of this idyllic day.

With a sudden, incomprehensible stab of fear of the unknown, Ruth slowly lifted the instrument off it's hook. 'Hello,' she said quietly.

Her single word was greeted with a strangled sob of despair, from the other end of the wire. Even though it had only been a soul destroying half word, half cry for help, Ruth knew immediately who it was, and her heart went cold. 'Hello, is that Enid?' she asked tentatively.

'Yes,' the voice was weak and trembling. 'Please help me mother, I — I don't know if I can cope on my own.' For a moment a spate of heart rending sobs crackled over the line and interrupted the conversation, then Ruth's worst fears were realised, as the tenuous voice continued, in little more than a whisper. 'I received a letter this morning, telling me that Brian has been killed in action, whilst fighting somewhere in France!'

As the voice faded, Ruth clung to the back of a chair, placed near the telephone, and sat down. After a moment, she spoke. 'Please try and be brave Enid, Rose and I will be there as quickly as possible.' Her words were greeted with another series of heart wrenching sobs, then a click as the line went dead.

One Sunday afternoon, a month after another memorial service, this one for the second of her three sons within a few weeks, Ruth was sitting quietly on the terrace with Miles, and her one remaining son Charles, each of them in their thoughts, dwelling upon the recent tragic deaths of their loved ones, though Ruth was also worrying about how the two, comparatively young widows, Joan and Enid were going to be able to bring up five children between them, and cope on their own.

Apparently, Charles was also thinking along similar lines, for suddenly he broke the silence. 'I say mother, wasn't Enid a school teacher before she married Brian?' he asked quietly.

'Yes, I believe she was. Why do you wish to know, my dear?' replied Ruth, endeavouring to sound interested.

Charles appeared pensive. 'I was just thinking how difficult it's going to be, for Joan and Enid to make ends meet,' he said thoughtfully. 'Then I remembered how Enid used to teach school, and I wondered if they would consider an idea I have floating around in my head.'

Miles roused himself, coughed loudly, and sat up. 'Now what might that be my boy?' he asked.

Charles looked at each of his parents. 'Well personally, I think it is completely unnecessary for those two to struggle to keep two homes going, especially when one is the size of 'The Gables'. So, my idea is, that Enid sells her house on the outskirts of Hull, moves in with Joan and her children, turns one of the many rooms into a schoolroom, and between them, they set up a private school together. I'm sure both Alan and Brian, left sufficient funds to enable them to buy desks and seats, blackboards and easels, slates and pencils, and any other books and writing materials they may require.'

For a full minute, complete silence reigned, then both Ruth and Miles exploded together. 'Sorry, you first my dear,' he said courteously.

For the first time since she had picked up

the phone on that dreadful day, Ruth smiled. 'Thank you kind sir,' she murmured. 'Well Charles, I think that's a marvellous idea,' she said enthusiastically. 'I suggest we telephone Enid right away, ask her to prepare herself and her children for a short journey, then go and collect them, and bring them over to see Joan at 'The Gables', though of course, before we do that, we shall have to inform Joan of the arrangement, just to make sure it's convenient.'

This was duly carried out, and culminated in Charles and Rose, dropping his parents off at Joan's house, then going on to Hull, to collect Enid and her two children. Ruth had warned him to be very careful how he approached the matter, for Enid was a very proud woman, and any vestige of a hint, that they were doing this as some form of charity, to help her and her family in their hour of need, would be decidedly frowned upon, and she would be instantly scared off. Bearing this in mind, Charles wisely decided to say nothing of the reason for this visit to 'The Gables', only murmuring something about a family get together.

When they were all comfortably ensconced in the large front room of the house, replete with tea and cakes, and the children were outside playing ball on the long sloping lawns, Miles broached the subject, which was uppermost in at least four of the minds of those present.

He coughed, unnecessarily loudly to attract the attention of his captive audience. 'We have brought you here today Enid, to talk over an idea which Charles had earlier. I have been given to understand, that at one time you used to teach school. Is that correct my dear?'

'Yes that is quite true father, though I'm afraid I would be a bit rusty now. Why do you ask? Has it something to do with Charles' idea?' she asked, her tone flat and uninteresting, her movements slow and languid.

Ruth leaned forward. 'Yes Enid, very much so, and personally I think it is a wonderful idea. You see my dear, we are all very worried about you and Joan, living on your own in two houses, with five children to look after, and no man about the house, to bring in a weekly wage. We have already discussed the idea with Joan, while we were waiting for you to arrive, and she is quite willing to cooperate if you are'

As Ruth paused for breath, Enid, who had listened attentively, and was now sitting up and taking notice of the proceedings, said rather coldly. 'I don't know about Joan, but

145

I can cope quite well on my own thank you, anyway please tell me. What is this wonderful idea, you all seem so excited about?'

'Well, as this was my suggestion, I suppose I should be the one to tell you,' said Charles quietly, for he knew how proud and independent Enid was. 'You see Enid, I can't see any sense in Joan continuing to live in this large house, with half the rooms unoccupied, when eventually the children will be leaving home to attend college and public school. Nor can I see any sense, in you continuing to live in your house, alone with your children.'

Joan held up her hand. Charles was her favourite brother-in-law, and though she was aware he had her best interests at heart, she was a little suspicious of his motives, yet she still wanted to know more. 'So, what do you suggest we do, both of us sell up, and move in with your parents at 'Mount Pleasant', and allow you and your father to support us all?' she asked facetiously, she would have continued, but he stopped her.

'No Enid, that is not what I had in mind. In fact exactly the opposite. I think it will make a lot of sense, for you to sell your house in Hull, and move out here to live in the country with Joan and her children. You can bring your school teaching expertise with you, and with Joan's help, set up school together. Apart from anything else, just think how much healthier your children will be, living out here with all this fresh air.'

The room was quiet, except for the muted sounds of the children at play.

At length, Enid turned to Joan. They had always been very friendly these two, there had never been any jealousy or animosity on Enid's part, because Joan was living in a far better and much larger house, than her and her family. 'Well, Charles has put forward a very strong case, but I still haven't heard a word from you. What do you think to this idea Joan?'

Joan stood up, and walked over to the window. 'Just come over here dear, and have a look at these children, I think they will answer your question.'

Enid complied, and moved across the room to stand by her sister-in-law. They stood side by side, and watched as the five children gambolled and played happily together, in the bright sunshine. 'Very well Joan, I see what you mean, and it would be very selfish of me, to deprive both our families of such a wonderful opportunity, when obviously, they get on so well together.'

She turned away from the window, and faced her companions. 'Yes, the answer is yes. You have all finally convinced me, that this is a very good idea. I will search out my old school books, and probably buy a few new ones. However, in the meantime Charles, will you please attend to the sale of my house, and make the necessary arrangements for us to move here to 'The Gables', if that is all right with you Joan?'

Joan hugged and kissed her affectionately. 'Yes dear, of course it's all right, the sooner you move in, the better it will be for both of us. In the meantime, I will contact a few of my friends, and see if I can induce them to send their children to our new school.'

Several weeks later, one lovely morning in late August, the new school was finally opened, amid much pomp and ceremony, with the help of the older generation, and all the remaining members of the Cartwright family being present on this auspicious occasion. Even Charlotte had volunteered to give up two of her mornings each week, to teach art, completely free of charge. However, this unprecedented gift of her time to the school, wasn't quite as unselfish or as generous as it seemed. For Charlotte was still carrying a torch for Charles, and in her peculiar twisted mind, she thought an action of this nature on her part, may just soften his attitude towards her, and possibly make him a little more pliable and caring in the future.

Two of Joan's children were old enough to start school, and both Enid's were eligible. Also Rose had managed to convince six other sets of parents, it would be a very good idea to send their offspring to the new school. Consequently, a total of fourteen pupils of mixed gender, ranging in age from five years to ten, attended for their lessons on that first unforgettable morning, at 'The Gables' school.

8

During August, when British, American, Canadian, Australian and French troops, went into action near Amiens, the enemy collapsed.

The whole character of the war had changed dramatically, for tanks and planes were being used in large and ever increasing numbers, and the enemy was being pushed back to the same position they held, prior to their great Spring Offensive.

Along the length of the ruptured front, small groups of Germans were found hiding in shell holes and blasted buildings. They all surrendered immediately, and the steady stream of prisoners captured daily, were obviously tired of the incessant bloodshed and death, and consequently were very thankful to be taken.

During September, the Allies were sweeping all before them along the entire Western Front, from the Scheldt in the north, to Sadan in the south. More than two hundred divisions attacked simultaneously, and delivered crushing blows in Flanders, where the war began.

As the Germans retreated through Belgium, they rounded up and took with them, all the men and boys, from sixteen to sixty, to be used as forced labour, to build emergency defences. For along the German Frontier, as elsewhere, all Germany's allies were collapsing.

By the end of October, Germany, in the shadow of defeat, appealed for an armistice, her allies had already quit the field, and the retreating Germans on the Western Front, showed very little resistance.

The end came, just before dawn, on the eleventh of November, nineteen eighteen, when a party of Germans, including two army Generals, entered a guarded railway carriage in the forest of Compeigne.

Six hours later, at eleven-o-clock on the eleventh day of the eleventh month, after four and a quarter years of the bloodiest war known to man, the guns fell silent across the battlefields of Europe, as Germany admitted defeat, and signed the armistice.

It has become known as 'The Great War', and certainly there had never previously been any war like it in history. More countries were involved, and more soldiers, sailors, airmen and civilians were killed, (over ten million in all) than in any other known conflict.

Throughout Britain, great jubilation marked the end of the war, as peace came at last to a war weary land. Victory day began quietly, then just before noon, as the armistice really took effect, church bells started to ring, and suddenly it seemed the entire population, as though controlled by a master puppeteer, rushed out on to the streets, waving flags and cheering vociferously.

In every town and city, the street lights were shorn of their sombre war time covering, blackout curtains were ripped down, and even during the day, shop windows were ablaze with light. Rigid licensing laws were forgotten, and all the pubs and inns were packed solid with boisterous inebriated customers, until they ran out of beer.

A more sobering thought, to which the populace quickly became accustomed, after the end of this war, ('To end all wars') apart from the death, destruction and devastation across Europe, was the huge number of unemployed ex-service men, seen begging on street corners, and busking outside theatres and cinemas, many of them maimed, with an arm or a leg missing.

It was sights such as these, which upset Rose more than anything else in the immediate aftermath of that terrible conflict. Consequently, she redoubled her efforts for the Red Cross, tirelessly organising soup kitchens and jumble sales, where the returning service men could obtain a reasonable free meal, and purchase good clean, cheap clothing.

★ ★ ★

During the early spring of nineteen hundred and nineteen, when Daphne, on one of her rare visits to the wing of Brackley Hall, occupied by her brother Richard, espied Michael just emerging from Charlotte's bedroom.

With a note of surprise, edged with typical feminine curiosity, she cried out, 'You there! Come here at once!'

Never having had the misfortune of meeting Daphne, Michael, slightly shocked by the sharpness, and resonance of authority behind her tone, turned quickly and walked towards her.

Taking him completely by surprise as he reached her side, Daphne grabbed him by the hand, opened the door to Richard's room with her free hand, and literally dragged him inside.

'I have just caught this lout, leaving Charlotte's room!' she cried triumphantly, as she released Michael's hand, and pushed him forward, further into the room.

Charlotte was in the process of giving Richard a thorough strip down wash, as he sat up in bed, when this interruption occurred, and for a few seconds, complete silence reigned in the room. Then, quite suddenly, whilst still holding the flannel aloft, she broke into raucous laughter, with Richard immediately joining in.

Daphne, now pale with anger, screamed furiously. 'What the devil are you two idiots laughing at?'

Richard at last managed to contain his mirth, and while Charlotte wiped away the laughter tears from her eyes, he addressed his volatile sister. 'My dear Daphne, if only you were to visit me a little more often, you would know who that very handsome young man is. Tell me, does he remind you of anyone?'

Still trembling with rage, for she abhorred being laughed at, Daphne gave only a cursory glance in Michael's direction. 'No, of course not,' she snapped. 'Why the devil should he?'

Richard smiled smugly to himself, enjoying to the full, the anticipation of the effect this bombshell, which he was about to deliver, would have upon his obnoxious sister, whom he knew, would immediately dash off and inform his wife, of this his latest escapade.

Doing his utmost, though not very successfully, to prevent a touch of arrogant satisfaction creeping into his voice, Richard replied nonchalantly, 'Because, my dear sweet sister, he should. That good looking young man, you so mistakenly called a lout, just happens to be, my only son and heir!'

For a full ten seconds, complete silence reigned in Richard's tranquil room, then this was suddenly shattered by Daphne's strident voice. 'What! You stupid bloody fool!' She whirled around on Charlotte. 'I suppose this is all your doing, you meddling bitch!' Then turning once again upon her brother. 'Oh! Richard. How could you be so gullible, as to be taken in by these two, who are both so obviously from a much lower class, than either you or I?'

Richard's original half amused look, was beginning to turn to one of anger, at his sister's vituperation. 'That's enough Daphne!' he snapped, his voice hard and cold. 'Charlotte is my friend, my confidante, my nurse and my companion. Michael, is beyond any shadow of doubt, my only son, and if you require any specific details, I can tell you exactly where and when, even to the hour, in which room of this house, he was conceived! So, I wish to hear no more of

155

your stupid, childish jealous carping, or I shall have no alternative, other than to ban you completely, from this wing.'

Daphne, beneath her immaculate make-up, paled at her brother's words, half turned as though to leave, changed her mind and faced him again, with something akin to triumphant hatred in her lovely eyes. 'As I approached your room just now, this er Michael person, was emerging from your dear Charlotte's bedroom, and was about to go skulking off along the landing. Does that mean anything to you, dear brother?' she ended silkily.

Only a very observant onlooker, would have noticed the brief sudden flash in Richard's eyes, or have heard the subtle change in his voice. 'Yes Daphne. That means, Michael is probably sleeping with Charlotte, and looking at her, who can blame him? For it is patently obvious, I can't do anything for her. Much as I would love to,' he couldn't avoid the bitterness, coming to the surface in his last sentence.

During this verbal diatribe between brother and sister, Charlotte had remained remarkably quiet, now however, she thought the time had arrived for her to join in. 'If you two have quite finished discussing my sex life, as though I wasn't here,' she said acidly. 'I will tell you now. I had no idea Michael was in my room, but even if he was, I fail to see what the hell it has to do with either of you, particularly you Daphne, you painted virginal apology for a woman! Why the devil don't you go out, and find yourself a real man, someone who can relieve you of all your pent up fantasies and frustrations?'

As usual, whenever these two met, Daphne always seemed to come off worse. Now she was even paler than before, and literally seething with rage. 'You — You unspeakable, horrible twisted guttersnipe!' she screamed. 'One day I'll have you flogged, for the whore you are!' unable to say anymore, because of her rage, on that last remark, she turned on her heel and left the room, slamming the door behind her.

After his sister had departed, Richard emitted a slow curious chuckle, but this failed to fool Charlotte, for only she had noticed the fleeting look in his eyes, and the subtle change in his voice, and now as he cleared his throat to speak, she thought she knew what he was about to say. What she didn't know however, and certainly had never expected, was what followed his opening gambit.

'So, Michael my boy, are you sleeping with the lovely, very desirable Charlotte?'

The question, gently put and softly spoken, caught the young man completely by surprise. However, correctly assuming his father would never tolerate lies or cowardice, he decided to take the plunge. 'Yes father I am, and have been doing so for some time,' he replied calmly, and even amazed himself by his sudden feeling of debonair self confidence.

To the utter astonishment of Michael, and particularly of Charlotte, who had been fearing an explosion after Michael's candid admission of their surreptitious love making, Richard laughed loudly and heartily, as much as his wretched condition would allow. 'Good for you my boy,' he reached out and grasped Charlotte by the hand. 'What did I tell you my dear? A typical Brackley, eh?'

Charlotte, wondering what on earth would happen next, squeezed his hand in return, and smiled. She didn't have long to wait, for Michael spoke again. 'I had no intention of mentioning this matter yet, but I don't think there will ever be a more appropriate moment than this. Father, may I please have your permission to marry Charlotte?'

Charlotte gasped audibly, yet quite uncharacteristically, said nothing.

Richard gazed upon this new found son of his with an appraising eye. He admired the broad shoulders and athletic form, his polite manners and his lucid spoken English, and he had to grudgingly admit to himself, that Peter Sinclair had done a first class job of bringing the boy up. He suddenly became acutely aware, that two people in the room, were breathlessly awaiting his reply. A sudden spasm of coughing, shook his pain racked emaciated body, and Charlotte immediately stood by, with a basin and a glass of water.

At length the spasm subsided, and Richard, turning once more to Michael, carried on the conversation, as though there had been no interruption. 'According to the way Charlotte reacted when you broached the question, it occurred to me, that you have not proposed to her yet. Am I correct?'

Michael blushed and looked decidedly uncomfortable. 'Well no — er yes. You are quite correct in one sense sir. We have discussed the matter occasionally, but thought it would probably be more appropriate if we waited a while. You see, we were a little afraid of what you might say father.'

Richard revelled in the way the youth said 'father'. 'Afraid? Of me? I can assure you my son, and you too Charlotte, there is and never will be, any reason why either of you should ever have anything to fear from me. However, enough of this. Will you Charlotte, accept the hand of my son in marriage? Go on my boy, ask her.'

Michael moved closer to the bed, and gently taking her hands in his, and looking deep into those beautiful, green hypnotic eyes, which at times seemed to glow from within, and which he had found so fascinating, right from the first time he had seen her, he softly spoke her name. 'Charlotte. Charlotte my darling. Will you be my wife?'

Charlotte, a plethora of mixed emotions churning around inside her, sat perfectly still on the edge of this man's bed. The same man, who had once made wild passionate love to her, when they had both stripped naked in a small wood, carpeted by lush grass, on the hill side just below Watersmeet. That memory seemed so long ago, as though in another life, for now here he was, no more than a pathetic shadow of his former self, and completely dependant upon her, for his every need.

And now, this handsome young man, at least three years younger than herself, who proclaimed to be the only son and heir of her former lover, had just asked her to be his wife! It took no more than the length of a single heart beat, for Charlotte's mercenary mind, to realise the full potential of the privilege, power and wealth this offer of marriage would mean to her, even so, before replying, she turned appealingly to her ex-lover and benefactor. 'Please Richard, tell me what you think I should do. After all, you are his father, and I would like to know if you think I am worthy of your son, and would make a suitable daughter-in-law, you being my employer and everything?'

Richard eyed her quizzically for a moment, then smiled. 'Yes of course my dear Charlotte, but really it is not for me to say. Apparently, Michael is desperately in love with you, and is confidant you will make him a wonderful wife, and that is the most important part. Also, this will be a sure way of keeping you in the family,' he added jocularly.

Still holding his hands, she turned again to Michael. 'Yes my darling, I will be your wife,' she said simply, her lovely eyes shining, but not as father and son thought, with love and adoration! Oh No! The light shining forth from Charlotte's eyes, was of pure unadulterated avarice! Her spine tingled, and a frisson of excitement coursed through her veins, as she contemplated the vast wealth and luxury which lay ahead, and which, if events went according to her master plan, would one day, all belong to her!

Michael, in reply to her acceptance of his proposal, suddenly lifted her off the bed, and taking her in his arms, crushed her to him. 'Oh Charlotte. Charlotte. When? When will you marry me?'

'Right away dear. Anytime you say,' she replied happily.

Richard, gazing fondly upon this happy couple, who were obviously so very much in love, quite suddenly experienced a kaleidoscopic cameo flash back, of a grass carpeted copse, and a beautiful, ravishing naked girl. Inwardly, he cursed how the war had scarred and ravaged his body, as a single unprecedented tear, cut a furrow down his emaciated cheek.

Michael, who was just coming up for air, after a rather extravagant lover's kiss, opened his eyes and glanced over Charlotte's shoulder.

'Father!' he cried, pushing her aside. 'Whatever is the matter? You look dreadful!'

Charlotte moved quickly forward, and bending over the bed, with a clean handkerchief deftly wiped away the offending tear. She then pretended to puff up Richard's pillows, to give him time to compose himself, for through her inherent woman's intuition, she had correctly suspected he was still in love with her, and this was the reason for his sudden spate of apathy, and his next words only added fuel to her suspicions.

Richard coughed slightly, just enough to clear his throat, then addressed his son. 'I'm sorry Michael, but seeing you and Charlotte together, so close and so young, with the world at your feet, made me realise how utterly useless and inadequate I really am. You see my boy, many years ago in another life, I once knew a lovely young girl, very much like your Charlotte. I loved her so much, I would have done anything for her. I think she loved me too, but then the bloody war came, and this is how it left me, a mere shadow of my former self. Of no use to man nor woman.'

On that last remark his voice broke, and Charlotte, with crocodile tears in her eyes, placed her arm around his skeletal shoulders and tried to comfort him. 'There there Richard,' she murmured softly. 'Please don't upset yourself, you know it only makes you worse.'

While Michael sat in a chair beside the bed, and watched this lovely girl, whom he had so recently asked to be his wife, and wondered. Little did he realise, that he was witnessing a supreme display of pure theatre, by a very beautiful, multi-talented consummate actress!

The village of Watersmeet had never, in all it's long and sleepy history, witnessed anything quite like the wedding which took place there during early May, in the year nineteen hundred and nineteen, between Charlotte Thornton, youngest daughter of the local miller, and a real genuine aristocrat, The Honourable Michael Sinclair-Brackley.

All the main streets were festooned with flags and bunting, from Mill House all the way down to the church, for everyone had become so weary of the austerity and rationing of the long war years, that the entire population saw this as a golden opportunity to let their hair down, and to celebrate in a really big way.

After much heart searching between the miller and his two daughters, it had finally been decided to hold Charlotte's wedding in the church. She was given away by her father, while her sister Rose played the organ, and Michael's little half-sister Sophia, looked resplendent, as the only bridesmaid.

Old George had brought his employer round by road from Hull, sitting in his wheelchair in the rear of a modified Bentley.

Richard couldn't help feeling a touch of sadness, tinged with bitterness, as Rose struck up the Wedding March, and he watched, as his beautiful ex-mistress walked down the aisle on the arm of her father, to be joined at the altar by his own, so recently discovered son.

It was at that moment, Richard almost succumbed to an outrageous fit of jealous rage at his own plight, and total lack of mobility, as he had to admit for the thousandth time, what an utterly useless wreck of a human being he really was, and that he would never again be able to hold and caress, or experience the closeness and physical love of a beautiful vibrant woman.

At last the wedding service ended, and the happy couple turned from the altar, and went to sign the register, as the church bells rang out their glorious joyous message.

The entire population of Watersmeet had turned out to be present on this wonderful occasion, to witness one of their own being married into the aristocracy, and many of them remembered, though no-one dare voice their thoughts, the previous promiscuous lifestyle of this beautiful, innocent looking bride!

Richard's uncle had allowed the lavish reception to take place in the grounds of Didcot Hall, where a massive marquee had been erected on the main lawn, immediately in front of the Hall. A dazzling array of wedding presents was on display, upon trestle tables inside the marquee, though the many guests who came to inspect them didn't stay long, because fortunately the weather had decided to be kind on this, 'The Miller's Daughter's' day, and the sun shone brilliantly.

Daphne, though invited, had deigned not to honour them with her presence, for she could not bear this common upstart, whom her brother had allowed his son to marry. However, because of her abrasive manner to all and sundry, and often embarrassing haughty disposition, no-one missed her, and the celebrations proceeded apace.

There were three tables running the length of the marquee, one containing the wedding gifts, and the other two groaning beneath piles of mouth watering food and culinary delights, the like of which hadn't been seen since before the war. There was also plenty of tea, lemonade and beer to drink.

Richard's uncle had a band stand erected in the grounds, and engaged the services of a very good local town band, which added greatly to the colour and gaiety of this special occasion.

Also, this being a Saturday, a cricket match was in progress in a field adjoining the Hall grounds, where cricket had been played on that same pitch, for more than a hundred years!

As Charles and Rose were leaving the marquee, after partaking of a rather scrumptious and very satisfying repast, they caught up with old George pushing Richard along in his wheelchair. Charles nudged George to one side. 'Go and have a rest, and get yourself a drink George. I'll push Richard for a while,' he said, taking over.

Richard half turned in his chair. 'Hello Charles, Rose, pleased to see you. I spotted you earlier, but couldn't get near enough to speak to you, because of the crowd. Thank you for playing the organ Rose, you play beautifully. Well what do you think of my recently discovered son Charles? Not much doubt about who his father is eh?' he asked with a chuckle.

'No, not really,' replied Charles slowly. 'If you remember, it was I who broke up that fight between you and Peter Sinclair. Strewth! What a night that was, though according to the result, Peter didn't find you soon enough!'

Richard laughed heartily at his friend's remarks. 'No, you're quite right Charles. For you see, had Peter arrived earlier, there probably would never have been a child with the name of Michael, who grew up to be a very handsome young man, and was eventually recognized by your sharp eyed sister-in-law, with whom he fell in love. And today Charles, those two lovely young people were married,' he ended, rather wistfully, Charles thought.

As the afternoon wore on, some of the guests with young children, began to drift away, however many more arrived to replace them. For the grounds had been thrown open to the public, and teas were being served in the marquee. There was also dancing on the lawn, scheduled for later in the evening, to a rather more modern dance band, completely different to the one engaged to play earlier.

However, after making the relevant excuses, first to Richard, then to Charlotte and her new husband, Charles and Rose left the happy couple, to go and help her father at the mill.

They approached from the rear, and as they came around the corner of the house, Edward had just finished pumping a tank like contraption on iron wheels, full of water, and was about to push it down Mill Road, to give to the poultry.

'Please allow me to take that for you,' said Charles, moving quickly forward.

'Yes father, let Charles push that heavy

tank. We will feed and water the poultry, and collect the eggs, while you attend to the pigs,' said Rose graciously.

'Thank you. Both of you,' replied the miller, wiping his glistening brow with a large red handkerchief, for it was a very arduous task having to pump that tank full of water, especially on such a warm day.

After they had filled all the troughs with water, Charles and Rose came back to the mill for some meal and corn, and as they entered this silent edifice, once again that same feeling of tragic violent death, assailed his being, and he found it utterly impossible to rid himself of the sense of foreboding, until he was once more outside in the fresh air and brilliant sunshine.

Rose commented upon his apparent lack of colour, but he could give no credible explanation for this unusual phenomenon, and shrugged it off with some lame excuse about the hot weather.

Though Rose did not really believe him, because it was comparatively cool inside the mill, she allowed it to pass as his colour returned, the moment they left the mill.

Had Charles Cartwright been able to see into the future, he would have treated that cold feeling of violent death, with much more than a mere casual shrug of the shoulders!

Didcot Hall had its own independent power station, generating sufficient electricity to easily supply the needs of the inhabitants. Because of this remarkably rare innovation, coloured illuminated Chinese lanterns, had been strung across the lawns and between the trees, and as evening approached, turning the whole scene into a veritable fairyland.

The lights were low, the evening was warm, and the music was soft, as Charles and Rose, having returned a few moments earlier, were enjoying a heavenly waltz to one of their favourite tunes, when suddenly Rose was rudely interrupted and shaken from her romantic reverie.

'Excuse me Rose. May I?' said Charlotte, as she tapped her sister on the shoulder, at the same time bestowing upon her, one of her most bewitching smiles, and making very sure Charles was included.

'Yes of course dear,' replied Rose graciously, as she released Charles and moved away, showing no sign of the hurt and frustration she felt, at her sister's untimely intervention, and unseemly behaviour.

For it had become patently obvious, no matter how many times Charles had rejected her advances, Charlotte had never given up hope of tempting him into a clandestine relationship with her, and used the full force of her very considerable sexual allure at every opportunity, even including this, her wedding day!

However, Charles was too well schooled in the wiles and fantasies of the opposite sex, particularly those appertaining to this young lady. For he had seen and experienced every facet of Charlotte's wild, unpredictable and volatile character, and could still vividly remember the imprint of that searing lover's kiss, she had so blatantly forced upon him in the yard, behind Mill House at Watersmeet, all those years ago.

She looked up into his eyes, with that haunting hypnotic expression he had tried so hard to avoid, ever since their meeting at Mill House, the first time he had taken Rose home.

He had never danced with her before, or held her so close, and the warm balmy evening air, coupled with the delicate intoxicating fragrance, which seemed to emanate from every part of her, were beginning to take their effect upon his senses, as through the almost transparent material of her dress, he became aware of the heat rising within her, and the sweat welded his shirt to his back.

Charles attempted to look over her head, and fix his gaze upon some point in the distance, but to no avail. For he didn't seem to be in control of his movements anymore, and inexorably his eyes were drawn ever downward, until finally they were locked upon hers!

A frisson of undiluted ecstasy coursed through the veins of Charlotte as their eyes met, for she suddenly had a wonderful feeling of euphoria, that at last she was beginning to break down the indomitable barrier which had been erected between them, by this man whom she loved with every fibre of her being!

Surreptitiously, and very gradually, as they danced, Charlotte began to manoeuvre him towards the darkened perimeter of the lighted dancing area, until they were in almost total darkness. It was then, Charlotte made her big mistake, for as she entwined her naked arms around his neck, and pulled his head down to crush his mouth upon her warm, moist sensuous lips, the music suddenly stopped!

As though coming out of a trance, Charles slowly lifted his head and looked around, then forcefully removing her arms from around his neck, he gripped her wrists and thrust her from him, holding her at arm's length. 'You two-timing little slut!' he hissed. 'For years you have been doing your best to try and seduce me. Well allow me to inform you madam, that after tonight's little exhibition, you have no chance,' he paused for breath, but quickly continued, every word dripping with vitriol. 'There is one small item which occurred today, that you appear to have very quickly, and very conveniently, completely forgotten about. Only a few hours ago you were married, and made your vows before God in church! All I can say is, instead of extending my congratulations to poor foolish Michael, I should be offering him my deepest sympathy!'

Charlotte glared at him. Her green eyes seeming to glow from within, with rage and frustration. She was so sure she could have tempted him to make love to her, if only the damn music hadn't stopped, and then for him to stand there and call her those dreadful names, and say such horrible things to her, in front of all her wedding guests, when, if only he knew it, she literally worshipped the ground he walked upon.

Suddenly, and very dramatically, something in Charlotte's make-up, snapped. Now it was she holding Charles by the wrist, as she dragged him into the circle of light, whilst hitting him repeatedly about the head with her free hand, and screaming at the top of her voice; 'You filthy philanderer! How dare you make suggestions of that nature to me?

And on my wedding day too. My God, you should be horsewhipped! Michael, Michael! Where are you?'

Then, as Michael pushed his way through the astonished, mesmerized crowd of onlookers. 'Please get me away from that dirty old man Michael! He tried to force me to go into the woods, to have his way with me, and him married to my sister. My God! our Rose, your husband makes me sick. For Heaven's sake take him to bed, and give him what he wants!'

It was then she began to cry, fooling everyone with her deep sobbing and shaking shoulders, everyone that is, except her sister. Rose stepped forward, and pushing Michael aside, she slapped Charlotte several times across the face, first one cheek then the other, she then proceeded to flay her with her tongue.

'You dirty scheming little whore!' she shrilled. 'You have been chasing Charles from the first moment you saw him, and tonight you thought you had succeeded. I watched, as you steered him from the light towards the shadows, beneath those trees, and I can well imagine what you said to him. Well our Charlotte, I thank God I have a husband who loves me, and one who is completely immune to your pathetic simpering, and stupid childish attempts at seduction. And now,' Rose stopped and looked around her at the bemused wedding guests. 'I think everyone here knows you for what you really are. So may I suggest Michael, you take your new wife indoors and give her a very cold shower, to see if that will cool her ardour, and if that doesn't work, then take her to bed, and endeavour to assuage her voracious sexual appetite.'

For several seconds after Rose had finished her tirade, complete silence followed this remarkable show of faith in her husband's love for her, and in his undoubted integrity, and the complete and utter denunciation of her sister. Then quite suddenly, everyone seemed to be talking and laughing at once. A few members of the crowd even clapped, and one or two were heard to shout. 'Good for you Rose.'

The result of this, was a furious and highly embarrassed Charlotte, grabbing Michael by the hand, and beating a hasty if somewhat shambolic retreat, into the privacy of the Hall, where they intended spending the first night of their marriage, before travelling to the South of France for a month long honeymoon.

Charles and Rose only stayed a short

while after that fracas with Charlotte, for the whole evening had been soured by her stupid jealous nature.

However, Richard didn't appear to bear any ill will, quite the contrary seemed to be the case, for he was very genial when they finally found him to bid their farewell.

Rose took her husband home to stay the night at 'Mill House', and when they came down for breakfast the following morning, Charlotte and Michael were already sitting at the table with the girl's father, carrying on a very animated conversation, at the same time attacking three piled up plates of eggs and bacon.

Charlotte lifted her head as they entered the room. 'Hello you two,' she greeted them cheerfully, the embarrassment and trauma of the previous evening completely forgotten. 'Had a little lie in did you? It's not like you our Rose to stay in bed till this time in a morning. By the way, didn't we have a wonderful wedding yesterday? Thank you Rose for playing the organ so beautifully, and you Charles, for acting the part of best man so elegantly. I think I'm very lucky to have such a clever charming sister, and such a handsome brother-in-law. Don't you agree Michael?'

Michael beamed upon his sparkling lovely

new bride, and acquiesced immediately. 'Yes darling, of course.'

Before anyone else had a chance to speak, Charlotte began again. 'Michael and I just popped in to say goodbye, before we leave on our honeymoon, but father insisted we stay for breakfast. Do cheer up Charles, and you too our Rose, remember, nothing is as bad as it seems. Please wish me well, and remember this is the first day of my life, and I do so need to make a success of it.'

Charles failed to register any sign of amazement at this little charade, only a slight half amused smile. For he had become used to Charlotte's violent mood swings, and he was beginning to treat them all with the contempt which they deserved.

However, Rose was of a more forgiving nature, and moving forward, she bent and kissed her sister. 'Oh! Charlotte my dear, of course we wish you both every happiness, and long may you live to enjoy it.'

Charles also moved to Charlotte's side, who, after finishing her breakfast, had pushed back her chair and was now standing, but as she moved to embrace him, he fended her off, and calmly held out his hand. 'Goodbye Charlotte,' he said with studied nonchalance. 'I simply reiterate my wife's words.' He then turned to Michael, and shook him by the hand, wishing him every success.

Later, the happy couple drove away, to begin, what Michael thought, as he gazed upon his lovely bride, would be the perfect marriage!

9

Five years had elapsed since Michael and Charlotte returned from their highly successful, blissfully happy honeymoon in the South of France. During which, Charlotte had revelled in the attention, deferential treatment and obvious respect, which her position as Lady Brackley, wife of Sir Michael Sinclair-Brackley demanded.

Five years, which had seen a love hate relationship develop between Charlotte and Richard Brackley, the father of her husband, and one of her many ex-lovers. Richard now secretly despised his illegitimate son for marrying the beautiful exotic Charlotte, with whom he was still so desperately in love, and he also cursed himself daily, for allowing the couple to marry, and to continue to live here at Brackley Hall!

For though he was painfully aware, he was of no more use to her as a man, he knew he could not exist without her tender care of his war torn body. Even though Charlotte had taught another woman how to treat him, he still required her undivided attention at least four days every week.

Richard knew this continuous treatment would eventually become self destructive, for though he could hardly bear the close proximity of her fragrant sensuous body, so near to his often naked one, life without her would be utterly impossible.

His long suffering wife, had finally been granted her divorce, and his sister Daphne, had fled his household in disgust, at the encroaching powers of Charlotte into all aspects of the Brackley Estates private affairs.

The snobbish aristocratic Lady Daphne, could no longer bear to be in the same house as that 'slut of a miller's daughter', who had so assiduously weaved her detestable silken thread of deceit around the heart of her brother, and had finally succeeded in persuading him to allow her to marry his only son and heir.

That last deplorable act, had been utterly unforgivable, and immediately after the wedding, Daphne had packed her bags and her trunks, and left Brackley Hall, bound for America for ever, or so she thought!

★ ★ ★

Charlotte was becoming increasingly bored, and sexually very frustrated, by the lack of male companionship in her life at Brackley

180

Hall. Some time ago, it had become apparent to her, that Richard wasn't quite as euphoric about her marriage as he had been, and with her acute womanly intuition, she had correctly assumed he still loved her, and that as time went by, he was becoming more obsessive, and ever more jealous of his son!

There was a tremendous amount of rebuilding work to be carried out in several towns and cities on the continent, for the destruction caused by the war, had destroyed very many factories, fine buildings and houses, and left thousands of people homeless, and unemployed.

Michael's father had a major share in a large construction company, and to get his son away from Charlotte, he had resorted to sending him to work on different sites in France and Germany, only in a supervisory capacity, because of course he knew no trade. However, what hurt Charlotte and her husband more than anything, was the fact that he was allowed a break of only one week at home, every three months.

Both Michael and Charlotte had protested most vehemently when this suggestion was first mooted, but Richard had been adamant, and now Michael was half way through his first stint abroad.

Charlotte was mulling over these thoughts, as her horse picked his way along one of the many paths which ran through Brackley's wood, and though it was a beautiful sunny morning in June, she felt dejected and trapped, as she cursed her present situation. For she knew that her wonderful carefree spirit, and her voracious sexual appetite were being stifled, and that eventually her enviable capacity for making love, would wither and die.

Her horse suddenly pricked up his ears, and Charlotte halted him and listened. She could hear the faint sound of someone chopping wood, interspersed with a man's voice singing, and Charlotte tilted her head, concentrating, as she tried to ascertain from which direction the sound was coming. It was then, as Charlotte gazed around her, that she discovered she was hopelessly lost, for she could see nothing which seemed familiar to her, and she realised that while she had been dwelling upon her miserable life, her mount had simply plodded on, and now they were deep in the forest. She vaguely wondered what time it was, at the same moment experiencing a sudden pang of hunger.

Having satisfied herself from which direction the sounds were coming, Charlotte selected one of the paths winding through the trees, and followed it.

As the sounds of singing and chopping became more pronounced, Charlotte's heart began to beat a little faster, until quite suddenly, she rode out of the trees and halted on the edge of a beautiful clearing, roughly the size of a tennis court.

At the far side of this clearing, stood the most exquisite log cabin, with a small porch and a surprisingly very pretty flower garden, surrounded by a white painted, low wooden fence.

However, Charlotte gave all of these a mere cursory glance, for her eyes were riveted upon the most magnificent specimen of English manhood, she had ever seen, and she had seen a few! He was stripped to the waist, his well developed, bronzed torso glistening wet with the sweat of his exertions, as he wielded his heavy axe.

Charlotte sat perfectly still upon her horse and watched, fascinated by this totally unexpected, yet wonderfully welcome scene, as the old familiar juices began to flow through her veins, and she felt the heat rise within her, as she began to tremble with anticipation, and allow her fertile imagination to run riot!

Gently, she urged her horse forward,

thinking the man wasn't aware of her approach because of all the noise he was making.

Actually however, he had known of her presence for some time prior to her appearance on the edge of his clearing, and though he had been waiting for this moment for many months, he was suddenly apprehensive, and thought perhaps if he ignored her, she may go away!

Such thoughts were really never a part of Charlotte's makeup, and as she halted two or three yards behind this brawny woodsman, she spoke softly. 'Good morning.'

He pretended not to hear, and continued with his singing and his chopping.

Charlotte was determined to make him turn and look at her, for she wished to ascertain if his looks matched the rest of that magnificent body. Quite undeterred she tried again, louder this time. 'I say. You there. Good morning.'

He abruptly ceased his singing, and with a flick of his wrist, his axe bit deeply into the log. Slowly he turned, and Charlotte caught her breath. Never in all her wildest dreams, could she have imagined a more handsome, more perfectly formed man, for there was no doubt, his looks certainly matched the rest of him!

'Good morning Miss Charlotte!'

She gasped. He knew her name, and even as he spoke it, the timbre of that rich baritone voice, thrilled her to the core. She tried to sound nonchalant. 'Good morning. You seem to have me at a disadvantage. Who are you? What is your name?'

He smiled, a lovely sunny smile, showing two rows of white even teeth. 'My name is Tom Laceby, my grandfather was the head keeper on this estate, until he shot himself accidentally with his own gun. I know you because I happened to be lying on the next stretcher following that of Bill Tate, when we were being carried to your ambulance. I heard him call your name, and have never forgotten it! That day Miss Charlotte, I fell hopelessly in love, and at a discreet distance, have worshipped you ever since!'

For a moment, Charlotte sat immobile and stunned, then her beautiful eyes softened, and her pulse quickened, as she absorbed this entirely unexpected revellation, from such a handsome stranger. Gracefully, she slid to the ground and handed him the reins, watching him as he tied them to a low branch, after making sure her horse was standing in the shade. 'How long have you worked on the estate, Tom Laceby?'

Again he smiled, he liked the way his name

fell from her lips. 'Since a week after you married Michael!'

She looked up at him, she was surprised how tall he was, now she was standing beside him. 'Do you know Michael?' she asked in some surprise.

'Not personally, no miss, but I do know of him.'

She tossed her lovely jet black ringlets. 'Why do you insist on calling me miss, when you know perfectly well, that I'm married?' She was sure she had detected a twinkle in those wide set, sea blue eyes, and wondered vaguely if all he was telling her, bore any resemblance to the truth!

It was then the real Charlotte surfaced, and she knew immediately, she didn't care a damn how many lies he told her. He was here! she was here! And from that first moment when she had emerged from the forest, she had wanted him! He interrupted her train of thought, he was speaking again.

'Because that is how I wish to think of you. Young. Innocent. Virginal, and Single!'

To his surprise, she turned away, and with a half sob in her voice, replied. 'I'm very sorry Tom Laceby, but I can't ever remember being any of those.'

Swiftly he moved forward, and gripping her by the shoulders he swung her round to face him. He was amazed to see tears welling up in those lovely eyes, and without a second thought, he put his strong arms around her slim pliant body, and crushed her to his naked chest.

Charlotte smiled wickedly to herself, as she thrilled at the strength of him, and tentatively she offered him her lips.

He kissed her, hungrily, longingly, yet with a gentle kind of burning passion, she for all her wild years of blatant promiscuity, had never previously experienced, and suddenly, for the first time in her short, yet chequered life, Charlotte knew she was losing control!

As he lifted the thick black tresses of her beautiful shining hair, and brushed his moist lips along the nape of her neck, a frisson of unprecedented longing seared through her entire body, as she felt the heat rise within her, and knew that once again, she had found a man who could satisfy her never ending voracious sexual appetite.

Gently he released her, and taking her by the hand, led her to the entrance of his log cabin.

Charlotte, who had never had any inhibitions about shedding her clothes in front of a man, suddenly sensed that Tom Laceby was somehow quite different, and she became rather reticent about flouting her naked charms.

Her apparent, shy innocent manner, endeared her to him more than ever, and slowly, yet showing great restraint and tenderness, he helped her to undress. Finally, she stood before him, naked as the day she was born, though looking vastly different he thought, as he allowed his gaze to travel over the length of that glorious body, and back again, his eyes washing over her and drinking her in.

'I have waited a long while for this moment,' he muttered hoarsely, as he lowered her gently on to his bed.

That morning, Charlotte relived once again, that day in another wood, many years ago, below the village of Watersmeet. At the time, Charlotte had never expected the euphoria she had experienced on that wonderful day, ever to be equalled, but on this particular morning, it was excelled!

With a tremendous feeling of exhilaration, Charlotte realised she had at last discovered another man who could lift her to those unsurpassed heights of satisfaction, which previously she had only been able to attain with Sir Richard Brackley!

She was content and happy now, and could easily have drifted off to sleep, when suddenly she had to bring all her concentration to bear, for this new man in her life was speaking to her.

'That was wonderful Charlotte, thank you.'

Her only reply was a contented sigh, as she snuggled closer to him.

After a while, he stirred and gently shook her. 'Come along Charlotte, it is almost noon, and if you don't return to the Hall fairly soon, they will be sending out a search party to look for you.'

She kissed him once more, then with a strangled cry, tore herself away. 'Oh! Tom, why can't I stay here with you, in this beautiful idyllic cottage, so we could make love, morning noon and night?'

Tom laughed as he struggled into his corduroys. 'That's a wonderful idea Charlotte, but if this morning's session is a portent of things to come, I think we should both probably be dead by the end of the first week.'

She flashed him one of her wondrous smiles, as she fastened her skirt, and murmured 'I know my darling, but what a way to go!' A sudden thought struck her. 'What did you mean Tom, when you said you had been waiting a long time for this moment'? she asked quietly.

He smiled. 'Did I say that? Well you see

my dear, after that first time I saw you, and then whilst I was in hospital, I used to sit in the grounds and watch you visit Richard Brackley. Unfortunately, I left hospital before he did, and consequently I lost you for a while, not for long though. I was sitting on a bench in the park, when wonder of wonders, you walked by, pushing a pram. I couldn't speak, I was too excited, then the moment had passed, and it was too late. Was that baby your's Charlotte?'

Charlotte didn't reply immediately, she was thinking furiously. Several times since those first few walks in the park, near the house Richard had given her, she had experienced a peculiar sensation of being watched, but could never seem to discover by what or by whom. She had a sudden thought. 'Were you watching, the day Charles and Rose came to visit me?'

First beginnings of 'crow's feet', wrinkled as he laughed with his eyes. 'Yes my dear, soon after you moved in, I took a room in a house on the opposite side of the park.'

'That was much too far away for you to see anyone very clearly.'

'Not with a good pair of binoculars it wasn't,' he replied with a smile.

They were outside now, and she gave him a hefty push. 'Oh! you little sneak,' she said facetiously. 'I could never have believed that of you, if someone else had told me.'

He untied her horse, then with his free arm, held her close and kissed her tenderly, before helping her to mount. Charlotte gazed down upon this handsome bronzed woodsman, she had so inadvertently stumbled upon on this wonderful morning, her beautiful eyes filled with obvious adoration. 'When may I see you again?' she asked.

He looked up at her, his own thoughts mirrored in his eyes. 'I will try and be here every Tuesday and Thursday morning.'

She appeared disappointed. 'Is that all you can manage darling?' she asked, her feelings apparent in her tone.

He laughed. 'Well, of course I am always here all day, Saturday and Sunday.'

Her whole demeanour had changed as he finished speaking, and she laughed with him. 'Oh! Tom Laceby,' she trilled through her laughter. 'You had better be very careful, for I could easily fall in love with you!' On that last remark, and after he had shown her the way, Charlotte dug her heels in, and galloped away.

One year after Charlotte had married Michael, and almost a year after she had met Tom Laceby, she presented her husband with a beautiful baby daughter.

Michael had never even thought of endeavouring to work out the date she must have conceived, which really was very fortunate for Charlotte, for he had been working in Germany, a further two months after she had first met Tom!

There was however, one person who had bothered to work out those all important dates.

Eric Teesdale, the head groom, was busy in his tack room one morning, when Milly came in and said Sir Richard wished to see him. On occasions Eric had taken his master for walks around the estate, and the two had become quite close, as he pushed the wheel chair along. So naturally, he assumed this to be the reason he was being summoned now.

He couldn't have been more wrong! Eric stood dumbfounded, as his employer issued the instructions which culminated in the head groom keeping a watchful eye on the beautiful Charlotte. And when, a month after her baby was born, she came to the stables, and asked for her favourite horse to be saddled, Eric saddled one for himself, and keeping a safe discreet distance, he followed her!

Only Richard Brackley was informed, of what Eric had witnessed taking place, in a certain clearing in Brackley's wood, on that particular morning.

Approximately three weeks later, Charlotte was quietly reading in her room, when she heard a car draw up on the gravelled drive, immediately below her window. Looking out, she was intrigued to see Richard's solicitor alight from the car, and walk towards the entrance to the hall.

Her feminine curiosity, and her inherent suspicious mind instantly aroused, Charlotte moved swiftly and silently, to the adjoining door leading to Richard's room, and very gently opened it, only slightly, but still sufficient for her to be able to overhear the gist of any conversation, which may ensue when the two men met.

A few moments later, she heard the solicitor enter Richard's room, and the greetings which passed between them. However, the conversation which transpired during the next half-hour, caused Charlotte to stand rooted to the spot. Apparently, Richard knew all about her illicit liaison with Tom Laceby, and their surreptitious meetings! He had also worked out where and when her baby had been conceived, and remarked upon the absence of Michael at the time.

It was then she learned the object of the solicitors visit. She was to be cut out of the will entirely, and upon Richard's death, her house would be restored to the Brackley family estate, and her husband was to be informed immediately by letter, of her adulterous behaviour, and of the consequence, namely a child!

Richard even told his solicitor how he had become acquainted with all these facts, and that if she disputed any of the allegations, his head groom, Eric Teesdale, would willingly corroborate the evidence, for on his (Richard's) instructions, he had followed Charlotte on several occasions to Tom Laceby's log cabin!

Long after she heard the solicitor's car drive away, Charlotte lay perfectly still upon her bed, going over and over in her mind, and sifting word for word, the damning evidence she had overheard that afternoon, all against herself.

Gradually, the fear and desperation she had at first experienced, began to evaporate, and as the old cold, hard cynical Charlotte resurfaced, she began to evolve a plan, which though fraught with a modicum of risk to herself, if successful, would instantly and irrevocably cancel out any future arrangements, Richard Brackley may have made with his solicitor, on that particular day's visit!

Actually, this was a plan Charlotte had been toying with for some time, it was just this matter of extenuating circumstances, which were forcing her hand, and causing her to bring the nefarious operation forward.

The following Saturday morning, dawned bright and sunny, and for late April was quite warm. After attending to Richard, and with no mention of the conversation she had overheard the previous day, Charlotte went to the nursery to see Milly. Half-an-hour later, Charlotte accompanied Richard down to the ground floor in the lift, and she sent for Eric to help her negotiate the broad stone steps leading down to the drive, with his wheel chair.

Milly was waiting for them, with Charlotte's baby in her pram, and Sophia standing beside her with her favourite dolly in her pram.

'Hello papa,' she cried excitedly, when she saw Richard. 'We are all going for a lovely long walk today. Well not you and my dolly, 'cause you two are going for a ride.'

Richard chuckled along with his daughter, and as his lovely companion came forward and tucked the rug more tightly around his legs, his conscience troubled him, and he wondered if he really should have sent for his solicitor yesterday. But then he remembered how this woman had committed adultery with Tom Laceby, a common woodsman, and had made a fool and a cuckold of his son, and his resolve hardened.

'Where are we going Charlotte?' he asked, in a friendly tone.

Charlotte smiled. If anyone had seen her, they would have involuntarily recoiled. For it was the kind of cruel smile the Romans must have worn, just prior to throwing those unfortunate Christians to the lions! 'I thought you may like to go and have a look at the lake this morning Richard, for the first time this year. It is such a beautiful morning, I wondered if there might be a few fish coming to the surface, trying to catch some insects.'

'Yes, yes, very good idea Charlotte. You certainly seem to know what I like, damned if I know what I'd do without you.'

The fresh air had quickly restored a little colour to Richard's cheeks, as Eric pushed his master across the sloping lawns towards the lake, and the others walked along beside him, Charlotte pushing the pram containing her new baby, and Milly keeping an eye on Sophia, as she pushed her doll's pram.

Just then the placid surface of the lake came into view. It was quite a large natural lake, approximately one mile long and half-a-mile wide, and Richard became more animated, as the small party progressed ever closer to the dark mysterious looking waters. They were quite high at that point, for the ground in front of them sloped very steeply, all the way down to the water's edge.

Suddenly, they were all startled by Charlotte's hair raising scream, for apparently she had slipped and fell, and the pram she had been holding, was speeding towards the black waters spread out below! 'Help! Eric! My baby. My baby!

Eric took in the situation in one glance, and in the same second, he slammed on the brake fitted to Richard's wheel chair, and tore after Charlotte's baby.

However, what Eric didn't know, was the fact that during the early hours of that morning, when the house was quiet, and everyone else was asleep, Charlotte had crept into Richard's room, and spent a few minutes working on the braking system of his chair! Consequently, immediately Eric released his hold upon Richard's chair, even though he thought he had applied the brake, his master went careering down the hill, in the wake of Charlotte's baby!

Of course Eric had never looked back, for he was too intent on catching the pram before it hurtled into the water, and consequently, was completely unaware of the drama unfolding behind him. Until that is, he heard the combined screams of Charlotte and Milly, but it was too late, for Richard's extra weight, combined with the weight of his heavy wheel chair, had added greater impetus to his downward rush, and as Eric grabbed the pram handle in time to prevent it hitting the water, he glanced round to see his employer, Sir Richard Brackley, just disappearing beneath the cold black waters of the lake, still strapped in his wheel chair!

The head groom only had seconds to stand and stare, for at that moment, Charlotte came tearing down the slope, screaming at the top of her voice. 'Richard! Richard!' and Eric only just managed to prevent her from flinging herself into the icy depths after his master, at the same time struggling to hang onto the handle of her baby's pram.

He managed to apply the brake to the pram wheels, then turn his attention to the screaming Charlotte. 'For God's sake stop screaming, and look after your baby,' he shouted at her, while shaking her violently by the shoulders.

Charlotte looked at her baby's saviour with glazed eyes, as though the shock of what had just happened, had affected her power to assimilate what the man said. Finally she seemed to visibly shake herself back to reality, and though her eyes were still wet with tears, she bravely bestowed upon Eric one of her most ravishing smiles, as she remembered the part he had played in this drama, and that he, apart from the solicitor, may be the only person alive who knew the name of her child's real father!

Slowly, Charlotte allowed her beautiful hypnotic, almost luminous eyes to wash over the countenance of Eric Teesdale, and immediately he succumbed to their power, and she knew then, come what may, this man would never testify against her!

With deep choking sobs, she helped him to pull her pram up the hill towards the stricken Milly and Sophia, who had just seen her father drown. The sobbing child ran to her side. 'Oh! Auntie Charlotte,' she cried. 'Papa has gone. I saw him fall into the lake sitting in his chair. What are we going to do?'

Charlotte handed her pram to Eric, and lifted the broken hearted Sophia up in her arms. 'There, there dear, we must all try and be very brave, please don't cry, look you are upsetting your dolly.'

The sad little procession wended it's way up the remaining slope towards the Hall, and one or two estate workers, who had noticed their employer was missing, came rushing to meet them. Consequently, within minutes of their arrival, everyone who worked on the estate, knew their master, Sir Richard Brackley was dead.

Charlotte made sure Sophia and her baby were safe with Milly, then slipped into the Hall to telephone her sister. She heard the receiver lifted off it's hook. 'Hello Rose, is that you?'

'Hello. Yes dear, you sound dreadful, what's wrong Charlotte.'

'Listen Rose. There is no nice way to tell you this, so brace yourself. Richard is dead! Drowned in the lake, while sitting in his wheel chair.'

There was silence for a couple of seconds, then. 'What? Richard dead? Drowned in the lake? However could that happen Charlotte? Someone must have been with him, to push him that far.'

'Yes I know. Milly, the head groom and I, were with him. I can't tell you what happened over the telephone. Please ring Charles, and ask him to come, and to bring two divers with him from the yard.'

'Yes dear, of course. I will come over myself, as soon as I have contacted Charles. Do try and be brave dear Charlotte, I suppose in some way, this could be a blessing in disguise. Just think that where Richard is now, he will be free of all pain and suffering, hold on to that thought dear sister, and your loss won't seem so hard to bear.'

The line went dead, and with a cynical half smile, Charlotte replaced the instrument upon it's hook. Then humming quietly to herself, she went up to her room, lit a cigarette and lay on her bed, awaiting developments.

An hour or so later, Charles turned up with his two divers. Meanwhile Rose had arrived, and Charlotte had told her the whole sad story, except of course, that bit about her tampering with the brakes on Richard's wheel chair.

The lake was quite deep, and a couple of hours had elapsed, before the divers, assisted by the head groom, and one of the gardeners, managed to drag the dead sodden body, still strapped in it's chair, from the hidden depths below.

Of course there had to be an inquest, at which all three witnesses were called to give evidence, and they all seemed so genuine and honest, it was obvious that no foul play had been committed. However, a lengthy discussion on the braking system attached to the late Sir Richard Brackley's wheel chair, caused Charlotte some concern, but finally no-one could decide definitely, that it had been tampered with, for the very fact that Eric had slammed it down so forcefully, could easily have caused a break in the linkage! So, the coroner declared a verdict of accidental death, was the only possible one he could bring.

When the small group were leaving the courthouse after the inquest, Charlotte silently heaved a sigh of relief as she tucked her arm through her husband's, and walked confidently, head held high, towards the Rolls.

As they turned into their drive, Charlotte's heart missed a beat, when she recognized the car just pulling up in front of the Hall, for it was the same one which had brought Richard's solicitor to see him, on the day before his unfortunate accident.

'Michael. What the devil is he doing here?' she asked sharply, turning to her husband.

Michael looked at her, and wondered why she sounded so concerned. 'What are you worried about Charlotte? He has to be here for the reading of the will.'

Quickly she realised how stupid she must have appeared, and decided she would have to be much more careful, otherwise someone was bound to notice her nervousness, and begin to wonder. With a great effort she smiled at her husband. 'Why of course darling,' she replied nonchalantly. 'It was just that I saw the same car here, the day before dear Richard — ,' she broke off, with a catch in her voice, and tears in those beautiful eyes.

Instantly he became the protective, sympathetic husband. 'There my darling, please don't cry. This won't take long, and then the man will be gone.'

Charlotte dried her eyes, and bestowed upon Michael a wan little smile. 'Thank you dear, I'm much better now, it's just that seeing the same car, brought everything back to me so clearly.'

By the time Michael and Charlotte entered the library, everyone else invited to the reading of this will, were already seated.

Charlotte almost cried out, when she saw Tom Laceby sitting at the table, next to Eric Teesdale! Fortunately she was placed beside her husband, at the head of the table, so it was impossible for either of them to have any direct eye contact with her.

As the dull monotonous voice of the solicitor dragged on, outlining the many small bequests, to various long serving members of staff on the estate, Charlotte had to make a Herculean effort to control herself, for she was becoming increasingly impatient to learn the real content of the will, regarding her and Michael. At long last, the man came to it. He announced that Michael and his wife Charlotte, apart from a trust fund set up for Sophia, were to inherit equally the entire Brackley Estate, including any stocks and shares which were relevant at the time of the reading of the said will, and also all monies deposited in various banks in the City of Hull, and in the City of London.

The air of expectancy which had prevailed earlier in the room, before the solicitor began reading the 'Last Will and Testament' of the late Sir Richard Brackley, had now completely evaporated, to be replaced by a low gentle hum of conversation, for all of those present, had received something, and though some more than others, everyone was very grateful, particularly Charlotte, and she silently congratulated herself upon Richard's early demise, before he had been given the opportunity to sign any new will!

Charlotte roused herself, for the solicitor had collected all his papers, and was replacing them in his case, and now she realised she must assume the mantle of responsibility, as mistress of this house, which had so suddenly been thrust upon her. She pushed back her chair and rose to her feet, then moved over to the fireplace and pulled the tassled cord which hung beside it. Almost immediately, a smartly dressed, very neat Milly appeared. 'Please show the guests to the dining room Milly,' said Charlotte quietly.

The young woman bobbed a small curtsy, and beckoned everyone to follow her, and they all complied, with the exception of Charlotte, Michael and the solicitor.

When the three of them were left alone in the library, the man turned to Michael. 'I was terribly sorry to hear of your loss sir. Of course you had no idea, but your father had just drawn up another will, unfortunately he never lived to sign the document. However, he did leave instructions for me to send you a letter, which I will do now the funeral is over.' He turned to Charlotte. 'Please allow me to extend my condolences to you too my dear. I am sure it must have been a terrible shock for you, being there at the time, and so soon after the birth of your baby. Tell me, does she look anything like her father my lady, a typical Brackley?' he asked silkily.

Fortunately for Charlotte, Michael chuckled aloud. 'Being a girl, I should hope not, though she does have my eyes, and her mother's hair and cute little nose, doesn't she darling?'

Michael never knew why his beautiful wife bestowed such a ravishing smile upon him that day, though in later life, he remembered it, and occasionally he wondered.

Charlotte then turned to the solicitor, and in a cool voice with a cut glass accent, she said. 'There you are my man, I think my husband has answered your superfluous question perfectly. And now if you require any refreshment, I think you had better wander off, and find the others.'

Without so much as a goodbye, the man huffed a 'tut tut', and left the room.

'I say darling, that was a bit rough on the old boy, he was only trying to be civil.'

'Trying to be civil!' Charlotte cried, 'the nasty little man, I can't stand him. Every time he looks at me, he gives me the impression he is undressing me, and then raping me with his eyes.'

Her husband allowed his own eyes to wash over her, and then remarked facetiously. 'Well, one can hardly blame him darling.'

10

The 'Gables Private School For Young Ladies And Young Gentlemen', run by the two Cartwright war widows, had continued to prosper, and now in nineteen twenty six, the year of the General Strike, they had an attendance of some twenty pupils of both sexes.

From the very beginning, Charlotte had suggested that Richard Brackley's daughter Sophia should attend this school, at which she herself taught art on two days a week. However, Charlotte could never by any stretch of the imagination, have foreseen what the result of her quite reasonable suggestion, would eventually lead to.

On that memorable day of the opening ceremony, the then dozen or so children who were attending for the first time, were all introduced to each other, and when James Cartwright, a mere boy, met Sophia Brackley, the beautiful golden haired daughter of Sir Richard, and almost a year and a half his senior, he was completely and utterly hooked!

James literally worshipped the ground

Sophia walked on. Over the years he had followed her everywhere, he had fought for her in the playground, he had sometimes taken the blame for her small indiscretions, and Sophia loved every moment of his undivided attention, and youthful adoration. For he was a fine handsome lad, and all her friends were extremely jealous.

The two young friends were out walking across the parkland belonging to Brackley Hall, one beautiful morning in late summer, nearly at the end of the school holidays. She was now fifteen years old, and he was almost fourteen, when she turned to him with sadness in her beautiful eyes. 'Oh! James, what are we going to do? You know I have to leave next week, to go to that awful finishing school for young ladies in Switzerland, and I may never see you again!' as she finished speaking, she flung herself down on the grass, and looked up at him, with tears in her eyes.

James, forever the young gentleman, and complete Knight Errant, particularly where Sophia was concerned, immediately threw himself down beside her, and in quite a manly way, he took her in his arms. 'Please don't cry Sophia. Of course you will see me again, and you know how it upsets me to see you unhappy. You will be home again for Christmas, I know it seems a dreadful long way off, but we shall just have to try and be patient. In the meantime, we can write to each other, and you can tell me all about your new life.'

As he stopped speaking, she pulled his head down towards her, and kissed him. 'Oh! my dearest James. I shall miss you terribly. You will wait for me, and not forget me, won't you?'

Showing surprising tenderness considering his youth, James gently brushed his lips against her cheek, then searched for her hand. Upon finding it, he gripped it tightly and held on. 'Dearest Sophia. There may be many things in my life I shall forget, but you should know, I will never forget you. And when you return, I shall be waiting. However, I hope with your fancy school, and your new kind of education, that in time you don't find me boring and uninteresting and grow away from me.'

She drew her body closer to his, placed her free hand beneath his head, and kissed him again full upon the lips. 'I think that should help to prove, I shall never grow away from you, dearest James,' she gasped, a little frightened and dismayed at the effect of that single kiss.

James gently eased himself away from her

lissom young body. 'I'm very sorry Sophia, but I think we should be getting back, Aunt Charlotte will be wondering where we are, and I don't want to be banned from seeing you, just before you leave.'

The following Monday morning, Michael, Charlotte and Sophia called at 'Mount Pleasant', to collect James in the Rolls, to take him with them to see Sophia off at Paragon Station, on the first part of her journey to Switzerland.

Both Sophia and James, were very brave that morning, having been brought up, never to show emotion in public, and at all times to maintain 'a stiff upper lip'.

All the same, James angrily brushed his sleeve across his eyes as the train pulled out, and unknown to any of them, Sophia was sobbing her heart out in the privacy of her first class compartment, and it had nothing to do with leaving Hull, Michael or Charlotte!

On the return journey, James turned to his aunt. 'Aunt Charlotte, why does Sophia have to go to a finishing school at her age, surely she is too young?'

Charlotte smiled upon the boy. 'Dear God, how like Charles he is', she thought. 'Well, you see James, this is a bit more than a finishing school. First of all, she will be having further education in all things pertaining to young ladies of her standing and background, also she is going to study foreign languages, hoping to become fluent in at least three of them, therefore James, you will have to work very hard with your own education, if you wish to stay the course with our Sophia, when she finally returns.'

★ ★ ★

A couple of years ago, Charlotte had managed to convince Michael, that Tom Laceby would be much happier and more civilised, if he was allowed to live in one of the estate houses in the village, instead of living in the middle of Brackley's wood, in an old log cabin.

She'd had rather an uncomfortable embarrassing moment, when her husband enquired how she knew so much about the woodsman's living accommodation. However, being Charlotte, she quickly lied her way out of the problem, by telling him that Eric Teesdale had informed her of the squalid conditions in which Mr. Laceby was living. Consequently, whenever Michael was away from home, or in Hull for some business meeting or other, Charlotte would make sure Tom was available!

This particular weekend, Michael had gone

to London, to stay over until Monday, and after taking him to the station, Charlotte had driven the Rolls back to Tom's house. She drove round to the back, and parked the car out of sight in an old barn, she then went to the house, and let herself in with her own key.

Tom wasn't at home, but this small fact didn't deter Charlotte. She, the Lady Brackley, of Brackley Hall, began to prepare lunch for her lover, the man employed by her husband, to tend the trees in Brackley's Wood! Charlotte found some cold pheasant in the meat safe, and was cooking potatoes and vegetables, when Tom arrived home.

He took her in his arms and kissed her. 'Now my darling, this is what I call a real homecoming,' he said, as he stood back, and ravished her with his eyes. 'Why don't we do this more often? much better than sitting down alone to bread and jam.'

Charlotte laughed with him, as she brushed a stray bit of her beautiful hair off her forehead. 'Now go wash your hands lover, then come and sit at the table with me.'

Tom needed no second bidding, and after clearing away, then both of them washing up, which in Lady Charlotte Brackley's life was completely unheard of, they spent the rest of their time together, making love and resting! Before Charlotte had left home that day, she'd had a word with Milly, and told her not to expect her until the morning, or probably late afternoon, and if anyone telephoned, wishing to speak with her, to tell them, she was out riding.

11

Unfortunately for Charlotte, and also for Tom Laceby, someone did telephone on that terrible, unforgettable Saturday afternoon, asking to speak to Charlotte, at about the same time as they went to bed together!

The caller was a very agitated Rose, needing to speak with her sister most urgently. Milly of course knew where her mistress was staying, and though the love of the girl for her employer was almost sacrosanct, she had to admit to the whereabouts of Charlotte, when Rose threatened, in no uncertain terms, to have her dismissed.

Milly stayed in the car, whilst Rose strode purposefully towards the front door. She banged upon the door with her gloved fist. At first there was no reply, then after the third attempt, she stepped back as an upstairs window was flung open, and the half naked body of Tom Laceby appeared.

'What the hell's going on? Oh! sorry Mrs. Cartwright. Do you want something?'

'Yes,' replied Rose coldly, her anger rising, as she saw the number of bedraggled onlookers, gathering round just to gawp. 'I wish to speak to my sister.'

The top half of Tom withdrew and disappeared. Moments later, the front door opened, and Charlotte invited her in.

'There had better be a damn good reason for this intrusion, our Rose. Tom and I were just about to enjoy ourselves, weren't we darling?' she winked at him, and smiled lasciviously as she crossed one shapely bare leg over the other. That was the last genuine smile the Lady Charlotte emitted for some considerable time!

Rose gazed upon her sister, with undisguised contempt. 'Yes, as it happens Charlotte, there is a damn good reason.' Her voice was cold and dispassionate. 'I just thought you ought to know. Our father is dead!'

For several minutes after that mind numbing statement, the silence which prevailed in the room, was almost tactile. It was broken at last, by a terrible scream from Charlotte.

'No! No! our Rose, I don't believe you. You have only come here today with this tale to try and break up Tom and me. Tell her it isn't true Tom,' she ended hoarsely, as she sank into the nearest chair.

'Don't be stupid Charlotte. If you have nothing better to do with your life than this, then I can't even begin to pity you.

215

Personally, I'm past caring what poor stupid idiot you take to your bed, I stopped worrying about that years ago. Now will you please gather up your things, and come with me? We have to go to Watersmeet right away.'

As though in a daze, Charlotte moved out of her chair. 'I can't come with you Rose. You see I came here in the Rolls, it is hidden in a barn behind the house.'

'Very well, get it out and then follow me. I will drive to the Hall, and wait for you to collect some clothes, and whatever else you may need. We shall probably have to stay over for at least a week. Well certainly until after the funeral anyway.' Upon that last remark, Rose turned, walked out of the house, and retraced her steps to the waiting fretful Milly.

As the two cars drew up in front of the Hall, Charlotte ran up the steps and indoors. A quarter of an hour later she reappeared with Milly and her beautiful five year old daughter.

'You can't bring Emma with you Charlotte,' said Rose shortly.

Charlotte immediately became abusive. 'Why the hell not? Are you ashamed of us?'

'Don't be ridiculous. There just won't be any time for you to play with her that's all. Also I don't suppose it will be at all convenient.'

'Well everyone will have to make it convenient, and anyway, Milly is coming with me, and I can assure you, she is quite capable of looking after my little darling.'

Rose could see it would be much easier to succumb to the wishes of her wayward volatile sister, than become engaged in a time wasting shouting match, out here on the drive.

When they were all settled comfortably in the car, Rose drove straight home to 'Mount Pleasant'. She then asked Alice, who had stayed with Rose and Charles after Charlotte had married, to pack a few clothes for her, while she telephone Charles, to tell him of her father's death. Of course he wanted to come home immediately, and take her to Watersmeet. At first she demurred, but quickly realised how important it would be, to have her husband along with her, at a time like this.

Consequently, another hour had elapsed before everyone was ready and seated in the big Bentley. 'Have you let Michael know about this Charlotte?' asked Charles, over his shoulder.

Even though Charlotte could only see the back of his head, and even on a sad journey such as this, she still couldn't help giving him one of her ravishing smiles. 'No dearest Charles, it was impossible for me to let him know. You see, he is away in London, and I received a message this morning, telling me he has gone to Germany for some important business meeting, and won't be returning for at least another week, so he may not be able to attend poor father's funeral,' she finished speaking, with a half sob in her voice, and produced a tiny handkerchief, to wipe away an imaginary tear.

Eventually, the big car pulled into Mill Road, round to the back of the house, and stopped in the yard. With much puffing and stretching of limbs, the occupants alighted. Though Rose had telephoned earlier to inform the housekeeper of their imminent arrival, no-one came out to meet them, so it was with some trepidation, that she moved towards the back door, and after knocking gently, opened it and went in.

The house was quiet, as though it knew The Grim Reaper had so recently paid a visit here. She went into the kitchen. Everything was neat and tidy, table scrubbed and all pots put away. There was a good fire burning in the grate, and though the kitchen was warm and inviting, Rose couldn't eradicate the presence of death which seemed to hang so heavily in the air.

She jumped involuntarily, and turned as Charles made a sound behind her. 'Sorry darling, Haven't you found anyone yet?'

'No, I don't like calling out, somehow it didn't seem the correct thing to do.'

Charles moved to the foot of the stairs. 'Hello. Is anyone there?' he called quietly.

A muffled reply came down from somewhere in the upper regions. Then a buxom middle aged woman appeared on the landing, and began to descend the stairs. 'Very sorry sir,' she gasped. 'I didn't hear you, I was preparing beds in the far bedroom for guests, as Miss Rose instructed. I beg pardon sir. Mrs. Cartwright, but you see we always knew her as Miss Rose.'

Rose was now standing beside her husband. 'Jane!' she cried. 'I had no idea it was you I spoke to this morning on the telephone, why on earth didn't you tell me?'

Jane smiled, a lovely sunny smile, which seemed to light up this house invaded by death. 'Because I wanted to surprise you Rose, how are you? I must say you look remarkably well, family life obviously agrees with you. I do wish we could have met under better circumstances, we must have so much to talk about.'

'Yes, I can believe that, you always were a good talker.'

'Charlotte,' the woman cried, as Charlotte appeared, hand in hand with the beautiful, doll like Emma. 'It is wonderful to see you, and I suppose this is your lovely daughter?'

Charlotte smiled, 'Hello Jane, yes you are quite right, this is Emma. Say Hello to the nice lady Emma.'

The well behaved obedient Emma complied, and everyone laughed, then in the length of a single heart beat, they suddenly remembered why they were here, and immediately they all became subdued and very quiet.

Rose moved towards the front room, and upon opening the door, said. 'Oh I say Jane, we can't have the curtains completely closed, we must let some light in, otherwise we won't be able to see.'

Jane followed her in. 'Yes I know, I was going to draw them back a little when you came. It was just to show some respect. You know how people talk in this village Rose.'

They were all shown to their respective rooms, and then changed into something more comfortable after travelling from Hull. Rose enquired where the body of her father was, and was informed he was at the undertakers, but they would be returning with the coffin later that day.

Charles, forever the practical one, spoke up. 'I say Jane, may I call you Jane?' without waiting for an acquiescence. He continued, 'Has anyone attended to the poultry or the pigs?'

The woman looked at him. 'Yes sir, of course you may call me Jane. No sir, I don't think anyone has.'

Rose immediately stepped forward. 'Don't you worry about it Jane, Charles and I will take care of everything. Come along Charles, a bit of real work for a change will be good for us both.'

They were pleased to get away from the shut in, claustrophobic atmosphere of the darkened house, and breathe the fresh air outside for a while. When they entered the mill, Charles once again had this dreadful premonition, that something terrible was going to happen within the walls of this towering edifice. Only this time the feeling was much stronger than before, and he had to call upon all his strength and will power, to stop himself crying out in despair, at the knowledge that whatever was going to take place, it was utterly impossible for him to prevent.

At last they were out in the open again, and he involuntarily breathed a sigh of relief. Rose glancing swiftly in his direction, noticed his lack of colour. 'What's wrong Charles, you look dreadful?'

'Do I? Sorry darling, I must admit I don't feel so good. It's that damn mill, I don't know what causes this phenomenon, but whenever I go in there, I always have this feeling that something terrible is going to happen near the centre of the mill, on the ground floor.'

His wife looked at him keenly. 'Have you ever had these feelings before Charles,' she asked, her smooth brow creased, and her concern reflected in her voice, for she knew her husband too well, to take this situation lightly. She knew he did not suffer from a fanciful mind, or a wild imagination.

'Yes, the last time we were here. I had a fleeting vision of a young woman lying on the floor, it was only transitory, and though I knew she was dead, for some obscure reason, I couldn't see her face! Just now when we were in there, I didn't experience a recurrence of the vision, but the feeling of death was much stronger than previously.'

Rose passed him another bucket of meal, and opened the gate. 'Well I really don't know what to say my dear, I can't think of any woman, apart from myself, who would wish to venture inside the mill, with all that dust and flour about. So I suggest that in future, when we come here, you stay outside, and just allow me to collect the corn and meal, for as you are well aware, I know everything there is to know, about the working of the mill.'

He smiled bleakly. 'Very well dear, if that is your wish, but I shall be worried sick, all the time you are in there. By the way, I wonder if your father made any plans regarding the running of the mill and the business, in case of an emergency, or accident.'

At that moment, while the gate was open, a large rough haired dog came gambolling through. The miller had bought him some three years ago as a puppy, and apparently had allowed the animal free rein, for as they proceeded further into the field he didn't bother the poultry, nor did they take any notice of the dog, with the exception of the geese, and they were prone to do a bit of snorting and hissing, however he didn't seem to mind.

Finally, all the chores were completed, and a tired Rose and Charles made their way up Mill Road to the house, with a bucket full of eggs. As they entered, Jane was just putting the finishing touches to a rather scrumptious tea. Immediately he saw the table, Charles couldn't suppress an exclamation of delight.

'I say Jane, that ham looks delicious. I don't know about you Rose, but all that walking, collecting and carrying has given me a tremendous appetite.'

Rose smiled fondly upon her husband, and nodded in agreement.

Next day, the majority of the two services held in chapel, morning and evening, were devoted to the life and times of the late miller, Edward Thornton. Apparently he had been responsible for many good deeds in the village, going about his work quietly and without fuss, and helping anyone he found in need, along the way. The minister said Edward would be sorely missed, and at the end of each service, there was hardly a dry eye in the chapel.

The following morning, the day of the funeral, dawned dull and miserable, a typical February morning, with heavy clouds scudding across the Heavens, accompanied by a biting wind and a faint drizzle.

Miles and Ruth, the parents of Charles, arrived at ten-o-clock, and were ushered into the front room for tea and sandwiches. 'Typical funeral weather Rose,' said Miles, endeavouring to make polite conversation.

Ruth glared at him. 'Miles! Surely you can say something better than that.'

He looked sheepish. 'Sorry my dear, I was

only trying to help you to cope with the awful sadness of this terrible occasion.'

Rose flashed him a wan little smile. 'I know father, and for that I thank you. At least you started people talking,' she said, as other mourners in the room, struck up a buzz of conversation.

At precisely two-o-clock on that unhappy afternoon, the body of Edward Thornton, the miller of Watersmeet, left Mill House for the last time, in a hearse drawn by two magnificent black horses. The mourners followed on foot, as the cortege made it's way to the chapel where Edward had been a life long member. Many tears flowed that day, and eventually everyone was gathered in the cemetery, for the final committal.

The majority of the population of Watersmeet had come to pay their last respects to the local miller, who had befriended, and helped so many of them during his lifetime, and consequently the tiny cemetery situated on the outskirts of the village, was filled to capacity.

As the minister came to the end of the short, sombre graveside service, with the words 'Ashes to Ashes and Dust to Dust,' Charlotte lifted her eyes towards the cemetery gates, then with a pointed finger, and a strangled cry of 'No!' she collapsed right on the edge of the grave, and if it hadn't been for the immediate reflex action of Charles, she would most certainly have crashed down on top of her father's coffin!

After pulling her clear, and seeing that the faithful Milly was already passing the inevitable bottle of smelling salts beneath the nose of her mistress, Charles stood up to see what all the hubbub was about.

He then, also nearly followed Edward into the grave! For a tall bean pole of a man, was cutting a swathe through the crowd of astounded gawping mourners, as he made his way towards those family members standing by the new grave.

Though the man had put on a certain amount of weight, Charles recognized him immediately, for this was none other than Charlotte's long lost husband, Halle Scroggs!! Charles moved forward, hand extended. 'Hello Halle,' he greeted, in a calm quiet voice. 'What a time to put in an appearance. Where the devil have you been for the last ten years?'

Halle accepted the proffered palm, and shook it warmly. 'Hello Charles, sorry about the timing. I can't tell you where I've been until we have a little more privacy,' he replied, looking round at the crowded cemetery, then added almost as an afterthought. 'Also a little more time. Believe me Charles, it's quite a long story.'

During the walk from the cemetery to Mill House, Charlotte moved as though in a trance. Afterwards, she could never remember how she arrived at her old home. She didn't appreciate the full impact of the disastrous effect Halle's resurrection would have upon her own life, until some time later, when they were all sitting in the front room, listening to the story of his wonderful escape, when her daughter Emma came in, hand in hand with Milly.

The child ran across to Charlotte and hugged her. 'Hello mama,' she cooed. 'We have been to see the mill, and thousands and thousands of chickens, haven't we Milly?'

Milly didn't reply, she was holding her breath, and waiting to see what effect the words of this innocent child, would have upon certain other people in the room.

For what seemed an Eternity, the room hung heavy with silence, then very slowly Halle raised himself from his chair, and moving as though just recovering from some kind of anaesthetic after an operation, he finally stopped in front of Charlotte.

The past ten years of his life appeared to be etched within the lines of his face, as his pain filled eyes washed over this beautiful

227

woman who was once his wife, and the angelic child clutching her hand.

Again this captive audience held it's breath, not daring to break the emotion of the moment. At last, Halle broke it for them. 'Did that.' the words stuck in his throat, he apologised and started again. 'Charlotte, did that child call you mama?' It was a very simple question, and he asked it in a quiet dignified way.

However, no reply was forthcoming, for Charlotte seemed incapable of speech. All she could do was sit and stare at this apparition, which had somehow returned from the grave, and which, though she would not admit it even to herself, she knew must be the man she had married, all those long years ago.

Halle seemed a trifle irritated, as he repeated the question. 'I asked you Charlotte. Did that child call you mama? and if so, who is the child's father?'

When Charlotte still seemed incapable of answering Halle's question, Charles, who sensed an atmosphere of enmity arising between the two, who after all were virtual strangers, thought the time had come for him to say a few words on Charlotte's behalf. 'Look here Halle, we all thought you were dead.'

Charles got no further, for the normally

volatile and vociferous Charlotte, who had been literally shell shocked into silence, by the appearance of her supposedly dead husband at the funeral of her father, suddenly snapped out of this unaccustomed role, and the Charlotte of old, resurfaced.

With her beautiful hypnotic eyes fixed upon those of her interrogator, she first addressed Charles. 'Dear Charles, I don't need you to protect me. I can fight my own battles thank you,' her voice began, soft as a silken thread, then gradually turned until it became comparable, only to a whiplash! Still with her eyes locked upon those of Halle, she continued.

'So, you think you can come back after twelve years, and just take over where you left off. Where the hell have you been all that time? Didn't you ever think of me and our baby?

'I joined the ambulance service to try and forget your loss, what a bloody fool I was. My God! Twelve miserable years you put us through, and now you come sailing back into our lives, and demand to know if this child is mine. Yes of course she is mine, why the hell do you think she called me mama? And don't you come to the conclusion she is a bastard, because you would be wrong. Surely you didn't expect me to live the life of a nun for the past twelve bloody years. When you were reported missing believed killed, after a while I began to look elsewhere, and eventually remarried. So you see, you can quickly forget any stupid plans you may have, of ever returning to my bed!'

Halle was stunned by her vitriolic attack, and the ferocious venom of her words. The rest of those present were also shocked, for some of the expletives Charlotte had allowed to drop from her slit of a mouth, they had never heard before, even from a man.

Rose was the first to break the ensuing silence. 'Charlotte, I think we should allow Halle to tell his side of the story before we condemn him.'

There were sounds of approval from around the room, so Halle, managing to break the magnet of those hypnotic orbs, which he had once found so fascinating, turned away from Charlotte, and seated himself in a chair, facing his captive audience. He spoke quietly, in soft cultured tones, very different to when he had first joined the army as a young man.

'We were under heavy artillery attack, late one afternoon in France, when a shell burst very near to three of us. My two friends were killed instantly, and I was blown into another empty shell hole. God knows how long I remained in that hole, but when I regained consciousness it was dark, and physically I seemed to be unscarred. However mentally, that was something very different. I had no recollection of who I was, or what I was doing hiding in that hole in the ground!

It was then I heard distant heavy gunfire, and realised I must probably have been hidden, and now apparently the war had passed on, and I was alone. Tentatively I climbed out of my hole, and began to walk away from the sound of the guns. Several hours later, I stumbled across an isolated farm, and crept into a barn, where I thankfully fell into a deep sleep, on a pile of wonderfully soft hay.'

Rose noticed Emma was becoming restless, obviously bored with all this grown up talk, so suggested Milly go and make them all a cup of tea, then take the child for a walk.

After this slight interruption, Halle continued, his avid listeners, hanging on his every word with bated breath. 'I was awakened by two very pretty young girls, who spoke to me in French. It was only then I realised I was in France, anyway they ran to fetch their grandfather, who fortunately for me, hated the Germans, and when he recognized my uniform, became most animated and very friendly towards me. He was amazed when I answered him in perfect French, so was I, for of course I couldn't remember that I had learnt French at college. Apparently one of the anomalies of amnesia, is that although one forgets everything which went before the loss of memory, one can often remember words. The problem was, and this was something the old chap found very difficult to comprehend, I had no idea who I was, and couldn't even tell him my name!'

At that point Milly returned with the tea, and Emma handed everyone a piece of seed cake, for which they all thanked her with smiles and a pat on the head.

Halle had a sip of his tea, and continued. 'Let me see, where were we? Ah yes, I remember. Well the man's son, who was actually the farmer, had joined the army, and was away fighting, therefore his wife and parents were trying to run the farm on their own, while he was away. Of course this was very difficult for an old man and two women, so really they welcomed me with open arms, saying they would hide me and feed me, if in return, I would help on the farm. Naturally I jumped at this idea, not knowing of anything else I could do, or of anywhere else I could go,' he paused for another sip of tea, and a bite of seed cake.

'Well eventually we received word that the war was over, and the village, which was only a mile from the farm, had no schoolmaster, he had been killed during the conflict. For some inexplicable reason, I could never fully understand why, though I think it must have been something buried deep in my subconscious mind, I felt attracted to the school, and applied for the position of schoolmaster, in which I succeeded, for I was the only applicant. However, during my years at the farm, I was of course living in very close proximity to the family, and right from the first day, when those two girls found me, the eldest one, Maxine, who was fourteen years old at the time, and very pretty, had become extremely fond of me. Her feelings were reciprocated, and in nineteen twenty, we were married!'

This quite unexpected, astonishing revelation, caused gasps of amazement from his listeners, and prompted Charles to ask; 'Halle, if as you say, you left the farm and went to teach in the village school, who replaced you, to help run the farm?'

Halle drained his cup, and placed it carefully upon the saucer. 'Good question Charles,' he replied with a faint smile. 'I was coming to that part. There was a school house attached to the school, so naturally when Maxine and I were married, we left the farm and went to live near the school. The girl's father was killed during the last weeks of the war, but fortunately Maxine's sister had fallen in love with a young farmer, and when we left, he moved in with a view to eventually getting married, which incidentally they did.'

If the news of his marriage had caused a ripple of gasps and whispered comments to fly around the room, the next part of this fascinating story, had them all struck dumb!

'After we had been married just over a year, Maxine presented me with a beautiful baby daughter,' he paused momentarily, to allow this monumental message to sink in, and when no reply was forthcoming, he opened his mouth to continue, when this time it was Rose, who suddenly interrupted.

'Excuse me Halle. Can you please tell us, when your memory returned, and what your reactions were?'

'Sorry Rose, I can't give you any specific date, but after I had been teaching at the school for about three years, I began to have kaleidoscopic flash backs of scenes from my childhood. The first one was of the vicarage at Watersmeet down Whitton Road, if you remember, I was born there. Then I had a momentary flash of the school which I attended, and later taught there. All of these were spread over a great many months, I think my recovery had something to do with my school environment, you see teaching was what I had always done in my past life, and I firmly believe that was the catalyst which finally triggered the return of my memory, which incidentally, only returned fully, two months ago!'

Rose thanked him. 'Now what about the second part of my question Halle, what were your first reactions, when you discovered your true identity?'

He was silent a moment, as though in deep thought, his eyes downcast, then he lifted his head and looked directly at Charlotte. 'Shock. Horror. There just aren't the words to describe how I felt. At first I couldn't believe who I was, the memories came flooding back far too fast for my tortured mind to assimilate. It was like a window opening on to another life, as though I had been dead for many years, and was born again. I know that may sound rather silly now, but in some ways I suppose that could be the only true metaphor. Of course, after much thought and heart searching, I told my wife what had happened, and everything about my life in England, and it was a joint decision, that I should return here and discover if you were still alive. Of course you are very much alive, so now I shall have to write a letter to Maxine, and inform her, that we were never really married, because I was already married to you,' his face was a mask, completely devoid of expression as he finished speaking, and no-one present, could even begin to guess his thoughts.

For several minutes, silence reigned supreme in that front room at Mill House, each member of the small funeral party going over in their minds, the words of that traumatic wartime story, they had just had the privilege of hearing from the lips of one of their own, no less a person than the local village school master!

Once again it was Rose who broke this all pervading silence, as she turned to Charlotte. 'Well dear sister, apparently your marriage isn't legal either. Dear, dear what a mix up. I'm afraid you are going to have to give up your lavish lifestyle, and revert to being the wife of Halle!'

Charlotte leapt to her feet, and for the first time since Halle had begun his dialogue, she spoke. 'If you think for one moment, our Rose, I am going back to live with Halle, and try to survive on the miserable wages of a village schoolmaster, you must be more bloody stupid than you look. My God, I would rather die!'

She then turned on Halle, her normally wide open eyes mere slits, as she vented her fury upon her hapless long lost husband. 'As for you, what the hell did you have to come back here for and spoil everything? After years of sleepless nights and worry, wondering if you were dead or had been taken prisoner, at long last I have been able to put all that behind me, and now have my life on an even keel, exactly as I want it, and believe me, neither you or anyone else is going to take this life away from me, or deprive me of any of the wonderful luxuries which have now become my right!'

'Our Charlotte!' the voice of Rose whipped across the room like a pistol shot. 'Please remember where you are, and why we are all gathered here today!' she said scathingly.

One of the small company of mourners, an old friend of the late Edward Thornton, rose unsteadily to his feet. 'Please excuse me Rose,' he said haltingly. 'If you don't mind, I am going, I don't think this is a suitable subject for anyone to discuss in public, I'm sure your father would never have allowed Charlotte to carry on like this. Good day to you all, and thank you Rose for inviting me and my wife. Come along Mabel.' A lovely sweet faced old lady, bestowed upon Rose a charming smile, as her husband took in the remaining members of the company, with a single glance from his alert, bird like eyes, and they left the room together, her arm linked through his.

The rest of the people present became aware of a hostile atmosphere being generated between the members of this family, with whom they had come to grieve over the loss of a very fine member of their community, and as one, they suddenly decided they had over stayed their welcome.

Immediately the family members were at last on their own, Charlotte once again tore into Halle. 'The best thing you can do, is return to your precious Maxine, and forget all about me, or that you were ever married in this country. Anyway, I have a headache, and am going to lie down for a while, don't you dare follow me into my bedroom, or have any fanciful ideas about sleeping with me tonight!' upon that last vicious remark, she flounced out of the room, and went upstairs to her own room.

However, before Rose retired to bed that night, she looked in to see her sister, and wasn't surprised to find her still awake. 'What do you want?' Charlotte greeted her sullenly.

Rose seated herself upon the bed. 'Now you just listen to me for a moment young lady. You may have married into the aristocracy, and no doubt think yourself a little above us normal mortals, but allow me to tell you something our Charlotte. This time, you are going a bit too far, for you have committed bigamy! I know you were not aware of it at the time, but ignorance is no excuse for breaking the law, and if you persist in this rebellious manner, you could finish up in prison! So just think about that tonight before you go to sleep, and then I hope you may see some sense in the morning.' Rose bent over the bed and kissed her. 'Goodnight dear,' she murmured, and left a very mollified sister.

The following morning during breakfast, to the surprise of everyone, and after helping to clear away and wash up, Charlotte suggested to Halle, that she would help him to feed the poultry, while Rose and Charles filled all the containers with drinking water. Had the others known of the devious, deadly plan, behind this apparent generous gesture, none of them would have complied.

After the work had been completed in the morning, they all sat down quite amicably to lunch, and then went for a walk up to the cemetery to freshen the flowers on their father's grave.

When they returned to Mill House, unfortunately Charlotte couldn't find her purse, and then she realised she may have lost it in the cemetery. Immediately she remarked upon this, Halle offered to go back and look for it, which of course was exactly what Charlotte had expected of him.

'Come along Rose,' said Charles, moving towards the door. 'While Charlotte waits for Halle, we will go and take our water tank down to the chickens. I filled it ready, when we finished this morning.'

After a few minutes, Charlotte ran down the garden path, and into the mill, and a short while later re-emerged, and returned to the house, again via the garden path. She waited another quarter of an hour, and Halle had still not returned, so she decided to make her own leisurely way down Mill Road.

Three years ago, Edward had purchased a large rough haired dog which was blessed with the name of Ben. Well during the last couple of weeks, this dog had suffered one or two slight fits. They didn't seem very serious, so no-one had bothered too much. However, the miller had always allowed any dog he had to accompany him, and run free among the poultry, which he was doing today with Charles and Rose.

Charlotte was half way down Mill Road,

when she heard the most awful sounds coming from the poultry runs. There were whining noises from the dog, interspersed with a single high pitched bark, and Rose screaming at the top of her voice; 'Help! Charlotte! Halle! Help!' She ran the rest of the way as fast as she could, and almost crashed into the gate with the force of her impetus.

On looking over the gate, Charlotte froze. The big dog was obviously having a fit of some kind, it was slavering and frothing at the mouth, and savagely attacking Charles, the only man she had ever really loved! and all he had with which to defend himself, was a pitiful short stick.

Rose saw her. 'Charlotte. Fetch the gun! Fetch the gun!' she screamed, 'The dog will kill him!'

Without a second's hesitation, or a single thought for herself, only for the safety of that wonderful man, whom she loved above all others, Charlotte tore across the yard, up the steps, and straight into the mill:

Halle, who was walking down Mill Road, and wondering what all the noise was about, coming from the direction of the mill, suddenly heard through that cacophony of sound, the beginning of a woman's high pitched scream, which seemed to be cut off,

241

almost before it began! He sprinted the rest of the way, and went straight to the gate. Taking in the seriousness of Charles' predicament in one single glance, Halle picked up a heavy shovel which was leaning against the mill wall, calmly opened the gate, shepherded Rose and then Charles, out through the open gate, closed it, and turning just as the animal attacked, dealt it a savage blow on the head, killing it instantly!

Thanking Halle as he ran, Charles rushed to the entrance to the mill, but even before he reached it, he had a terrible feeling he knew what lay inside.

All that could be seen of the once beautiful Charlotte, was the soles of her shoes, sticking out from beneath a sixteen stone sack of corn! She had set a trap for Halle, and in the excitement of the desperate situation facing the only man she had ever really loved, had forgotten all about it, and now lay still and silent, with the life crushed out of her!

12

Almost five years had passed since the traumatic events at Watersmeet, when Rose had lost her two remaining close relatives, both within a week of each other. During which, for the first six months, she was bordering very close to the brink of a nervous breakdown, and if it hadn't been for the love lavished upon her, by her wonderful husband, there was no doubt, she would probably have succumbed under the effect of that terrible double tragedy, and gone to join her beloved father and sister Charlotte!

Of course there had been an inquest into the death of Charlotte, and though she had died in extremely suspicious circumstances, no incriminating evidence or motive could be discovered or proved, so the only possible verdict the coroner could bring, had been; Death by Misadventure!

Charles of course, suspected what the real cause of her death had been, but he refrained from telling Rose or Halle, though sometimes he wondered if Halle had worked it out for himself. Halle's son Richard, had dropped out of college, and gone to help his father run the mill at Watersmeet. For Rose being the only survivor, had inherited everything, and not wanting any part of it for herself, had allowed the mill and the land, to go to Halle and his son, for a peppercorn rent.

In the meantime, Halle had written to his wife in France, explained everything to her, and asked her to join him here in England, but unfortunately she had declined, on the grounds that they were not properly married, and she couldn't speak the language, but the biggest hurdle of all, was the English weather! So, considering the amount of luck he'd had with his previous lady friends, Halle had decided to remain a bachelor for the rest of his days, and simply hire a housekeeper to tend the requirements of himself and his son Richard.

★ ★ ★

Michael had returned in time to be present at Charlotte's funeral, and having completely broken down in the cemetery, had reached for the strong arm of Charles, to help him remain upright.

Halle also attended, but managed to avoid Michael, chiefly through the expertise of

244

Charles, in keeping them both well apart. For he could see nothing to be gained by the two widowers knowingly attending the funeral of the same wife!

Fortunately, Michael refused an invitation from Rose to go with the assembled mourners to Mill House, saying he wished to return home before dark. So it was, he just sat outside in the Rolls, waiting while Milly packed her own and Emma's suit cases, then they bid Charles and Rose, a tearful goodbye.

The following afternoon, Charlotte's solicitor called at Brackley Hall and was taken immediately to the library, where a strange assortment of expectant legatees awaited him. With a cursory nod to the assembled company, the man opened his small case, and spread some important looking documents upon the table.

After thoroughly cleaning his spectacles, he began to read the 'Last Will and Testament of Lady Charlotte Brackley'. The reading did not take many minutes, for there were few recipients, even so, it contained quite a number of surprises. Her house overlooking the park, she had bequeathed to Tom Laceby! (Whom she stated, had been a very good friend. Many years were to elapse, before Michael discovered how good!) Charlotte had also left Tom an annuity of Three Thousand Pounds, to be paid out of her share of the Brackley Estate.

Eric Teesdale inherited Two Hundred and Fifty Pounds. (For services rendered) To her sister Rose, she left her fur coats. To Alice and Milly, the choice of any clothes in her wardrobe. There was also, One Hundred Pounds for George. (Her dear friend and chauffeur) Unfortunately, old George had passed away some months ago, so Michael suggested the money should go to George's nearest relatives.

There was also Two Thousand Pounds for her son Richard, and a large sum set aside for her daughter Emma, the interest to accrue, and she was to inherit the money, when she attained the age of twenty one. Any balance outstanding, after the foregoing had been expedited, was to go to her beloved husband Michael.

Amidst a low excited buzz of conversation, the solicitor gathered up his papers, picked up his case, and was on the point of leaving, when Michael invited him to stay for a drink. However, the man declined on the pretext that he had another client waiting, and a few moments later he had left.

Miles had finally retired from attending the shipyard, in what he called a supervisory capacity, and had died peacefully in his sleep, adding more pain to the catalogue of suffering Ruth had lived through in her lifetime. She was now approaching seventy four years, and though occasionally she felt a little more tired than usual, she was still very fit physically, and her ready wit, coupled with her wonderful capacity to solve most mental problems, was the envy of all the younger generations, including her two remaining children Charles and Debbie.

The year was nineteen hundred and thirty four, and Richard Brackley's daughter Sophia, was approaching twenty one. She had finished her college days some time ago, and the love she and James Cartwright had shared through their childhood years, had never waned.

James had inherited the exceptional looks, build, and almost equalled the strength of his great grandfather, Thomas Cartwright, and Sophia, the daughter of Sir Richard Brackley, had the poise and beauty of a true aristocrat. Many of their envious contemporaries had to admit, they made a very handsome couple, but no-one could truthfully speak ill of either James or Sophia. For he remained cool, and in complete control in all situations, and her whole personality exuded charm and love of the only man in her life.

Thus it was, one beautiful soft evening in the middle of July, by sheer coincidence, James led his beautiful partner to the same idyllic rose covered arbour, in the gardens of Mount Pleasant, that his grandfather Miles Cartwright had taken the exquisite, innocent Ruth, all those years ago, with similar intentions, and exactly the same result!

'Oh! James, what a beautiful place,' murmured Sophia, her eyes filled with love and adoration, as she gazed upon her lover. 'Why have you never brought me here before?' she asked, as she seated herself upon the clean white handkerchief, he had spread upon the seat.

He took her in his arms and kissed her. The evening was warm, there was no sound of wind or of birds in the trees, the moment was perfect for lovers. Very gently he released her, yet still holding her close, and looking directly into her eyes, he spoke the words she had so longed to hear for many months past. 'Sophia,' strangely his voice sounded slightly high. He began again. 'Sophia, will you marry me?'

She linked her fingers behind his neck, and pulled his head down towards her, and kissed him, passionately, longingly, completely different to any kind of kiss they had ever previously experienced.

James suddenly realised he was beginning to lose control, and with a Herculean effort of sheer will power, he very gently but firmly, eased her warm pulsating body, slightly away from his.

'Why did you stop kissing me James?' she asked, an injured air of innocence flooding her lovely features.

'Sorry my darling. I had to,' he gasped, producing another handkerchief, and wiping the perspiration from his glistening brow. 'I'm afraid I was allowing the situation to get a little out of hand. You still haven't answered my question. Please Sophia, will you marry me?'

Sophia locked her beautiful deep blue, almost violet eyes upon his, and in a low voice vibrant with emotion, she murmured, 'Yes of course I will my darling James.'

Once more he held her close and kissed her, being careful not to betray his true feelings this time. 'Thank you my dearest Sophia. When?'

'When what?'

'When will you marry me?'

She laughed, a happy girlish laugh. 'Oh! you silly man. Any time. Just now, if you wish.'

For some considerable time, the two young

lovers sat locked in each other's arms, until finally, James glanced at his watch. 'Darling, it's half-past-seven, we shall really have to be going, dinner is at eight. Come along, let's go tell everyone our fantastic news,' he said, as he released her, and standing up, helped Sophia to her feet.

Hand in hand, the happy couple ran all the way to the house, hot and gasping for breath, they charged through the open French window, which led off the terrace, straight into the drawing room.

James's parents and sister Marcia, were sat reading and listening to dance music on the wireless. They all looked up, startled at this unseemly intrusion.

'What's all the rush for my boy?' asked Charles rather coolly.

James, still holding the hand of Sophia, drew himself up to his full height, and addressed his parents. 'I thought you should be the first to know, Sophia has just consented to be my wife. We are to be married during the last week in August!'

His captive audience gasped, then all began speaking at once. Rose however, leapt to her feet, and embraced the joyful blushing Sophia. 'Oh! My dear. Congratulations. You have no idea how thrilled Charles and I are. We were only wondering the other day, how much longer it would be, before James popped the question.'

Charles was on his feet. 'Well done my boy,' he said, giving James a bear hug, and shaking him by the hand. 'We always hoped you would, but one can never be really sure you know, until you tie the knot.' On that profound remark, he turned and kissed Sophia on the cheek.

After Marcia had duly bestowed her congratulations upon the happy lovers, and Charles, after sending for a bottle, had poured each of them a glass of sparkling champagne, as she lifted her glass, a sudden thought struck Rose.

'James, did you say the last week in August?' she asked, now they were all seated.

He smiled, and gave Sophia's hand a squeeze. 'Yes mother, that is exactly what I said.'

'But James, that is only six weeks away! We can't possibly have everything ready in so short a time.'

Irritatingly, he continued to smile. 'Yes of course you can mother, there's nothing to it. All we have to do is see the vicar, book the church and the organist, and then book an hotel for the reception. I'll take care of the honeymoon arrangements,' he added, as an afterthought.

His mother looked at him askance. 'And you think that's all there is to worry about, do you?' she asked scornfully. 'What about your brides dress, the bridesmaids and their dresses, the scores of invitations which will have to be posted, the wedding cake, the flowers, the presents, and hosts of other things.'

Marcia stepped forward. 'Please don't fret yourself mother. I'm sure Sophia and I will be able to cope, won't we dear?' she said, turning to her future sister-in-law.

Sophia laughed happily, and replied in the affirmative. They were the best of friends these two, having known each other since Marcia first started school at 'The Gables', and Sophia, for all her aristocratic lineage and fine finishing schools for ladies, was really a very down to earth young lady, and a lovely person to know. In fact, Marcia could not think of anyone, whom she would rather see marry her beloved James, than her best friend Sophia.

Rose, resigned to the inevitable, raised her glass along with the others, in response to the toast by Charles. 'Very well,' she said, after a sip of her champagne, and taking out a minuscule handkerchief, for the bubbles tickled her nose. 'If you girls think we can manage this tremendous task, and be ready by the last week in August, then so be it. For I am not one to pour cold water upon the wedding aspirations, of so handsome a couple, particularly when this could turn out to be the highlight of this year's social calendar!'

A column appeared in the London Evening Telegraph, during the heady days leading up to the wedding, which few people seemed to read, or if they had, they took very little notice.

★ ★ ★

President Hindenberg of Germany aged eighty seven years, had died on August the second, and three hours later, at noon, an ex-corporal who was in the German army during the Great War, announced that the title of President was being abolished, and that he was to be known as Fuehrer and Reich Chancellor. After styling himself as Supreme Commander of the Armed Forces, he exacted from all officers and men 'a sacred oath of unconditional obedience', not to Germany but to himself personally!

The name of that man was Adolf Hitler!

On August the nineteenth, he cleared the last remaining hurdle to total power, when an unprecedented thirty eight million Germans gave him a remarkable ninety per cent vote of approval, for his decision to become head of state as well as Chancellor.

Only four million Germans said No!

However, irrespective of the war mongering signs coming from abroad, all plans for the wedding of the year, proceeded apace. For many months past, the Cartwright's yacht 'The Maria', had been in dry dock, undergoing a complete refit, and a week before the wedding, she had just returned from her maiden voyage. Much heart searching, and midnight oil had been spent, on trying to determine a new name for the boat.

Charles had wanted to call her 'The Rose' after his wife, but she would have none of it. Finally, after several other weird attempts had been discarded, he persuaded her to accept 'The Charlotte Rose'. This inference to her late younger sister, had thrilled Rose to the core, for of course now Charlotte was dead, she was prone to remember only the best things about her short, yet very colourful life.

On that last Saturday of the month, the twenty fifth of August, nineteen hundred and thirty four, James William Cartwright and The Honourable Sophia Penelope Brackley, were joined together in Holy Matrimony, at the same church in which his great grandfather, the legendary Thomas Cartwright, had married his beautiful elegant Kate.

★ ★ ★

The snobbish, aristocratic Lady Daphne Brackley, still unmarried, having been informed of the impending wedding between Sophia and James Cartwright, had immediately packed, and made all haste to leave America, and arrive in England as quickly as possible. Unfortunately, she was delayed, and a fuming Daphne reached Brackley Hall, only to find everyone had left, and gone to the wedding! She ran outside again, but her taxi was fast disappearing down the drive, in desperation she hurried through the house, and out to the stables.

Daphne burst into the tack room, to find two young stable lads playing cards. 'Are you two supposed to be working?' she shrilled, as they jumped up, knocking over the card table. 'If there isn't a car available, one of you saddle me a horse, and be bloody quick about it.'

The eldest of the two, stared at her. 'I'm sorry, I can't do that madam, I don't know who you are.'

Daphne was quickly losing what little

patience she had. 'I'll tell you who I am, you stupid boy,' she was almost screaming now. 'I am Lady Daphne Brackley. I was born in this Hall, and have just arrived from America for the wedding of my niece, so saddle a horse for me. Now!' she shouted, 'Before I take a whip to both of you!'

The stable lad needed no second bidding, and as she followed him outside, Daphne noticed a powerful looking Norton motor cycle, propped up on it's stand a few yards away. 'I say lad, who owns that machine?'

The youth stopped, and turning, walked back to her. 'I do my Lady,' he said proudly.

A few minutes later, The Lady Daphne was riding pillion, hanging on for dear life, as they went hell for leather, down country lanes and across fields, taking the shortest route he knew to get her to the church, before it was too late! At last the church loomed ahead, and Daphne slid off the back of the motor cycle, almost before it skidded to a shuddering halt.

Without so much as a 'Thank you,' or a backward glance, Daphne dashed into the church, just as the vicar was saying; 'If there be any person present who knoweth of any just cause or impediment why these two should not be joined together in Holy

Wedlock, let him speak now, or forever hold his peace.'

There was a second's deathly silence, and then that terrible thing happened, which every couple who were about to be married, had dreaded down the ages.

The silence was suddenly and dramatically shattered, by a high female voice, which Rose instantly recognised. 'Stop this wedding! Stop it now! Those two are half brother and sister!'

There was another silence, more pregnant than the first, but it lasted less than the length of a heart beat, then the whole congregation turned as one, and the church was filled with an excited buzz of conversation, as a red faced, hatless bedraggled Lady Daphne walked unsteadily, (because she was still suffering from the effects of her hectic ride) the length of the church. Her face was grubby, and her dress was torn where it had snagged on thorn bushes during her onward rush.

At last she reached the astonished, bemused bride and groom, not to mention the shocked vicar. 'Upon what do you base this scandalous accusation madam?' asked the minister loftily, as he allowed his piercing eyes to flicker over the hot wretched Daphne, while the crowded church had fallen silent, as everyone strained their ears, trying not to miss one syllable

257

of the conversation, as this unprecedented drama unfolded before their eyes.

Daphne wished now that she had never come, that she had allowed this stupid wedding to go ahead, and that she had remained safe and out of reach in America. As these thoughts were skimming through her mind, she searched for a way out of her self induced predicament, but quickly realised there was none, and she knew that everyone present was expectantly waiting for her answer.

Finally, Daphne lifted her head, squared her shoulders, and turning, looked directly at Rose. 'I base this accusation on the fact, that while Rose and her sister Charlotte, were both confined to their beds, having each given birth to a son on the same day, that I bribed one of the maids to let me see the new babies in their cots. Well I had a score to settle with Rose Cartwright, and knowing that my brother was the father of her sister's child, I exchanged the two babies. You see the cots were both in the same room, so it was quite a simple matter really to change one for the other. I now realise what a stupid thing I did that day, and when I heard these two were getting married, I just knew that somehow I had to try and prevent the wedding taking place.

I'm dreadfully sorry Rose, please forgive me,' Daphne had begun her mind numbing revelation with a low voice, but when she finished it was little more than a whisper.

To the amazement of those who could see her, and particularly to Daphne, Rose was actually smiling. 'I'm very happy to tell you dear Daphne,' she said quietly, yet in a voice tinged with something which sounded remarkably like triumph. 'That I am afraid your journey from America has been totally unnecessary. You see, my baby had a small birth mark on one shoulder, so of course when the nurse brought him for his next feed, I realised immediately what had happened, and after a few words with the maid you so callously bribed, I discovered the whole sordid truth of the matter. I then asked for my baby to be brought to me, and decided to say no more about it.'

A very angry, highly embarrassed Daphne had great difficulty keeping her temper in check, particularly when, much to her chagrin, a low hum of approval swept through the church as Rose finished speaking, and the two lovers standing at the altar, embraced each other.

'You mean to tell me, you have known about this all these years, and never said anything,' she hissed, through a slit of a mouth.

However, the vicar having seen and heard enough for one day, cut across Daphne's vilification of Rose, and holding up his hand, pronounced that the wedding service would now continue.

After all the photographs had been taken, on this lovely sunny day, amidst the roars of appreciation from the hundreds of people who had gathered just to see this spectacular wedding, and as the bells rang out their joyous message, and James walked with his beautiful bride, of but a few moments, beneath a canopy of crossed whale bone, held aloft by the boys from Trinity House, Charles, who was following in the wake of the retinue, wondered if the ghost of his grandmother Maria, was standing by the churchyard wall, watching this colourful procession!

As in the days of Thomas and Kate, all the streets surrounding the church were packed with vehicles, only this time they were not horses and traps!

Rose had decided to hold the reception at home in the great hall of Mount Pleasant, and exactly as some eighty years ago, twin trestle tables ran the length of the hall, the same candelabra, the same phalanx of polished silver cutlery, and the same brilliant cut glass, decorated the snow white table cloths, though the light this time, came not from hundreds of candles, but from four huge cut glass chandeliers, holding scores of electric light bulbs.

As the convoy of cars drew up outside the imposing front entrance to Mount Pleasant, and began to disgorge their elegantly dressed passengers, James and Sophia had already run the gauntlet of two rows of cheering servants, and after he had scooped her up in his arms, and carried her over the threshold, to even more cheering, they were waiting just inside the great door, to welcome their guests.

Some one hundred and fifty had been invited, and according to the hubbub of conversation which echoed round the old hall, everyone must have accepted. Richard, who was the son of Charlotte, and James's best friend, the two having grown up together at 'The Gables' school, was the groom's 'best man', and when the guests had finished eating, though many of them were still drinking, he pushed back his chair, and standing up then thumping the table with his clenched fist, he shouted 'Order! Quiet please!' to which most of them acquiesced, though a few, not quite immediately.

Richard proceeded to read out several telegrams and cards from well wishers, made a short speech, during which he mentioned what a handsome couple James and Sophia were, and then went on to stress what a wonderful wedding they had all enjoyed that day, particularly after that rather unfortunate incident at the church.

When Richard finished speaking, Charles stood up and informed the assembled company, that regretfully he would have to bring the proceedings to a close. However, those who wished, could stay, because there would be dancing after the tables had been cleared away, but anyone who so desired, was quite welcome to accompany the bride and groom to the docks, where their yacht was waiting to sail on the evening tide.

A small crowd of slightly inebriated friends and relatives had followed the wedding car, and were now assembled in the Yard of Shipbuilders, Earnshaw & Cartwright, cheering vociferously as James and his lovely Sophia went aboard.

The 'Charlotte Rose' looked like a new ship, and really was a magnificent sight, dressed overall as she was for this very special occasion, with her sparkling new paintwork, twin masts and single funnel, and as she pulled away from the quay side, quite a crowd had joined the wedding guests, and all added their voices to the cheers which rent the air, and sent the happy couple on their way, to enjoy a wonderful honeymoon, cruising around the Mediterranean, for the next four weeks.

13

After the reading of his late wife's will, and Michael Brackley first realised how important Tom Laceby had become to Charlotte, even though he did not understand why she had bequeathed her house to Tom, he had sent for him a couple of months after Charlotte's funeral.

Slightly apprehensive, Tom had been shown to his employer's study, where Michael awaited him. 'Good morning Laceby, er let me see, Tom, isn't it?'

Tom removed his cap. 'Yes sir. I understand you wish to see me.'

The man waited a moment before replying, for he was busily engaged studying the appearance of his stalwart visitor. Of course he had met him before on the estate, and in the woods, but had never bothered to notice him, until now! He judged him to be about two or three years older than himself, easily a six footer and broad with it. Also he noticed a certain kind of outdoor animal magnetism, which he knew would have immediately attracted Charlotte. It was then Sir Michael Sinclair-Brackley, suddenly remembered all those months he had spent working abroad, and how his wife had hated the long separations. And he wondered!

Finally, he broke the silence, which to Tom had seemed an Eternity. 'Yes Laceby, I do wish to see you. I am aware my late wife bequeathed to you her house overlooking the park, and also a considerable sum of money. Can you give me any explanation, or any reason why she did this?'

Tom, far from being overawed in the presence of his Lordship, or embarrassed by these questions from the bereaved husband of his late beautiful mistress, actually smiled. 'No sir, I'm afraid I can't,' he replied calmly. 'You see, I only met her two or three times in the wood, and even then, on those rare occasions, we only exchanged half-a-dozen words.'

When Tom had finished speaking, Michael looked at him keenly. 'I say Laceby, your accent isn't that of a woodsman, or of a labourer. What was your profession before you came to work on this estate?'

For the first time, Tom hesitated, but only for a moment. 'I was a major in the Grenadiers sir!' he said quietly.

A stunned Michael was saved any further embarrassment by a light knock on the door, and his beautiful daughter came tripping in.

'Hello daddy. Oh! Hello Tom. Sorry daddy I didn't know you had company,' she turned and was about to leave, when her father stopped her.

'Emma,' he spoke her name softly. 'How do you know Laceby well enough to call him by his first name?'

Again she turned and faced him, surprise in her sparkling eyes. 'Laceby! Father, how could you? When you know perfectly well, his name is Tom!' with that wonderful explanation, she turned on her heel and left the room.

The two men looked at each other, then they both burst out laughing. Michael stood up, stepped forward and held out his hand, which Tom immediately accepted. 'I say La — , sorry, better call you Tom in future, for if Tom is good enough for my Emma, then Tom is good enough for me. I had the germ of an idea before you arrived this morning, and now we have met, I think the time has come to tell you about it. As you are probably aware, my agent left last week and I have no-one to help me with the affairs of running this estate. He occupied a cottage in the grounds, which now of course is vacant. So, if you could see your way clear to letting your house to a decent tenant, and move in to the cottage, then the job of Land

Agent to the Brackley Estate is your's!'

A myriad of thoughts rushed through Tom's mind. Why would his employer want him living so close to the Hall? Did he suspect him of seeing Charlotte? Anyway it was too late now, for she was gone, but that only made the offer more mysterious. At last he allowed a smile to touch the corners of his strong mouth. 'Thank you very much sir, it will be nice to get out of that house in the village, I have always been a bit of a loner, and would much prefer living in your cottage on the estate, though there is no need for me to worry about looking for a new tenant sir, you see even when Ch — , your wife left me the house, I still continued living in the village.'

Michael poured each of them a glass of port, and after one or two more cordial exchanges, they parted on very amicable terms.

Within a week of that interview, Tom Laceby had moved all his furniture and the rest of his personal belongings to his new home, only a short distance away from the Hall. During his move, he was helped, or perhaps hindered by the bubbly effervescent young Lady Emma. Over the weeks after Charlotte's tragic death, a strange but wonderful rapport had developed between the ex woodsman, and the young aristocrat, and at every opportunity, or on the slightest pretext Emma would excuse herself and dash off to be with 'her Tom'!

Though Michael had upbraided his wayward daughter on numerous occasions, and Tom had also mentioned the fact that some people would think she was peculiar, wanting to spend so much time with an old 'codger' like him, she had gazed at him with her almost deep sea blue eyes, identical to his own, simply smiled her lovely sunny infectious smile, which reminded him so much of his beautiful Charlotte, made some light hearted reply, and continued to visit him.

Emma, had now grown from a beautiful angelic child, into a very beautiful precocious, provocative young lady, with an apparent, much older outlook upon life, than her fifteen years. In another two weeks she would be going away to school for the next three years, so Michael wasn't unduly worried about her seemingly obsessive attachment to Tom Laceby.

During the course of helping Tom move his personal belongings from his house in the village, to his new home in the grounds of Brackley Hall, Emma had accidentally dropped a drawer filled with all kinds of bric-a-brac, and whilst picking them up to replace in the drawer, had suddenly stopped in amazement. For gazing up at her, from a photograph she held in her hand, was her mother Charlotte holding a baby, and on the back was written, in her mother's handwriting, Me and Emma nineteen twenty!

Emma was crouched down staring at the photograph, when Tom returned for another load. 'Come along Kitten, we still have an awful lot of stuff to shift — .' He broke off in mid-sentence, when he noticed what she was holding.

She looked up, her clear intelligent eyes searching his countenance. 'Tom, why do you have this photograph of mummy and me, in your house?'

For the first time in his colourful career, Tom Laceby was utterly bereft of speech. He knew this lovely innocent young lady was the result of his and Charlotte's clandestine affair, and he couldn't lie to her! Yet how else could he talk his way out of this impossible situation?

'I'm waiting Tom,' she spoke softly, almost purring, just as her mother had, when she wanted something.

At last Tom Laceby squared his shoulders, looked her straight in the eye, and spoke. 'I'm sorry to have to tell you this kitten, well

I'm not really. Actually, I'm very proud. You see, I once met your mother in the woods, and fell hopelessly and irrevocably in love with her. Well to cut a long story short, somehow she realised this, and after you were born she gave me that photograph. Of course you must never mention this to your father, you do realise the furore that would cause, don't you?'

To his astonishment Emma leapt to her feet, flung her arms around his neck and kissed him. 'Oh! Tom Laceby, I love you!' she cried. 'How very romantic, fancy you and mummy, though I must say, it makes me feel terribly jealous of mummy. Did she love you Tom?'

The question, was softly spoken, and delicately asked, yet it caught Tom completely off guard. 'Yes, I think so,' he replied, after a moment's hesitation.

'You hesitated Tom. Why did you hesitate?'

He couldn't seem to think of a suitable reply.

She spoke again. 'You know why, don't you Tom? You just don't want to tell me, because you think it may somehow tarnish my memory of mummy. Well I think she did love you Tom, and far from tarnishing my memory, it will only enhance it, because I think you are wonderful Tom Laceby, and if I had been around at the time, your Charlotte wouldn't have had a look in!'

He started to smile, but quickly realised she was quite serious, so decided to humour her. 'Yes kitten, you could be right, for you are going to be just as beautiful as your mum was. I mean when you grow up of course.'

She pouted. 'Oh! Tom, sometimes you make me that mad, as I keep telling you, I am grown up. My breasts are almost as large as mummy's were.' She caught hold of his hand, and before he could stop her, had lifted it to her bosom, 'Here feel these Tom!' she murmured seductively. 'This will prove it!'

Not wishing to upset her, Tom allowed his hand to remain there for a second, then casually removed it. 'Yes Emma, I believe you are quite right, it really is amazing how you have developed over the past twelve months. Now look my dear, if I intend moving into that cottage sometime this year, you will really have to stop all this philandering, and help me, otherwise I shall have to send you home.'

For a long moment, she allowed her deep blue, smouldering eyes to lock onto his, and in a voice which was little more than a whisper, she murmured, 'I am not philandering Tom Laceby, and I will remind you of this conversation, when I return home from college in three years time. In the meantime, please try not to forget me.' On uttering that last remark, Emma stood upon her tip toes, flung her arms around his neck, kissed him full upon the lips, and fled, little knowing what fate had in store for them both, as early as tomorrow!

The following day dawned grey and miserable, with a slight drizzle blowing in off the North Sea. Emma, after looking out through her upstairs window, suddenly had an idea. She'd had very little sleep, being unable to eradicate from her mind the memory of that kiss she had planted upon the lips of Tom Laceby, or the photograph of herself as a baby with her mother, in one of Tom's bedside drawers!

Emma knew her father had gone to the city for the day, and after a quick breakfast, she returned upstairs, and with a key let herself into Charlotte's old room. This room had never been disturbed, since the day Charlotte had walked out to visit Watersmeet, to attend her father's funeral, and had never come back.

The room felt cold and damp, and crossing swiftly to the tassled rope hanging by the fireplace, Emma gave it a sharp tug. Minutes later, an astonished maid entered the room.

'Oh! Miss,' she exclaimed 'You give us all quite a turn. For a minute, we all thought the mistress had come back to haunt us!'

Emma laughed softly to herself. 'No Eva, nothing like that. Just little old me, wanting a fire in here that's all.'

Within a quarter of an hour, much to the comfort of her mistress, Eva had a good fire blazing away in the grate, and after bringing up another bucket of coal, she left the room, closing the door behind her.

Emma, her heart beating a little faster than usual, though not knowing why, then began searching through everything her dead mother had owned. Her whole lifetime was here within these four walls, and Emma was filled with an excited, though poignant curiosity as she flicked through various cards, envelopes and letters. Suddenly she stiffened, she was holding in her hand, an opened envelope addressed to her father. Slowly she removed the letter. It was from her father's solicitor, and dated the day Sir Richard Brackley had died!

It was on that day, the young Lady Emma Brackley, born with a silver spoon in her mouth, learned the cold hard facts of life!

She sat transfixed, with her legs tucked beneath her, in the middle of the bed, the same bed her mother and Michael had shared so many times, before they were married, and she read that misguided missive over and over again. 'So', she murmured softly to herself. 'I am not a Brackley after all! No, I am a Laceby! And wonder of wonders, Tom is my real dad!'.

Emma suddenly felt her cheeks burning, as she remembered the intimate kiss she had bestowed upon the lips of Tom Laceby, just before she left him last night. 'No daughter should ever kiss her father like that,' she said aloud. 'Dear God, no wonder I love him so!' then with tears pricking behind her eyelids, she carefully replaced the letter in its envelope, and stowed it in a safe place.

Many young women, much older than Emma, would have been completely devastated by the revelations she had so recently discovered, but not Emma, for she was first and foremost, the daughter of Charlotte, and it would take much more than the mere fact that she had been conceived out of wedlock, to cause her a great degree of distress. The tears she had felt, were not tears of shame or anger, they were simply the tears of a young woman desperately in love with the wrong man, for she knew now, that she could never be more to Tom Laceby than a daughter!

With a sigh, Emma eased herself off the bed, and humming softly, continued rummaging through her mother's effects, when she suddenly came across a portfolio of Charlotte's paintings. Examining each one it turn, she finally stopped as she came to an oil painting of a wonderful rustic looking log cabin, with a very pretty garden, surrounded by a small white wooden fence, set in a beautiful clearing in Brackley's wood!

'I know that place!' she ejaculated, as she looked closer. Then she remembered her mummy had taken her there, when they were out riding one day, and she couldn't have been more than eight years old. She suddenly remembered something else, something she had never been able to understand until now. Her mother had looked at her, with a far away look in her eyes, though tinged with sadness, Emma had thought at the time. 'One day my darling,' she had said. 'When you are older, I will bring you here again, and explain to you what a wonderful part this place has played in both our lives!'

Emma glanced out the window, and much to her delight she saw a weak watery sun, just beginning to break through an ever thinning cloud bank, and with the abrupt decision making of youth, she knew exactly what she was going to do, for the rest of that momentous day.

Crossing swiftly to the bell rope, she gave it a sharp pull. In less than a minute, Eva was in the room. 'You rang miss?' she asked, followed immediately by a small curtsy.

'Yes Eva. I shall be going out shortly. Please keep an eye on the fire for me, only don't put any more coal on. Also send Milly to me, I will leave the key with her. That will be all, thank you Eva.'

The maid silently withdrew, her mind in a whirl. 'Please, Thank you', those were words she had never heard the young mistress use before!

Another couple of minutes passed, and Milly came in the room. Much to her astonishment Emma flung her arms around her. 'Oh Milly,' she cried, a half sob in her voice. 'I have so much to tell you.'

Milly led her to the bed. 'Now sit down Miss Emma, and tell me all about it. Nothing is as bad as it seems.'

Silently, Emma produced the letter and handed it to her friend. Milly was much more than a nanny or a servant, she really was her friend. She had cared for and cherished Emma from the day she was born, and the love she felt for the child, with the passing years had deepened and become something almost tangible, particularly when Charlotte had suffered such an early demise. The wonderful part was, her love was reciprocated, and now Emma almost looked upon Milly as her mother. Her countenance was devoid of expression as she slowly folded the letter, and carefully replaced it in the envelope.

To Emma, the ensuing silence was agonising. Finally she could wait no longer. 'Well Milly, don't you have any comment to make?' she asked, rather impatiently.

Milly turned, and with her clear grey eyes she looked at her dear young mistress. 'What can I say darling? Except how very sorry I am that you have found this letter.'

The young intuitive Emma had been studying her friend carefully. 'None of this came as a surprise to you, did it Milly?' she asked quietly.

There was another long pause, and Emma was on the point of repeating the question, when Milly handed back the letter. 'No dear it didn't, not really. Of course that part referring to the money and Charlotte's house, I knew nothing of, but I had suspected right from the day you were born, who your father was!'

'Oh! Milly, and you never breathed a word to me about your suspicions. Why didn't you tell me Milly?' she asked, a single tear rolling down her youthful, satin smooth cheek. 'As you are well aware, I love Tom Laceby, and now I can be no more than a daughter to him. What shall I do Milly? Please tell me.'

Milly took the tearful Emma in her arms, and gentled her, as she had a thousand times before. 'There there my darling, don't be sad, I'm sure you and I can overcome this small problem between us! I suggest you do nothing, except inform Tom of the contents of this letter, or better still, take it to him, and ask him to read it.'

Emma stared at her friend in amazement. 'But Milly, if I do that, then Tom will know that I'm his daughter!'

Milly smiled. 'I should think he already knows that Emma,' she replied.

Emma appeared to be thinking deeply, then she said. 'Yes he probably does, but he isn't aware that I know, not yet anyway.'

'No of course not. All the same, I think you should tell him, and show him the letter.'

Emma slid gently off Milly's knee, and ran to the window, she turned with a new light in her beautiful eyes. 'Right Miss Milly, I want you to go and ask cook, to prepare two scrumptious hot meals of pork chops, two for Tom and one for me, complete with all the necessary vegetables, and a lovely jam roly poly for dessert. That is Tom's favourite,' she added, almost as an afterthought. 'Oh! and tell cook to send the meal over to Tom's cottage, at precisely half-past-five, then prepare a couple of sandwiches and a flask of tea, because you and I are going for a ride in the woods, my precious.'

Fortunately, Charlotte had once taken Milly to visit Tom's cottage, just to show her where it was, in case of a riding accident, and she needed help at some time in the future, for Emma had no idea which of the myriad of paths to follow through the wood.

Eventually they arrived at the cottage, and after dismounting, Emma walked straight in, for there was no lock on the door, only a bolt on the inside. Someone had left a small pile of dry sticks on the hearth, and Milly soon had a good fire burning in the old range.

While her companion was busy with lighting the fire, Emma lay down upon the bed, staring up at the roof, her mind trying to visualise what had happened in this room, between Tom Laceby and her mother! Finally, she sat bolt upright, convinced she was lying on the bed, where fifteen years ago she had been conceived!

'Whatever is the matter Emma?' asked Milly, turning from the fire, now she had managed to get it going so well. 'You look as though you have seen a ghost. What's wrong my dear, don't you feel very well?'

Emma stretched luxuriously, and laughed, a happy tinkling infectious laugh, so much so, that Milly had to smile. 'Yes thank you Milly, I feel wonderful, I was a bit shaken earlier, but I'm all right now. You see, dear Milly, I'd just had the most wonderful feeling, that it was upon this bed I was conceived!'

'Emma!' cried a rather disturbed Milly, 'What a shocking thing to say.'

'But why Milly? If it's true, and I feel certain that it is, I think it's wonderful, and terribly romantic. I bet there aren't many of my friends, can say they were conceived in a log cabin in the middle of a wood!'

'Emma! Now stop talking like this, you're incorrigible, you know perfectly well you shouldn't say such things, even if they are true.'

Emma gripped the arm of her friend and companion. 'You believe it too, don't you? You knew mummy used to come here to meet Tom, and conduct a secret clandestine love affair, didn't you Milly?'

Milly held the hands of this beautiful young girl, looked deep into those wonderful sea blue eyes, and knew she could not lie. 'Yes, dear Emma. I believe it too!'

Emma leapt off the bed, and flinging her arms in the air, danced round and round her astonished companion. 'Oh! Milly, Milly!' she cried ecstatically. 'How wonderful. To think mummy and Tom used to lie on this very bed, and make love, and that I am the result of that passionate liaison.' Suddenly she appeared to lose a little of her euphoria, and ceased her dancing.

The ever watchful Milly, immediately noticed the change in her companion's demeanour. 'What's wrong darling,' she asked. 'Why are you suddenly looking so sad.'

Emma didn't reply immediately, but continued to stare out of the only window. When she turned, her expression was an amalgam of sadness mixed with a modicum of euphoric excitement. 'Milly' she began quietly. 'If what we are saying is true,' she stopped.

Milly looked at her encouragingly. 'Yes Emma? What is it my dear?'

Again Emma began speaking in the same subdued tone. 'If what we are saying is true Milly, then it means that I'm a child born out of wedlock, in other words, a bastard! Oh! Milly, what am I going to do?'

Milly placed an arm around the girl's slim waist, and drew her gently down on to the bed. 'Now don't you be thinking such things Emma dear. No-one else knows about Charlotte and Tom, and there is no reason why they should.'

'One other person knows Milly,' replied Emma, with a half sob in her voice. 'Eric Teesdale, he knows!'

Milly removed her arm, and stood up. 'Well show your letter to Tom tonight, and let him worry about Eric. Now what about this flask and some refreshment young lady,' she finished lightly.

Emma had taken her camera with her, and as they were leaving, she paused on the edge of the clearing, and took a photograph of her father's log cabin, then they both turned their mounts and headed for home.

After having a bath, Emma spent the rest of that afternoon, fitting Charlotte's oil painting of Tom's log cabin into an attractive old fashioned gilt frame, complete with cord, ready for hanging in his cottage. A little after five-o-clock, Emma and Milly made their way to the cottage, Milly carrying the picture, and Emma a hammer, and after considering several different positions in the room, they finally decided to hang it immediately above the fireplace. When this task had been successfully completed, Milly lit a fire in the range, and placed some plates in the oven to warm, ready for when cook sent Tom's dinner over.

It was almost six-o-clock, and Milly had been gone for some time, when Emma heard Tom open the cottage door, and her heart beating a little faster than usual, she moved quickly to stand by the fireplace, smoothing down her dress, while she waited expectantly for him to enter the room.

The door opened, Tom stood a moment and allowed his eyes to wash over this vision of beauty standing by the fire. 'Hello Emma, this is a sur — ,' he stopped, as his gaze lifted and caught the painting. He just stood and stared at it, apparently completely bereft of speech or movement, until finally Emma could bear the silence no longer.

'Yes Tom, this is a surprise, isn't it? In more ways than one I imagine,' for her age, she was calm, her voice was level and clear. She had got over her earlier bout of self deprecation, and was now completely at ease with the current situation. For Emma had realised, all she had before was a young girl's teenage crush on an older man. She had actually smiled and thought how ironic, when Milly had told her she had been looking for a 'father figure'.

At last he found his voice. 'Where the hell did you find that?' he asked harshly.

Emma paled. Tom Laceby had never spoken to her in those tones before. 'In my mother's room,' she replied quietly. 'I thought you might like it hanging in your cottage, father!'

A log crackled and sent out a spark from the fire. It sounded like gunfire in the ensuing silence, which followed Emma's earth shattering remark, and for the second time that afternoon, Tom Laceby could find no words. So Emma, with the impetuosity of her youth, pulled out the letter from a fold in her dress, and silently passed it to him.

With tight lips, and his eyes devoid of expression, Tom jerked the missive from it's envelope. He held it near the window, and began to read. Then he leaned against the wall, apparently for support, until finally almost collapsing in the nearest chair. 'My God Emma!' he cried hoarsely. 'What are we going to do? Has Michael seen this?' his final words were hardly coherent.

For one infinitesimal breath of time, Emma felt ashamed of Tom Laceby. But then, in less than it takes a falling star to shoot across the Heavens, the feeling had passed. 'No fa — . I must stop wanting to call you father, otherwise I might just do it one day in the wrong place. No Tom, Michael hasn't seen it, and Milly and I can think of no reason why he should. For of course if Michael does see the letter, then you will lose your house by the park, your annuity, your job and this cottage. I also will lose everything. My Title, my name. I shall be cut out of mummy's will completely, and receive no money, even when I reach the age of twenty one! So, I think you will agree Tom, that it is in both our interests to keep very quiet about this letter, and just hope Michael doesn't find out from anyone else.'

Tom remained seated, and read the letter again. After a few minutes he looked up. 'Eric Teesdale knows about Charlotte and me, and you have already told Milly. Who else knows about us Emma?'

'So far as I know, no-one,' she paused a moment. 'Except of course the solicitor who sent it, I imagine he knows, but he may have completely forgotten all about it by now, after all it is many years since Sir Richard's death, though I suppose he could have a copy of this letter somewhere in his office.'

Tom moved towards the table, he seemed to have accepted the position, as if he had known that eventually Emma would discover her true identity, and now she knew, in a weird kind of way, he felt a sense of relief and began to feel more at ease in her presence.

For some time now, he had realised she was falling in love with him, but hadn't known what to say to her, or how to handle this very tricky state of affairs. Several times during the past few weeks, he had awoke in the middle of the night in a hot sweat, because of Emma's obvious attraction to him, and had cried out in anguish, demanding of his God, why Charlotte had been taken away from him so early, and actually asking her for help!

He pulled out a chair and sat down. 'Daughter of the house!' he boomed, now a completely changed man. 'Did I smell food when I came home, and if so, can you please bring some for your old dad?'

With a cry of delight, Emma flung her arms around his neck. 'Oh! Tom,' she cried excitedly. 'Thank you so much for taking it like this, I was so scared you might deny everything. You see the trouble was, I was completely infatuated, and so much in love with you. Then when I discovered this letter, I realised immediately why I found you so devilishly attractive, and now I can kiss you anytime, without any feeling of embarrassment or constraint, except of course in public.' She removed her arms and kissed him on the cheek, then straightened up. 'Yes Tom, there is some food, lots of it, I asked cook to bring it over earlier, just for the two of us, and if you can curb your voracious appetite a moment longer, I think you will be pleasantly surprised.'

With a happy chuckle and a light step, Emma brought the hot loaded plates and placed them on the table. 'There you are Tom, our first meal together as father and daughter!' she declared happily, as she seated herself.

After the meal, they cleared the table, then Emma helped him with the washing up, and later they sat in front of a log fire, and discussed their present situation. It was finally decided that Emma would speak to Eric Teesdale in the morning, for they thought it might sound better coming from her as the 'innocent party'.

When they parted that night, as Emma gave Tom a good night peck upon the cheek, for a moment her own were burning with the memory of that other kiss, she had so blatantly planted upon his lips, and she ran all the way back to the Hall. As she burst through the back door, the ever faithful Milly was waiting for her.

'Steady Emma,' she whispered fiercely. 'You will disturb the whole house. Well what happened my darling?' she asked, after leading Emma into the warm kitchen.

'Oh! Milly, Tom was marvellous,' Emma enthused. She then proceeded to give her friend a resume, of the events which had taken place on that memorable evening, and it was nearly midnight before they finally retired to their respective beds.

The following morning Emma was up early, and after breakfast she changed into her riding clothes, then went out to the stables. As she hoped, Eric Teesdale was in his tack room, repairing a bridle. 'Good morning Eric,' she greeted him graciously. 'A fine morning for a ride. Will you saddle my horse for me please? and one for yourself? I would very much like you to accompany me this morning. We need to talk Eric,' that was all, no hint as to what the conversation was to be about.

With a feeling of foreboding, yet not knowing why, the head groom obeyed the instructions of his young mistress, and after leading the two horses out of the stable, helped Emma to mount. As they were leaving the courtyard, Eric turned in his saddle. 'Where do you wish to go Miss Emma?' he asked politely.

Emma bestowed upon him a ravishing smile. 'I understand Tom Laceby used to live in a log cabin, somewhere in Brackley's Wood! Can you show me where please?'

though her voice was low, Eric couldn't help but notice a resonance of authority behind those few words, which had sounded very much like a command, rather than a request.

He hesitated. 'Er, I'm not sure I know the way Miss Emma, can't we go for a ride in some other direction?' he asked, falteringly.

Quite suddenly, this young beautiful girl he had known since she was a child, completely changed! 'No! Teesdale. We cannot go in any other direction. You are going to lead me to Tom Laceby's log cabin, and it's no use bothering to lie to me, because you see I know that you do know the way!'

Eric's outdoor leathery features paled, as he froze in the saddle. 'How do you know that Miss Emma?' he asked, in little more than a whisper.

Her countenance hardened, and her appearance in one so young was frightening. Her lips hardly seemed to move, as she answered him through her slit of a mouth. 'I know, because you followed mummy there on more than one occasion!' she replied sharply, her voice like a whip lash.

Eric stared at her, open mouthed. 'Who told you that?' he managed to gasp.

She spurred her mount forward. 'Come along Eric,' she flung over her shoulder. 'I will answer your question when we get to the cabin.'

That morning, as Eric Teesdale followed in the wake of his young mistress, it slowly dawned upon him, that she obviously knew the way to Tom's log cabin! Now how the devil did she come to know that? he asked himself, and why had she asked him to accompany her, for she definitely didn't need him to show her the way?

Finally, the two sweating horses galloped across the clearing approaching Tom's old home, and slithered to a halt by the small white fence, which by now was sadly in need of one or two coats of paint.

Emma slid from the saddle, looped her reins over a fence post, and walked confidently up the path and straight into the cabin.

With an uneasy feeling in the pit of his stomach, Eric followed her. She was sitting at the table, calmly awaiting him. 'Now pull up that other chair Eric, and sit down.'

The pleasant beautiful, innocent young girl he had known, even as recently as yesterday, had somehow gone, to be replaced by this hard faced arrogant, older looking miss, who seemed devoid of all manners and scruples. And yet physically she was the same Emma he had always known, but something was very different. Eric sensed that in some way she had changed dramatically, apparently overnight, and he could think of no reason for this. Not yet anyway!

When he was seated, Emma withdrew an envelope from a pocket of her riding jacket, and slid it across the table towards him. 'What's this?' asked Eric, cautiously.

'Open it and read it man!' she snapped. 'That is if you can read,' she added brusquely.

His face a mask, Eric Teesdale removed the letter and began to read. Showing no emotion, he finally replaced the missive in it's envelope, and handed it back to Emma. 'So, if you already knew I'd been out here before, why all that stupid charade earlier?' he asked quietly.

Emma was slightly taken aback, momentarily she wished she had allowed Tom to handle this part of their plan, as he had wanted to, but then unknowingly, she suddenly drew upon unplumbed depths inherited from her mother Charlotte, and whirled around on the hapless Eric. 'Because there is something I want to show you.' She stood up and moved over to the bed. 'You see this bed Eric Teesdale? Well this is the bed where Tom Laceby seduced my mother, and where I was conceived! Do you know what that means?' she asked harshly.

As no reply was forthcoming, Emma continued. 'No? Then please allow me to tell you. It means that I am a bastard! That's right. A Bastard, with a capital B. It means I have no birthright, no name, nothing. Can you begin to understand what this means to me?' she demanded shrilly.

Now he knew. So that was the reason for this remarkable change in this lovely young lady, he had watched grow from an infant to the beautiful person she undoubtedly was, until today! She had discovered from this old letter, exactly what her mother had been, and that she, Lady Emma Brackley, was a bastard!

Eric's first reaction was one of sadness. 'Miss Emma,' he said quietly. 'This is no fault of your's, and please don't judge your mother too harshly, she was a very beautiful woman, and your grandfather forced Sir Michael to spend too much of his time abroad.'

In the old chameleon style of Charlotte, Emma changed immediately to her normal charming, charismatic self. 'Why thank you Eric. I do believe you also had a crush on mummy.'

For all his years, and his tanned features,

Eric Teesdale blushed, though he smiled when he spoke. 'Yes Miss Emma, I certainly had. Any red blooded male who met Charlotte, sorry, who met your mother, couldn't help himself. She was very beautiful Miss Emma, and if I may be permitted to say so, you are heading the same way.'

Emma laughed aloud. 'Oh! Mr. Teesdale, do you mean in looks, or behaviour?'

He appeared hurt by her remark. 'You know I mean your looks, Miss Emma,' he replied stiffly.

Again Emma laughed. 'Oh! Eric, you silly man, I was only being facetious.' Then she was quite serious. 'Is that true Eric, what you said about grandfather sending Michael abroad to work?'

He sat back in his chair, and appeared to relax a little. 'Yes miss, it is quite true, and sometimes for as long as three months at a time. You see miss, your mother was a very attractive young woman, possessed of a very impetuous nature, who needed a lot of love. Well, when she wandered down here one day, and met Tom, and with your father being away so much, you can't really blame her. I think if she had not met Tom, or someone else, in time her love would have withered on the vine!'

Emma gazed upon Eric Teesdale with a

293

new look of respect in her beautiful eyes. 'Why, Eric. 'Her love would have withered on the vine'. Wherever did you find that gem?'

For a moment, the head groom appeared quite embarrassed. 'Well I read a fair amount of books my Lady. I must admit I can't remember everything I read, but I do remember quite a bit, especially silly unimportant things like that.'

Emma smiled. 'Dear Eric, don't ever deprecate phrases such as those, it really is quite romantic, and personally I do believe you are an old romantic yourself.'

Her voice was almost a caress, and suddenly Eric Teesdale felt his loins begin to stir. He was only thirty eight years old, still in his prime, and really quite handsome. Eric had never married, and lived alone in a flat above the stables, even so, like all men, he had always had his dreams and fantasies!

As Emma allowed her eyes to wash over her companion, a tiny latent seed inherited from her provocative wayward mother, and previously completely unknown to her, suddenly began to propagate itself, with far reaching, fascinating results!

She moved closer, and placed her arm across his shoulders, with her fingers lightly stroking his cheek. 'Eric,' again that same soft purr of a voice. 'Eric, would you like to make love to me? on this same bed where I was conceived!'

It was warm in the cabin, and the sweat was beginning to weld Eric's shirt to his back. For a long moment he didn't reply, strangely his only thought being, if he had been a stronger more positive man, he could have become the father of this lovely girl! He had always thought a man has only one chance in a lifetime, but now had no intention of allowing this one to pass him by! Slowly he turned and faced this seductive young temptress, locking his eyes upon her's. 'Yes My Lady, I will make love to you on this bed, which Tom Laceby and your beautiful mother Charlotte shared!'

They quickly undressed, and rolled naked on the bed together. And so it was, on that lovely early autumn day, Emma, the daughter of Charlotte, lost her virginity to the head groom of Sir Michael Sinclair-Brackley's stables, and revelled in the experience, enjoying it to the full, just as Charlotte had, so many years before, in the middle of another wood, carpeted by lush green grass, below Watersmeet.

Emma, whether through sheer instinct, or because of what she had read, seemed to know what she was doing and had insisted when Eric had to stop, because, as she stated, she had no intention of having any little Emma's!

When they had finished dressing, and were about to leave, Eric placed his arm around her and attempted to kiss her. 'Stop that Eric!' she protested vehemently, as she again reverted to that strange other person, leaving him in no doubt as to what his position was in Emma's scheme of things. 'Just because I allowed you to make love to me, that in no way gives you the right, either to maul or to kiss me, whenever you feel like it,' she said coldly.

He remained silent, astonished by her peculiar attitude, and finished fastening his riding jacket, prior to walking out the door.

'Teesdale!' she called loudly, when he was outside. 'Come here at once,' and as he turned and moved back inside the cabin. 'Don't ever walk out on me again, without my permission,' she snapped.

A smile just touching the corners of his strong mouth, Eric doffed his hat and bowed low. 'I beg pardon My Lady. I will never allow it to happen again.'

Immediately she relented. On this very first meeting, Eric had found her 'Achilles Heel', for Emma, unlike her mother, could never remain angry with anyone who humoured her.

'Very well kind sir,' she replied graciously, returning his smile. Then picking up the envelope which had been left lying on the table, and placing it in her pocket, she again looked up. 'I have just remembered the reason I asked you to accompany me today Eric, it was to ask you to promise, never to divulge to anyone the contents of this letter, or the fact that you were instructed to follow mummy here, to Tom Laceby's Cabin. Because if you do, I shall lose everything, and be thrown out of my home, so will you, and so will Tom. Also, if this became public knowledge, all the monies which were bequeathed to us three, would have to be repaid. Of course I don't receive any of mine, until I'm twenty one, but I would very much like to be sure that I am going to get it then.'

Eric gazed into her deep blue eyes, and his own never wavered, as he said quietly. 'Of course I promise not to say anything to anyone about this matter. My dear Emma, even though I like my work and my living quarters very much, I value your friendship far more, and would never risk losing that, for any reason whatsoever.'

'Thank you Eric. Now I have one more

small request. Will you please stand just outside the cabin door, and allow me to take a photograph of you? You see, I would like a memento to keep, of the day I lost my virginity!'

He chuckled aloud, and reciprocated immediately. 'Yes Emma, indeed I will. What a wonderful thought, thank you.'

Poor old Eric, he had no idea how very much Emma was beginning to follow in Charlotte's footsteps. The only reason she required that photograph of him standing by the cabin doorway, was proof, just in case she ever needed it, that he had once brought her here against her will, taken her inside the cabin and ravished her!

They were able to indulge in very little conversation on the return journey, for the narrow paths only allowed them to travel in single file. However, as they approached the Hall and the wood became thinner, he spurred his mount forward, and as he drew level with her, she turned her head.

'Eric,' she said softly. 'You say you live in a flat above the stables. If I should happen to get the urge one night, please may I come and visit you?'

The head groom nearly fell off his horse! 'Yes, dearest Emma. Yes most definitely, only make it soon.'

She smiled serenely to herself. 'Listen carefully Eric, don't you be harbouring any fanciful ideas about us, because there isn't, and there never will be any us. Do you understand?' he nodded vigourously. 'You see Eric, I only intend to use you when the need arises, but in the meantime, for Heavens sake go out and buy something to wear, so that we may be safe at all times!'

He stared at her, and as his eyes drank in that superb young figure in her riding habit, he couldn't believe his luck. 'Yes Emma,' he replied, unable to keep the excitement out of his voice. 'I will go for a hair cut, and buy some tomorrow.'

They had now reached the stables, and as they both dismounted, Emma handed her reins to her companion. 'Thank you very much Mr. Teesdale,' she said loudly. 'For a very interesting day, we really should do it again sometime.'

Eric doffed his cap, and led the horses away.

Milly met Emma on the landing, as she was going to her room. She stopped her. 'Hello, why are you looking so happy today Emma? What's happened? You look like the cat that swallowed the cream.'

Emma chuckled. 'Actually I feel like her

Milly, come to my room and I'll tell you all about it.'

Milly obediently followed in the wake of her young mistress. 'Now tell me,' she said, unable to contain her curiosity any longer, immediately the door was closed.

Emma jumped upon her bed, and sat in the middle of it, with her legs tucked up beneath her. 'Are you sure you want to know what has happened to me today Milly?' she asked, tantalizingly, her eyes sparkling and her cheeks flushed.

'Yes. Yes of course I do. Now please tell me quickly Emma, before I burst.'

'Very well, though I'm not quite sure you're going to like what I have to say,' she paused a moment, chiefly for effect, smiled and then continued. 'This morning my dear Milly, I asked Eric Teesdale to saddle a couple of horses, one for himself and one for me. Then I told him to take me to the log cabin, where Tom Laceby used to live in Brackley's Wood.'

'Whatever for?' interrupted Milly.

'Because I wanted to let him know, that I knew he followed mummy there on several occasions, just to spy on her and Tom. I showed him the letter, and informed him in no uncertain terms, what the result would be if he ever told anyone of their clandestine meetings. After that we became quite friendly, and I asked him to make love to me, on the bed where I was conceived!'

Milly leapt up off her chair. 'You did what?' she shouted. 'You silly stupid little idiot. My God! Eric Teesdale of all people. I suppose you realise you could now be pregnant just like poor Charlotte was!' she said heatedly, as she began to pace the floor.

However, Milly was not prepared for what happened next. 'Milly! Stop your stupid pacing and sit down!' screamed Emma. 'Don't you ever call me an idiot again you old cow, or I'll bloody well sack you, go on get out of my room!'

Milly had stopped, frozen to the spot, and now with a finger of ice cutting a trace along her spine, she recalled seeing Charlotte behaving in just the same way. For the lovely young girl of but a few seconds ago, had suddenly aged ten years! She had changed so completely, her features were bitter and twisted, she was an entirely different person, and her eyes seemed to glow with a luminosity from within! With a shudder, Milly shook herself and threw off this yolk of terror, which had so suddenly almost engulfed her, and without another word, or a glance in the direction of that beautiful young body, with such an old face, she left the room.

Later that evening, when Emma thought he would have finished his meal, she again went to visit Tom Laceby. He was sitting by the window, reading a magazine. 'Good evening Tom,' she said politely, bending low and giving him a peck on the cheek. 'Are you fully recovered from the shock of my news of yesterday?'

He looked up, then apparently resigned to the inevitable, closed his magazine, and placed it on the table, turning to gaze upon this lovely young creature, who proclaimed to be his daughter. 'Yes thank you my dear, though I must admit, sleep seemed to be a long time coming last night.'

Emma chuckled. 'I really don't know why Tom, we have nothing to worry about. No-one is ever going to discover our little secret. I think you will be alright, when you become accustomed to the idea of our special relationship. You are not sorry, are you Tom? I mean, I don't disappoint you in any way, do I?' she spoke like a child pleading for another sweet, and he could not resist the sudden urge to reach out and pull her on to his knee!

With a low cry, Emma flung her arms around his neck, and once more pressed her warm sensuous lips firmly upon his!

At that precise moment, there was a knock upon the door of Tom's cottage. Emma quickly slipped off his knee, and calmly seated herself on a chair by the window, picking up the magazine Tom had discarded. She could hear the murmuring of low voices, then the door opened, and Tom ushered Michael, her father into the room!

For no more than the length of a single heart beat, Emma froze. Then, quickly reasserting herself, she jumped up and moved towards him. 'Hello daddy, what a lovely surprise. Fancy, I now have the two men I love most in all the world, both together in the same room!'

Michael smiled. 'Hello my dear. You're looking very well,' he turned to Tom. 'I know this may seem amazing Tom, but even though we both live in the same house, I very rarely see her.' His gaze shifted to the magazine Emma was holding. 'I didn't know you were interested in the Farmer and Stock Breeder Emma,' he remarked quietly.

Emma's eyes dropped to what she was holding in her hand, and with a short embarrassed laugh, she quickly placed the offending magazine on the table. 'No I'm not daddy, it had dropped, and I had just picked it up,' she lied easily.

At that moment Michael lifted his gaze and peered over the head of his daughter. 'I say Tom, isn't that your cottage in Brackley's Wood? what a lovely painting.' He moved closer, to enable him to read the signature, then stood perfectly still! In a voice devoid of any emotion, he read it aloud, and his words seemed to ricochet off the stone walls of this old cottage. 'To Tom, With Love, Charlotte'.

For what seemed an interminable length of time, though actually it lasted only thirty seconds, complete silence reigned in the room, broken at last by the irrepressible Emma.

'Yes daddy, isn't it marvellous, I think mummy copied those autumnal tints beautifully. Milly went with her on two occasions, she had to visit the place twice, just to make sure she got it right. Then she added that little message, just to show her thanks to Tom, for allowing her to paint such a lovely subject.'

Slowly Michael turned and faced his two companions. 'Is that correct Tom?' his tone was rapier sharp, but his agent didn't flinch, or drop his eyes for a second. 'Ah, yes I see it is. How stupid of me, please forgive me Tom. I must be forgetting Charlotte's little idiosyncrasies!'

Emma breathed a sigh of relief, then a silent prayer.

'I suppose sir, over a long period of time, it might be possible to forget, but you know your wife really was a rather remarkable woman, and of course it was entirely her own idea to paint my cabin in the woods.'

'Yes Tom, I'm sure it was. Please don't worry anymore about it, personally I think it looks quite charming, hanging over your fireplace. Now let me see, what did I come here for? Ah yes, I remember. Now Emma, you will be leaving shortly to go to that school for young ladies, and Milly tells me you will be needing lots of new clothes. So I suggest that you ask Tom nicely, and then he just might be willing to take you and Milly into Hull tomorrow, for a day's shopping.'

Emma flung her arms around his neck, and kissed him upon the cheek. 'Oh! daddy. That's wonderful idea. Thank you very much.' Then turning to Tom. 'You will take us, won't you Tom. Please?'

He laughed. 'Yes Emma. How could I refuse such a request, from such a lovely young lady?'

Michael smiled lovingly upon his daughter. 'There you are my dear, at least you have one good friend. I'll see you later. Thanks Tom, you're a good man, I can let myself out.

305

Good night,' and with that he was gone.

When Michael had left the cottage, Tom emitted a long low whistle. 'Whew! Emma, that was close. I really thought I was for it, when he noticed Charlotte's painting. I think you were marvellous with your tale about how she came to paint it! It was a damn good job you were here, I couldn't say a word, I was absolutely flabbergasted.'

Later that night, when Tom Laceby went to his bed, he enjoyed less sleep than he had the previous night, for he could still feel the impact of Emma's warm sensuous lips upon his own, but every time he closed his eyes, he saw the naked body of his beautiful Charlotte, lying on his bed in the log cabin, yet when his eyes had trawled the length of her, and finally reached her shoulders, the face staring out at him from the darkness, was not Charlotte's, no it was the face of Emma! and try as he might, he could not seem to eradicate that lovely vision!

The following morning instead of going shopping, Emma decided to visit Mount Pleasant, to see her Aunt Rose, so after sending Milly to ask Eric Teesdale to saddle her pony for her, she dressed in her riding habit, and then ran outside to the stables.

Eric was standing by her pony's head. 'Good morning Lady Emma,'he greeted her, then in an aside. 'Did you sleep well?' he murmured quietly.

'Perfectly, thank you Eric,' she replied shortly, as she waited for him to help her mount. It was a beautiful autumnal morning, and sometime later, after a very enjoyable ride, Emma was cantering along the drive towards the house. Apparently Rose had either seen her, or had been told of her approach, for she came out of the front door, just as Emma halted by the steps, leading up to the entrance.

'Hello my dear, how lovely to see you,' cried Rose, as she ran down the steps to greet her niece. 'How are you? I was only saying to your uncle Charles yesterday, that we should really make an effort to come and see you, before you leave home for that young ladies college, don't worry about your pony darling, I'll send one of the stable lads to collect him. Now do come along inside and tell me all your news.' With that remark, Rose gripped Emma firmly by the arm, and ushered her up the steps and indoors.

There was a small room, quite compact and cosy, which Rose frequently used for her own use, and also if she had only one or two guests. This was the room she took Emma to now, and though the day was comparatively warm for the time of year, a fire was burning brightly in the grate. Immediately they entered, Rose moved to the fireplace and gave a pull upon the tassled cord hanging there, and when the maid came in answer to her summons, she asked for the proverbial tea and scones to be brought right away.

When they were finally seated comfortably upon two of the easy chairs, Rose turned to her niece. 'Now Emma my dear, what do you have to tell me,' she asked, good naturedly, never for one moment, expecting that such a perfectly harmless question would result in the staggering, mind numbing revelations which followed.

The previous night, after Emma had gone to bed, she had lain awake for quite some time, going over and over in her mind, what to do about her present unenviable situation. Finally, she had arrived at the conclusion, that she must tell someone closely related to her mother, and of course the obvious choice had been her Aunt Rose, the sister of her dead mother.

Emma gave her aunt a wan little smile. 'I'm afraid you are not going to like what I have to tell you Aunt Rose,' she said quietly, giving no hint of what was to come.

Rose smiled fondly upon her favourite niece, thinking as she had on countless occasions, how very much Emma reminded her of her younger sister, Charlotte. 'Very well Emma. Now what are you about to tell me my dear, that is so terrible?'

Emma visibly braced herself. 'I have recently discovered Aunt Rose, that Michael Brackley is not my true father!'

The features of her aunt turned to stone, as she fixed an accusing eye upon her niece. 'What in Heavens name has given you such an appalling idea Emma?' she asked, in a flat emotionless voice.

Emma withdrew an envelope from her jacket pocket, and silently passed it over to her shocked aunt.

Rose spread out the offending letter and read it, twice, she then calmly folded the paper, and replaced it in the envelope. Slowly she raised her eyes, to lock them upon her companion. 'How did you come by this letter my dear?' she asked quietly.

'I found it among some of mummy's things. Oh! Aunt Rose, you must promise not to tell anyone about this. You see if Michael hears of it, I shall lose everything, also Tom will lose his house and his job, and I just couldn't bear that.'

'Don't be stupid child, I'm hardly likely to tell anyone about a scandal such as this within our family,' replied Rose.

Suddenly Emma was on her feet, and the quiet charming young lady Rose had known since childhood, was now standing over her, her features horribly contorted into someone or something utterly unrecognizable.

At that moment, Rose had a chilling memory of her sister Charlotte, for on certain occasions, she would behave and appear exactly like this!

'Don't you ever again refer to me as a child or stupid, you old cow. I'm a grown woman now. Yesterday I was ravished upon the same bed where I was conceived, in Tom Laceby's cabin! So just think about that, when you go to your bed tonight, aunt.'

Rose had paled before this verbal onslaught by her niece, but now she had quickly recovered. 'My God', she thought. 'When Emma had spoken, she had sounded just like Charlotte! Had the devil that was in her, been reincarnated in her own daughter!' She turned to Emma. 'I believe it is you who needs to think about that my dear. I mean, is there any chance that you may be pregnant?' she asked quietly.

To the complete astonishment of Rose, Emma smiled, as she suddenly reverted to her sweet charming self. 'Oh! No, dear aunt, absolutely not. How gracious of you to think of me, after an admission as serious as that.

Thank you, but really you have no need to worry, I do know about these things you know aunt. I'm terribly sorry, but I shall have to be going now, I only popped over to say good bye, before I go off to that silly ladies college.'

She stepped forward, and embraced Rose, then after kissing her affectionately, walked out the back way to the stables, and waved as she went past the window. As Rose watched her receding figure disappearing down the drive, she involuntarily shivered, as though someone had just walked over her grave! And try as she might, she couldn't eradicate from her mind, the terrible similarities between her niece Emma, and the girl's dead mother Charlotte! For a few seconds after her initial vile outburst, Emma had carried on the conversation as though nothing untoward had happened, and as Rose reflected, that is exactly how Charlotte had behaved!

It was at that moment, Rose remembered the letter that Emma had shown her, addressed to her father, Michael Brackley, the letter he had never received! Because Charlotte must have intercepted the mail that morning, taken the letter, read it, and then hidden it. Now her daughter had very unfortunately found the missive, and through her discovery, had realised Michael wasn't her real father, but Tom Laceby was! The awful realisation, that she was born out of wedlock, in fact a bastard, had somehow triggered off this latent desire to behave as Charlotte had behaved, apparently with dire consequences!

Rose sat a long time mulling over her thoughts, confident she was correct in her assumptions, because as she explained to Charles later that evening, it was less than a fortnight since they had seen Emma, and she was perfectly rational then.

However, as Charles had been quick to point out, Emma would be leaving home shortly, and it would be quite some time before they saw her again, and in the meantime, she may have grown out of these silly fantasies, and though that is what Charles had said, Rose never believed it!

14

Just before Christmas, and when Emma had been away from home approximately three months, Eric Teesdale, totally out of character, was on a drinking spree in one of the local pubs.

Being unaccustomed to too much alcohol, having imbibed far more than was his wont, and quite obviously drunk, he was overheard boasting about the number of times the gaffer's daughter had visited him at night in his room above the stables, and of what a wonderful time they had enjoyed in bed together.

No-one could have imagined, least of all Eric Teesdale, the repercussions which were to evolve, because of that one night's innocent drinking spree! A fellow stable hand who had accompanied Eric to the pub that night, finally persuaded him to curb his drinking and his tongue, but unfortunately he was proved to be too late.

One other, a po faced, miserable, sneaky looking individual, who also worked at the Hall as a labourer, had witnessed and overheard, the whole appalling revelation

313

of Eric's conquest, and fornication with the beautiful, young and very desirable Emma! Having fancied her himself, and been most definitely rejected on more than one occasion, and threatened with instant dismissal, if he should cause any further annoyance, 'Greasy', (that was his nickname, and apparently a very apt one) suddenly saw a window of opportunity opening up before him, whereby he would at last be able to wreak his revenge, upon those who had so delighted in belittling him, sometimes in front of his peers.

The morning following Eric Teesdale's uncharacteristic bout of heavy drinking, he was ordered to report to Sir Michael Brackley's office. Feeling more than a bit 'under the weather', and not having a clue as to why he was being summoned before his Lordship, Eric ambled steadily across the courtyard, through the rear door of the Hall, down a very long corridor, and stopped at a door marked Office. After removing his cap, and running his fingers through a mop of tousled hair, he knocked on the door and waited. Almost immediately, a sharp voice bade him enter.

Eric, with a half smile just hovering upon the corners of his mouth, nonchalantly bid a pleasant 'Good morning sir.'

Michael was sitting behind a solid oak

knee hole desk of gigantic proportions, and as he looked up, Eric's half smile was quickly wiped out. For his employer was glowering at him from beneath lowered beetling brows, and his whole demeanour was one of loathing and hostility. It was then, Eric discovered why!

'So, Teesdale, where were you last night?' the voice was soft as silk, yet the question was rapier sharp, and Eric felt a sudden frisson of fear shoot down the length of his spine.

Even so, Eric managed to smile. 'I was out at the pub drinking sir, though I'm afraid I may have had just a little too much.'

'Why Teesdale, what makes you think that?' the voice was still soft, but Eric thought he had detected a slight irritation creeping in.

Again he smiled. 'Because when I woke up this morning sir, I was still fully dressed, boots an all. I can't even remember coming home and going to bed.'

'I see,' slowly Michael rose to his feet, and came from behind the desk. Suddenly he grabbed Eric by the throat and slammed him up against the wall, and as he hit the startled, bemused head groom flush upon his mouth, he began shouting and swearing, until finally Eric began to get the message through to his befuddled brain, and realised the enormity of the situation and the trouble he was in.

Eric was only of normal stature, but the years he had spent around horses, had made him exceptionally tough and wiry, and now he began to fight back. Finally he knocked his employer to the floor, and then sat upon him. 'Right Sir bloody Michael, now listen to me,' he snarled through bloodied lips. 'So some lousy rat heard me sounding off in the pub last night, and couldn't get here quick enough to tell you what kind of a daughter you have. Well I don't think you need to worry that much, you see she ain't your daughter!'

For a moment, Michael was silent, until that earth shattering remark finally penetrated his mind. 'What the hell do you mean man, not my daughter?' he shouted, as he struggled in vain, to throw off this offensive antagonist.

Eric held on. 'If you promise not to try anything stupid, when I let you up, I'll tell you,' he muttered grimly.

After mouthing a couple of expletives, Michael acquiesced, and scrambling to his feet, staggered to the nearest chair.

Eric was already seated. 'I know your father Sir Richard, used to send you abroad quite often, sometimes for as long as three months at a time. Well Lady Charlotte, who incidentally was a very beautiful woman, and because of her loneliness, owing to the fact that you were away so much, took to riding in Brackley's Wood. To cut a long story short, one day she stumbled across Tom Laceby's log cabin, and he being such a strapping young fella', she was instantly attracted, and later took to visiting him when you were away.'

Michael was sitting pale and rigid. 'How the hell do you know all this Teesdale?' he suddenly blurted out.

Unabashed, Eric continued. 'Because your father sent me to spy on them, and report back to him everything that happened.'

Michael leaned forward. 'Even so, How can any of this prove that I am not the father of Emma?'

Eric shrugged. 'I don't know. You'd best ask Emma or Tom.'

'Very well. Just one more question Teesdale. Why were you boasting in the pub last night, about being in bed with Emma?'

Eric coloured, and lowered his eyes. 'Sorry sir, I didn't know I said anything like that.'

'Well apparently you did. Now I want to know, on what grounds you could make such a vile, preposterous statement as that?'

Eric hesitated, he didn't want to stir up any more trouble for Emma, than he

317

already had. 'I don't know sir, I suppose it was the drink talking. Honestly, I can't remember saying anything about Emma or anybody else.'

Michael was calmer now, and for a long moment was silent. Finally he stirred himself and stood up. 'All right Teesdale. This time I will give you the benefit of the doubt, but if I ever hear even a whisper about your behaviour in future, I'll have you horse whipped off the estate.'

Eric thanked his employer profusely, and quickly left the office, heaving a huge sigh of relief as he reached the outer door, and thought how very fortunate he was to still have a job!

Just before noon, Tom Laceby, completely unaware of the furore which had transpired earlier, knocked upon the door of his employer's office, opened it and nonchalantntly walked in.

'Morning Michael,' he said amiably. 'How are you this morning?'

Michael calmly replaced the cap upon his fountain pen, closed the ledger in which he had been writing, pushed it aside, and looked up. 'I'm very well thank you Laceby. Tell me, how is your daughter?'

Tom had nearly reached his employer's desk, but now he suddenly froze, and the silence following Michael's question, was almost tactile. In a remarkably clear cameo flashback, when time seemed to stand still, he saw once again, the beautiful face and naked body of Charlotte, lying upon his bed in that cabin in the wood, and as this vision of her beauty faded, though he knew he had only been in the office a matter of minutes, it felt like hours. Showing tremendous strength of will, and a character with which he had been born, yet ultimately had been honed to perfection during his years in the Grenadiers, Tom Laceby drew himself up to his full height, and faced his employer.

His face was a mask, completely devoid of expression, as he looked down upon the husband of his late mistress. 'You have obviously heard of this matter from someone else, and for that I'm very sorry,' his voice matched the coldness of his eyes. 'Only one other person knew of my relationship with your late wife, Eric Teesdale! So I presume I am correct in my assumption that it was he who told you?'

As Michael didn't reply, Tom hesitated a second, and then continued. 'Ha, I thought so. Very well, now you know, there is no point in my denying I am the father of Emma! I will write out my resignation immediately, and then move out of the

319

cottage this afternoon. If that is what you wish.'

Michael leapt to his feet and sent the chair crashing to the floor. 'So, Laceby!' he shouted. 'Do you think just by handing in your resignation, and getting out of my cottage, that is the end of it? Because if so, then you must be more stupid than I thought. I began to suspect something that night when I found Emma in your cottage, and saw a painting of Charlotte's hanging above the fireplace. But I simply thought Emma just had a teenage crush on an older man, and had given you that painting of her mother's, I never dreamt for one moment, that she could possibly be your daughter!'

He began to walk from behind his desk, and moved towards Tom, adopting a threatening attitude. 'I wouldn't attempt anything stupid, if I was you,' murmured Tom softly. 'I think you might find you have bitten off more than you can chew!'

With a snarl, Michael hurled himself at this usurper, this man, to whom he had given work, food and hospitality, and later, the hand of friendship. Only to be repaid by treachery, and cunning, during the seduction of his wife. What hurt him most, was the fact that he, Sir Michael Sinclair-Brackley, had been made a cuckold of, by a common labouring woodsman, and apparently, Charlotte had gone quite willingly, to join her lover, and to lie with him, in the log cabin which her husband had provided, solely for the comfort of the woodsman!

In a mad frenzy, and almost inarticulate with rage, he began shouting and cursing, as he tried in vain to hit Tom with his fists. Finally, Tom could see the only way he was going to restrain Michael, and stop this frenzied attack, was to give him a taste of his own medicine.

Holding off the flailing manic aristocrat with his left hand, Tom delivered a crushing blow to Michael's chin, with his right. His eyes glazed over, and his legs crumpled, as he collapsed into Tom's arms! Uttering a grunt of satisfaction, Tom heaved the inert body of his ex-employer behind his desk, and deposited him unceremoniously in his chair. He then pulled up another chair, seated himself the other side of the desk, calmly lit a cigarette, and waited for some sign of life from the unconscious man.

After some minutes, Michael began to stir and show signs of returning to the land of the living. His eyes flickered open, and as he looked around the office, he suddenly sat bolt upright. 'What the hell hit me?' he asked thickly, rubbing his chin.

Tom smiled, as he calmly blew a perfect smoke ring into the air. 'I did,' he replied nonchalantly. 'And if you attempt anything rash, I shall do so again. I am extremely sorry for what has happened, and now I know you're all right, I'm going to write out my resignation, then start moving my things out of the cottage.'

Now fully recovered, though with an ugly swelling on the side of his jaw, Michael emitted a harsh guttural laugh. 'And where do you intend taking them Laceby?' he snarled.

'To my house beside the park of course,' Tom replied, in some surprise at the question.

Again Michael gave the same laugh, though this time he accompanied it with a sneer. 'Oh! I see. Well you had better think again you bloody philanderer! Your house was given to you as part of my late wife's will. I often wondered why. Now I know. Anyway, after what has transpired, from today her will is null and void, so I require you to vacate that property immediately, and return all monies paid to you out of Brackley Estates. Emma of course, will have to be treated in the same way.'

For a split second, Tom Laceby experienced

the breath of fear, but in less than a single heart beat, it had vanished. He had not been concerned for himself, only for his daughter, yet now as he faced his accuser, the man whose beautiful wife he had stolen, and had made pregnant, eventually presenting him with the delicious Emma, his eyes crinkled, and the corners of his strong mouth, actually curved upwards into something resembling a smile. 'I don't think so,' he said softly. 'If you make the slightest move, to carry out such a threat, I shall return here one night, and break every bone in your miserable body! My God! There's no wonder Charlotte left you, and came looking for me!' on that remark, Tom Laceby turned upon his heel, and left the office.

15

The Lady Emma Brackley smiled, as she alighted from the train in Paragon Station, and sniffed the old familiar smell of the sea and fish, being wafted towards her from the Humber Estuary. A youngish man, whom she didn't recognise, probably in his mid-twenties, dressed in the uniform of a chauffeur, moved across the platform and touched his cap. 'Good afternoon my Lady. I hope I am correct. You are the Lady Emma?' he asked politely.

To his instant relief, Emma smiled. 'Yes, indeed I am. Have you come to meet me?' she asked, as he organised a porter to collect the masses of luggage.

'Yes My Lady. The Rolls is parked just outside the station.'

As they approached the car, Emma turned to her escort, a puzzled frown upon her otherwise satin smooth brow. 'Are you alone? Where is my father? He normally comes to meet me at the station.'

The young man hoisted the heavy cases into the car boot. 'Sorry my Lady, he never mentioned anything about meeting you, he simply told me to bring the car, and pick you up here.'

That same frown still continued to pucker Emma's brow, as the car pulled silently away from the station forecourt, and it was still in evidence, even when her driver opened the rear door for her to alight, on to the gravelled drive outside the imposing entrance to Brackley Hall.

Leaving her cases to the young man, Emma ran up the steps, through the open doorway, and straight into the hall. 'Hello,' she called. There was no reply. Again she tried, louder this time. 'Hello, is anyone there?' still no answer to her call. The place was silent as a tomb, she shivered at the metaphor, and was on the point of returning to the car, when a shadow appeared at the far end of the hall.

'Hello Milly. Is that you?'

The shadow materialized into a form which Emma recognised as belonging to her life long friend. Milly came quickly forward, and with stifled sob, engulfed the astonished Emma within her open arms.

Finally, with more than a little difficulty, Emma managed to extricate herself, and held a very distressed Milly at arm's length. 'Milly!' she cried, when at last she saw her tear stained face. 'Whatever is the matter? you look awful.'

Immediately tears began to run down Milly's cheeks. 'Oh! Miss Emma,' she sobbed. 'There was a terrible row this morning.

Somehow the master discovered Tom is your real father, I think Eric Teesdale told him, because 'Greasy' was in the office, and then Eric followed him a bit later. Well just after that there was the most fearful racket, shouting and cursing, and I'm sure they were fighting. Anyway, Eric came out and went straight back to his stables, then sometime later, Tom went to the office, and again there were sounds like a fight going on. About half-an-hour later, Tom came out looking like thunder, went straight to his cottage, and began packing, as though he is leaving!'

Emma had listened open mouthed to her distraught friend, but now, her puckish features set and grim, she released Milly and began walking towards the door, saying over her shoulder, 'Please don't worry Milly, I'll sort this out.'

Emma made a bee line for Tom's cottage, and as she went in, he was just staggering downstairs with his arms full of clothes. She hung back and waited until he had deposited them upon the kitchen table.

'Hello father!' she said quietly.

Startled, Tom turned, and as he did so, Emma rushed forward into his open arms. 'Oh! Daddy, what has happened. I have just been speaking to Milly, and she told me some garbled version about Eric Teesdale telling Michael the whole truth about you and I. Then later, you went to see him, and a further fight ensued, with much shouting and swearing, after which, you came straight here, and began throwing furniture around the place. Please tell me if all this is true daddy, and if so, what we are to do.'

Tom soothed his trembling daughter, and tried to sound cheerful, as he realised the tears were about to tumble down her cheeks. He held her close for a moment, and enjoyed the rich youthful fragrance of her, then very gently released her. 'Yes, my dearest Emma, all that Milly has told you is quite true. However, please do not worry your pretty head about any of this. In some respects I am happy Michael has finally learned the truth, for I was utterly fed up with all the lies, and now we can face the world as Father and Daughter!'

Emma, her eyes sparkling, and her face radiant, looked up at this wonderful man, with whom she had fallen so desperately in love, only to discover, he was her real father, and that she could never be more to him, than a dutiful daughter. 'Oh! Daddy, I think you're wonderful. I always feel so safe when you are near. If Michael has ordered you to vacate this place, then he is bound to throw me out. That being the case, where can we go father?'

Tom Laceby gazed upon this beautiful creature, and found it very difficult to believe she had been conceived in sin, and that he was her father, and his heart went out to her, for she was here in this world through no fault of her own. That day, Tom made a silent vow, that come hell or high water, his beloved Emma would never want for anything for the rest of her life. Suddenly he realised she was still awaiting his reply.

'Fortunately my darling Emma. The house your dear mother bequeathed to me, has recently become vacant, and I wasn't going to let it again until after Christmas. Well now, I don't think we have any need to look very far for another tenant, do you?'

Once again Emma flung her arms around his neck, hugged and kissed him. 'No daddy, I don't think so either. It will be wonderful us two living together in the same house mummy used to live in, and which she eventually left to you,' she stopped for a moment, and appeared to be thinking, then. 'Daddy, can we please take Milly with us. She can act as housekeeper, and will be able to look after you, while I am away, it won't cost much to feed and keep her, and I know you have quite a bit of money salted away.'

Tom saw the pleading in her eyes, and smiled, for he knew he would never be able to refuse his lovely daughter anything.

'Yes my darling. That is, if she wishes to leave here and come with us, of course we will take her.' The look he received from Emma spoke volumes, and was all the thanks Tom needed. 'Incidentally, what makes you think I have money salted away, as you put it?' he asked, with a smile.

Emma chuckled. 'Well father, I know you were an officer in the Guards, and was invalided out during the war, so you must have saved some money, apart from your pension.'

Tom laughed aloud. 'My dear Emma, I won't bother to tell you what magnificent sum my pension amounts to. Now go find Milly and tell her the good news, then please come and help me with my packing, and by the way, I wasn't invalided out of the army. I was wounded in France, but didn't recover in time to rejoin my unit before the end of hostilities.'

As Tom was emptying a chest of drawers, he heard a horse go galloping past his cottage, and slide to a halt in the cobbled courtyard. Seconds later he heard Emma scream.

Dashing outside, and tearing round the corner into the courtyard, he was amazed by the scene which met his eyes. Emma was pressed back against the stable wall, as Michael slid off his lathered sweating mount, and advanced towards her, his riding crop held aloft, ready to strike.

Again the terrified Emma screamed, as the man whom she had looked upon until recently as her father, advanced remorselessly forward, staring at her from hate filled eyes.

'Yes, go on scream, you little bastard!' he shouted, his whole being bent on wreaking his revenge upon this product of his late wife's infidelity. 'You can scream your bloody head off, it won't do you any good. There's nobody here who will dare to save you now, you bloody daughter of a whore and a fornicating labourer!'

He had reached the petrified girl, and as she lifted her arms to try and protect her head from the lash of that wicked looking crop, something happened, for it never fell, and Emma opened her eyes just in time to see Sir Michael Brackley hurled through the air, and slammed up against the opposite wall of the courtyard.

Tom, his fury almost out of control, strode across the yard, gripped the hapless Michael by the front of his shirt, hoisted him to his feet, and holding him upright with his left hand, continued to smash his right fist into the already bruised and bleeding face of this aristocrat, who had dared to take a riding crop to his Emma. Finally, as he allowed the dishevelled crumpled, semiconscious body to slowly collapse to the ground, through gritted teeth, Tom Laceby spoke. 'If you ever lay a finger on my daughter, I'll kill you!' and though Michael was barely conscious, the cold hard words penetrated his throbbing head, and he shivered, for he knew they were no idle threat!

Tom moved over to Emma and just caught her as she almost collapsed in his arms. 'There there my dear. Please don't cry, I'm here now. It is over, and we're getting out of this place as soon as possible.'

Emma lifted a pale, frightened face and looked upon her father. 'Oh! Daddy, I really don't know what I would have done if you hadn't come along. Did you hear his foul language, and the name he called me? It was horrible,' and she trembled as she clung to him.

At that moment Milly came running from the Hall. 'Oh! my darling baby, are you badly hurt? I saw some of what happened from a bedroom window, and then dashed downstairs and straight out here.' While she was speaking, Milly had relieved Tom of his charge, and was now stroking and caressing Emma, as though she was still a child. 'My poor baby. What a nasty bully he turned out to be. Anyway, he certainly made up my mind for me. I wouldn't stay here and work for him, even if he doubled my wages, that I wouldn't. Not after what he was going to do to you. What a good thing your real father came along. If your offer of that job as housekeeper to you and Tom is still open, I shall be pleased and proud to accept.'

Emma, who had been trying so hard to maintain the English 'stiff upper lip', was suddenly engulfed in tears, as the flood gates opened, and she sobbed her heart out in the arms of her confidante and friend and the wise and efficient Milly, knowing this outburst to be a reaction from what had recently transpired, allowed her to get it out of her system. In the meantime, simply stroking her hair, and murmuring soothing words of comfort, whilst dabbing her eyes with a miniscule handkerchief.

Some four hours later, Tom Laceby carried

the last item of furniture from the Brackley Estate lorry, which he had borrowed, into his house, overlooking the park. The same house Richard Brackley had given to Charlotte, all those years ago, and where she had first seduced Dr. Peter Sinclair, and then his supposed son Michael.

Of course none of the three new occupants, were aware of any of the shenanigans which had taken place within these walls, consequently there were no ghosts to haunt them from the past, on that first unforgettable night of freedom, (at least, that is how Emma and Tom saw it) or on any of the many subsequent nights which were to follow.

Of course with the house being vacant, at this time of year it seemed very cold and damp. However, Milly soon had a couple of good fires blazing away, in the front room fire place, and the kitchen range, and by the time Tom came back, after returning the lorry, the whole place had taken on a new identity. For as he walked down the front path, a welcoming glow of firelight flickering through the downstairs windows greeted him, and he smiled appreciatively, when he walked in, and a rush of warm air greeted him immediately he entered the room.

The lights were switched on, and the table

was laid for three. He stood amazed when he saw the plates laden with mouth watering culinary delights, which he supposed Milly had purloined from the Hall's larders. 'I say, what a spread,' Tom commented, as he seated himself. 'Wherever did all this food come from? Not from his Lordship's pantry I hope,' he said facetiously.

'Whatever makes you think that father?' asked a shocked Emma. 'Actually I do believe you're right. Milly didn't tell me, but I thought I saw her sneaking out the back way once or twice, carrying mysterious bundles wrapped in muslin. I dare not ask what they contained, however, I had my suspicions and now I think they have been verified,' she ended with a chuckle.

'Ooh! You do get me in trouble my Lady — .'

Emma held up her hand. 'Milly, I don't ever want to hear you say 'My Lady' again. Please remember, all that is over and finished with. So in future you will always address me as Miss Emma. Of course when we are alone, you will just say Emma, you do now anyway, so I don't think our lives will be that much different. Now what were you about to say?'

Milly gazed upon her mistress a little wistfully, Tom thought. 'I was going to say my L — , sorry, miss Emma, how much trouble you try to get me into. You know that pilfering, and fetching all this food from the Hall, was entirely your own idea.'

Emma laughed aloud, as she passed her plate to Tom for another slice of that lovely home cured, succulent ham. 'Yes, dear Milly, it was my idea, and though you objected, I'm very pleased you went along with it, and helped me. Cut her another piece of ham Tom,' she chuckled, with a twinkle in her eye.

After the meal, when all the pots had been cleared away, the three of them were sitting comfortably before a blazing log fire, when their thoughts, and the silence of this homely room, were suddenly shattered, by the strident ringing of the telephone in the hall. Being the youngest, and consequently the quickest, Emma was the first to leap to her feet, and dash out of the room.

Tom and Milly were subjected to a frustrating few minutes of muffled conversation, during which they were quite unable to make out any part of what was being said, when just as suddenly as she had left, Emma burst back into the room, her face alight with excitement. 'Neither of you, will ever guess what that telephone call was all about, or who it was ringing us,' she chortled, as she danced around the room.

As no-one spoke, Emma continued in a very excited manner. 'That person on the telephone was Aunt Rose, and you'll never believe it, but she and Uncle Charles have invited the three of us to 'Mount Pleasant' for Christmas!' she finished with a smile, and an impetuous hug for each of her bemused audience.

Tom was the first to recover. 'When are we going Emma? Did your aunt say which day she will expect us?'

'Yes daddy, tomorrow the twenty second, which just happens to be Saturday, and we are invited to stay for the whole of Christmas, even after the New Year, so we shall be away until Wednesday, the second of January, nineteen thirty five. Isn't that just marvellous you two?'

Tom caught his daughter's infectious mood, and was quick to realise, that this holiday, this complete change of environment, could be exactly what Emma needed to take her mind off the recent horrendous developments, which had so suddenly affected her young life.

'Yes Emma, that is marvellous. Your aunt must be a very forgiving person, if she is aware of the circumstances regarding our relationship, and yet, she still insists on

336

inviting me to spend Christmas with her family.'

'Oh! Tom, she is. She's a wonderful person is my Aunt Rose. I'm sure you will fall in love with her, immediately you meet her. Darling daddy do you mind if I call you Tom? It sounds so much more grown up, and could save some embarrassing questions, particularly when we're among friends.'

Tom Laceby smiled lovingly upon this beautiful delicious young product, of his illicit relationship with the wonderful Charlotte, and for a brief moment, experienced great sadness, that her mother had been taken whilst still so full of life, and had so much love to give.

'Did you hear what I said Tom? and why are you looking so sad?' asked Emma abruptly, causing Tom to jump a little, as she brought him out of his reverie.

'Sorry darling. Yes, I heard what you said. No, I don't mind in the least, I would love you to call me Tom. Sorry if I appeared a little sad Emma. I was just reminiscing a bit, and thinking how much Charlotte would have loved to have shared this Christmas with us, and to have seen us two together at last, especially in this house, which of course originally she owned, and actually lived in for a while.'

The tears pricked behind Emma's lids, as she put her arm around Tom's neck, and kissed him. 'Dear Tom,' she murmured. 'I think you're a wonderful father. I can easily understand mummy falling in love with you. Oh! if only you two had been married, and everything was legitimate, including me! Wouldn't it have been marvellous?' she ended with a heartfelt sigh.

Suddenly Tom jumped up, and tried to sound cheerful, in an endeavour to break this aura of sadness which seemed to have so quickly engulfed them. Turning to Emma's companion. 'Right Milly. There is a fireplace in each of the two main bedrooms. You take some paper and sticks, and lay a fire in each, while I go and see if there's any coal.'

'And what pray, shall my duties be, My Lord?' asked a much revived, exuberant Emma.

On his way out of the room, her father turned and smiled. 'On this occasion, I think it will be best if you help Milly, My Lady,' he replied facetiously.

Laughing happily together, the older maid and companion to the former Lady Emma Brackley, and the now just plain Emma, began collecting some old newspapers, and searching for a few dry sticks, while Tom Laceby took a torch outside to the coal

338

house. And soon after staggering upstairs with two buckets of coal, a good fire was burning in each of the bedrooms, and this house where Charlotte had resided, once again began to have a 'lived in' look and feel about it.

They awoke to a clear blue sky, and a world hiding beneath a covering of frost. Tom was the first downstairs, and quickly had a couple of fires burning brightly in the front room fireplace and the kitchen range, he also liked an occasional pipe, and while Emma and Milly were finishing the washing up, he sat by the fire, enjoying his first smoke of the day.

'Is that all you have to do My Lord?' asked Emma scornfully, as she hung a tea-cloth on the fireguard to dry.

'At the moment. Yes,' replied Tom, gently knocking out his pipe into the fire. 'Though I have been doing an awful lot of thinking, while you two were in the kitchen.'

'Why, that's wonderful Tom!' cried Emma. 'Did you hear that Milly? Our lord and master has been doing an awful lot of thinking, while you and I were slaving away in there. Isn't that marvellous? What a terrific help you are Tom,' she added, as she collapsed in peals of laughter upon the sofa.

After waiting patiently for Emma to cease her bout of youthful hilarity, Tom spoke again. 'Now if you have quite finished, I think we may have some serious spending to cope with.'

'Why? Whatever do you mean Tom?' asked a baffled Emma.

'I mean, my darling daughter, exactly that. Later today, we are expected at Mount Pleasant. Well I think, if your Aunt Rose is as generous as you describe her, then I firmly believe that us three, will be the happy recipients of some Christmas presents on Christmas Day. That being the case, I think it only right and proper, that we should be prepared for any such contingency, and go into Hull this morning, to buy a few gifts for them.'

Emma, with the impetuosity of her youth, flung her arms around his neck and kissed him. 'Darling Tom!' she cried ecstatically. 'That's a really brilliant suggestion, don't you think so Milly?' she asked, turning to her companion.

'Yes I do. Will I be able to come along with you Tom?' she asked quietly.

However, Emma didn't wait for Tom to reply. 'Of course you will Milly. We wouldn't dream of going shopping without you, would we Tom? Anyway, however will you be able to buy me a present, if you don't come with us?' she asked, with laughter in her beautiful eyes.

So it was, for the first time ever, Tom Laceby took his new daughter Christmas shopping, and with Milly to help, they had a wonderful time, and happy and glowing with health in the cold frosty air, they returned laden with parcels just before lunch, the three of them extremely hungry.

After partaking of a succulent beef pie, which Milly had mysteriously conjured up from somewhere, (neither Tom or Emma dare ask where) and a glass of sherry each, they proceeded to wrap their presents, for the host and hostess at Mount Pleasant, and for each other.

Though unknown to any of them, someone else would be joining the family tomorrow, someone Emma had never met before, and one who would have a far reaching effect upon her young life!

Soon after lunch, James came to collect them in the Rolls, and after much bantering and laughing together, they were all seated in the car, with their parcels safely stowed beside Emma and Milly, upon the rear seat. Lights were shining from several of the downstairs windows as they came down the drive, giving a most welcome aspect to the front of the old house.

'Oh! Tom, doesn't it look lovely?' breathed Emma, as James drew up at the front entrance, and opened the car door for her and Milly to alight.

Tom didn't have an opportunity to reply, for at that moment, the massive oak door swung open, and Charles and Rose came down the steps to meet them. After the kisses and vociferous Christmas greetings were over, James proceeded to empty the car of wrapped mysterious Christmas gifts.

'Good Heavens Emma!' cried her aunt in astonishment. 'Whoever are all those presents for?'

Emma smiled. 'I know aunt, there does seem to be rather a lot, but they didn't cost so much, not really. Anyway, all of this was Tom's idea. He said we were invited here to spend Christmas with you, so therefore we should show a little appreciation, and bring a few presents. Tom also said something about, 'Peace On Earth And Goodwill To All Men', I don't know what he meant by that, but he never mentioned Women!'

All laughing together, the happy party relieved James of several parcels, and carried them indoors, to place carefully beneath the huge Christmas tree, standing in the hall.

Of course Rose had previously met Tom

some years ago, well the top half of him anyway, when he had appeared half naked at his bedroom window, on that unforgettable rather unfortunate encounter, at his house in the village, when he was entertaining her sister Charlotte! However, Rose didn't appear to bear any malice towards him, in fact quite the contrary seemed to be the case, as though she was somehow sorry for the lie he'd had to live with for so many years.

Yet inwardly, Rose blamed her wild unpredictable sister Charlotte, for this present situation, for she knew that no man had been able to refuse to help satiate her voracious sexual appetite, no man that is, except one. And for the thousandth time, Rose thanked God, she had married Charles Cartwright!

16

Charles had immediately struck up a real rapport with Tom Laceby, and they sat talking together far into the night, long after the others had retired to their beds, and though Charles was well aware of his companions adulterous affair with the late Charlotte, and that the beautiful wayward Emma was the product of that illicit liaison, he was however, very pleasantly surprised to discover many facets of Tom's character, which far outweighed any misdemeanours he may have committed in the past.

It was with a feeling of self disgust, Charles remembered the wonderful sexuality and charisma that Charlotte possessed, and how he himself had almost succumbed to her womanly wiles, on more than one occasion! Also, he experienced a sudden cameo flash back of a certain curly haired boy, sitting on a bench in the park, with his mother only a few yards away talking to Rose, and he quickly realised he was in no position to pass judgment on any man! So Charles decided, 'Let he that is without sin, cast the first stone', and turned to his companion.

'Tom, I'm in desperate need of a farm manager and land agent. My wife tells me I must learn to delegate more, and if you have been running the Brackley Estate, well I can't think of a much better recommendation than that. So I will appreciate it if you will consider accepting this position, and come to work for me, here at 'Mount Pleasant', starting in the New Year.'

Tom Laceby sat quite still, thinking deeply and staring into the fire. He had only met Charles Cartwright that afternoon, yet what he had seen and heard, had somehow caused him to feel perfectly at ease in his presence, and he was convinced that he would make a very good employer, and that if they continued to get on as well together in the future, as they had during the last few hours, then he could very probably have a job here for life!

Tom was still in deep thought when Charles spoke again. 'Look Tom, I don't want to rush you into giving me an answer immediately. I am quite prepared to wait for your reply until Monday morning.'

Tom emitted a deep throated chuckle, and standing up, held out his hand. 'Thank you very much for the offer of this job Charles. I can assure you there is no need to wait until Monday morning, I can give you my

345

reply now. Yes, the answer is yes. You have no idea what a load you have taken off my mind, I really didn't know how I was going to be able to keep Emma in college. Once again I thank you, and I promise to try and fulfil all my obligations to your complete satisfaction.'

Charles was also standing now, and extended his own hand. 'Thank you Tom,' he replied, as he vigorously shook hands with his new agent. 'There is a three bedroomed cottage on the estate which is now vacant, and is yours if you wish. I'm very pleased you have accepted this situation Tom, you see we have so much work on at the yard, I really don't have the time to concentrate on farming or estate management,' then with a smile, he added. 'It is rather ironic what a wonderful good turn, Michael Brackley did for me, when he sacked you!'

Charles poured each of them a good measure of whisky, and the two men laughed as they touched their glasses. 'Yes,' agreed Tom. 'I would love to be a fly on the wall, when one of his lackeys runs to him, with this snippet of information.' Then in more serious vein. 'Incidentally Charles, how many acres do you farm here?' he asked.

Charles thought a moment. 'Seven hundred and fifty,' he replied. 'Five hundred arable, two hundred grass, and fifty odd is taken up by the gravel quarry.'

Tom gave a low whistle. 'By heck, that should be enough to keep me busy for a while.' Then after a moment's thought. 'Surely I'm not responsible for the quarry as well, am I?'

Charles laughed. 'No, don't worry Tom. The quarry is a separate entity, with its own manager. I suppose I could get rid of him though, if you think you will have some spare time,' he added facetiously.'

Tom smiled as he caught the twinkle in his new employer's eye. 'No! Keep him on please,' he pleaded. 'And if he has any time to spare, ask him to come and help me.'

The two men laughed heartily together, shook hands again, and bade each other good night.

When Charles entered their bedroom, Rose was still awake, but before speaking she glanced at the clock. 'Good Heavens Charles! just look at the time, it's after two-o-clock, whatever have you two been talking about until now?'

'You may not believe this my dear,' he began in a placatory tone. 'But I have found in Tom Laceby, a new agent and farm manager, and we have been discussing work!'

Rose sat up in bed. 'Tom Laceby!' he echoed. 'After what he did to our Charlotte. Charles, how could you?'

He moved to the bed and took her hands in his. 'This isn't like you Rose, normally you are always on the side of the under dog. Anyway, to begin with, I thought as you are thinking now. Then quite suddenly I had a vision of a certain little boy with his mummy in the park, his mummy's name was Dorothy, and he was called Paul! Well after that, I knew I was in no position to judge Tom Laceby, or any man. Consequently, I gave him the job.'

For a long while after he had finished speaking, Rose remained silent. At length, gripping his hands more tightly, she spoke. 'Sorry my darling, you make me feel so ashamed. I wasn't thinking clearly. Of course we must give Tom all the support we can, for after all, he is the father of my niece, and should be welcomed into the family, particularly now he has been sacked,' she kissed him. 'I'm so pleased you have made him your agent darling, I'm sure he will never allow you to regret this decision. Now please come to bed Charles, and let's try to sleep.'

After James had married his childhood sweetheart Sophia, his parents had invited them to come and live at Mount Pleasant, for as Charles had said. 'There is plenty of room for us all, and also for any children which may happen to come along!'

However, as yet they had not been blessed with any grandchildren, and they were not getting any younger. Also, apparently Marcia never intended to marry, for she had never at any time, shown the slightest inclination towards the opposite sex, and because of all this, Charles was beginning to worry about the Cartwright name sinking into oblivion!

The following morning dawned bright and crisp, and being Sunday, of course everyone had to attend church. However, when they returned home, a small sports car was parked outside the front entrance, and as no-one recognized it, they were all agog with excited curiosity, wondering to whom the car belonged, as they pushed their way through the front entrance into the hall.

As the butler relieved Charles and Rose of their coats and hats, their curiosity was heightened. 'A young gentleman came to the door asking for you sir,' he said quietly. 'So I took him to the library, and told him it wouldn't be very long before you returned.'

Charles thanked him, then he and Rose proceeded to the library, to discover who their mystery visitor was, while all the younger members of the family, went upstairs to put away their outdoor clothes.

Charles registered no surprise, as the tall broad shouldered young man, turned and walked towards them hand outstretched. Rose however, showed no sign of recognition. Charles shook hands with the stranger, then turned to his wife. 'Come along darling, you must remember who this is,' With a blank expression, and a murmured 'Good morning,' Rose accepted the proffered hand. 'No Charles, I'm sorry, I have no idea. Should I know?'

Charles and the young man smiled. 'No probably not,' replied her husband. 'Remember going to visit your sister one day several years ago, when she lived in that house overlooking the park, and then later, going for a walk with a young woman and her little boy?'

Still Rose said nothing, so Charles continued. 'Well, this my dear is that same little boy, and his name is Paul!'

Then it all came flooding back, and in an instant cameo flash back, Rose saw once again, the curly haired little boy sitting on that park bench, swinging his legs, and chatting animatedly with her husband.

All of this had only taken a split second, and now with a myriad of thoughts swamping her mind, and an amazed expression upon her countenance, Rose almost shouted 'Paul! Well I would never have believed it. I most certainly would never have recognized you. My, what a fine young man you have turned out to be. Surely Charles, you didn't expect me to know who he was, good Heavens it must be almost twenty years since I last saw him. Anyway, how did you find him?' As she finished speaking, Rose in the endearing way she had, moved forward and embraced Paul, kissing him on the cheek.

Behind her, Charles chuckled. 'Well I have been saving this as a surprise for you for some time my dear. I didn't have to find him. You see, I sent him to Trinity House for his schooling, and he has been working at the yard for a number of years now.'

Slowly Rose turned, and smiled lovingly upon her husband. 'Oh Charles, what a wonderful thing to do.' Then turning once again to the young man. 'By the way Paul. How is your mother Dorothy?'

Paul smiled, he now seemed more relaxed. 'Very well thank you.'

Rose suddenly had a thought. 'Paul, where is your mother spending Christmas?' she asked quietly.

'At home,' he replied shortly.

'Alone?' queried Rose.

'Yes,' came the reply.

Rose glanced at Charles, though he had already correctly assumed what was coming next.

'Darling,' she began gently. 'Have you invited Paul to stay over for Christmas?'

'Yes, as I said, I wanted to surprise you. Why do you ask?'

'Well I think it would be a wonderful gesture if you were to send the Rolls, to collect Dorothy and bring her here, to stay for the Christmas holiday. That is if she will come of course.' Then again in that wonderful endearing way she had, Rose turned to Paul. 'I know you drive Paul, but do you think you could drive the Rolls?'

The young man smiled. 'Yes Mrs. Cartwright. I have driven your husband on several occasions.'

Rose returned his smile. 'I see. I think I shall have to keep an eye on you two. Very well Paul, if you think your mother will return here with you, will you please take the Rolls and go fetch her?'

He was on the point of thanking them both, when the door suddenly opened, and Emma burst into the room. 'Hello, this is where you are hiding our mysterious visitor Aunt Rose, well are you going to introduce me?' she asked flippantly. She then turned to have a good look at their guest.

It was at that moment, the young beautiful, extremely desirable, Emma Laceby knew she was lost. It was also at that moment, she regretted bitterly her experience in her father's log cabin, with Eric Teesdale!

For these two young people, each of them a product of lust and an illicit liaison, yet neither knowing of the other's origin, were instantly and irrevocably attracted one to the other.

Emma, the unprecedented thrill of this first encounter with a complete stranger, coursing unchecked through her veins, was drawn as with a magnet, as she extended her hand and accepted the proffered palm, and when she looked into those kind brown eyes, she instinctively knew, there could never be another! She was also made immediately aware, that touch of promiscuity, endeavouring to follow the lifestyle of her mother, was at an end, and that interlude with Eric had been no more than an act of rebellion, on discovering she was conceived out of wedlock.

All of this had flashed through the mind of Emma in less time than a single breath, and now she was being introduced.

'Emma,' began Rose, stepping forward. 'This young man is Paul Hunt, Paul meet

Emma Laceby, my niece.'

They shook hands. Emma smiled automatically, and murmured something like 'Pleased to meet you,' though upon reflection later, she couldn't be really sure what she had said, for her mind was in a whirl, and his reply seemed very faint.

At last Paul and Emma broke off this handshake, which seemed to have continued for several minutes, whilst they simply stood and allowed their eyes to wash over each other. Finally Paul turned to Charles. 'I say sir, your Emma is beautiful, wherever have you been hiding her?'

If any other stranger had made such a remark, Emma would have bridled instantly, but somehow she didn't seem to mind, and accepted it as the compliment it was intended to be.

Charles laughed heartily. 'I'm pleased you can appreciate real beauty when you see it Paul. We haven't been hiding her, she just happens to be home from finishing school in Switzerland for the Christmas holidays, and she will be returning in the New Year,' he added quietly. For the instant rapport these two had shown for each other, had not escaped the sharp eye of Charles or his wife.

At that moment, the others came bursting

into the library and joined them, and the eye contact Paul and Emma had held for several minutes, was broken.

When the introductions were over, Emma drew Charles aside, and asked him quietly, if she could accompany Paul in the Rolls, when he left to collect his mother. Charles promised to have a word with his wife, but could think of no reason why not. That was when all other conversation had abruptly ceased, for without warning Emma suddenly flung her arms around his neck, and said quite loudly. 'Oh! Thank you Uncle Charles, I think you're wonderful.'

Fortunately, saving Charles having to answer any embarrassing questions, the dinner gong reverberated around the old house, and everyone was ushered into the dining room, for what turned out to be, a sumptuous repast.

Emma had manouvered herself into a position, where she was sitting next to Paul at the dining table, and wonder of wonders, he occasionally held her hand, beneath the table! All through that meal she was deliriously happy, and hardly aware of what she was eating or drinking, until Rose stood up and Thanked the Lord for what they had received. Then everyone pushed back their chairs, and prepared to leave the room, everyone that is, with the exception of Emma and Paul.

They both began speaking at once. Paul stopped, and smiled. 'Sorry Emma, you go first.'

She hesitated, then replied. 'No, you first Paul.'

He turned to Charles. 'Sorry to interrupt sir. I only wish to know where the Rolls is garaged.'

Having told him. Charles turned to Emma. 'Now my dear?'

'I think you know what I want uncle. Did he have a word with you Aunt Rose?'

Rose smiled upon this ravishing offspring of her dead sister, as she thought of how quickly her and Charles had fallen in love, probably in less than an hour, and their age difference had been just as great! and of how Charles had agreed to humour Emma's request. She had also pointed out to Charles how many years their marriage had lasted, and what a wonderful life they had shared together. Had either of them been allowed to see into the future, and learn of the tragedy and horrors, these two young people would live through during the coming years, they may have hesitated, and possibly refrained from giving their consent for Charlotte's beautiful daughter to go in the Rolls with

Paul, this love child of Charles Cartwright!

While Paul went to fetch the car, Emma ran upstairs to her room, and Milly was just hanging some clothes up in the wardrobe. 'Oh! Milly, Milly,' cried Emma as she danced into the room. 'I'm so happy, I could burst!'

Milly gazed upon her young mistress, with a look of apprehension. 'I should hope not, after all you ate, not on this carpet anyway, young lady.'

For a fleeting moment Emma looked at her life long friend and companion uncomprehendingly, then her countenance cleared, and she laughed uproariously. 'My sweet dearest Milly,' she said, drying her eyes, and gasping for breath. 'You are not funny very often, but when you are, you're absolutely hilarious.' Again she danced around the room. 'Can't you see Milly? I'm in love! Desperately. Wonderfully. Exquisitely in love, with the most deliciously handsome young man, I have ever met in my life!'

Milly couldn't help but smile at the exuberance of her young companion, for her mood was infectious, and of course she had noticed how Emma had no eyes for anyone at the dining table, other than Paul. However, bearing in mind, the wilful promiscuous extravagances of her late mother, Milly thought she should issue a word of warning, but then refrained, when she remembered Emma would shortly be returning to Switzerland.

'Why that's wonderful news darling, this handsome young man, wouldn't just happen to be Paul, that nice young gentleman you were sitting so close to at the table, and couldn't take your eyes off, would it?'

Emma looked appalled. 'Oh Milly! You noticed. Well if you did, do you think anyone else would!'

Her companion laughed. 'Yes, I think they probably would, if not, then they must be completely blind.'

'Dear Milly, surely I wasn't that obvious, was I?'

'Yes my poppet, I'm afraid you were. Though I shouldn't worry unduly, for you see Paul was equally enraptured over you, and just as obvious.'

Emma blushed a deep pink. 'Oh Milly! Was he really?' she then hugged her life long companion, and kissed her affectionately. 'I'm so pleased Aunt Rose invited us here to stay for Christmas Milly, otherwise I may never have met my brand new delicious young man!'

'Where are you going darling?' asked Milly curiously, as Emma picked up her hat and coat, and proceeded to put them on.

Her young mistress chuckled, and then adopting a pompous attitude. 'Just out with Paul, for a run in the Rolls my dear. We are going to collect his mother, and bring her back here to stay for Christmas,' she said in her best cut glass accent. Then in her ordinary voice. 'Oh Milly. Do you think his mother will approve of me?'

'Approve of you! By, she had better, otherwise she will have me to answer to, and so will that Paul!'

Emma gave her friend another hug and a kiss, and laughing, ran out of the room, leaving Milly wondering a little apprehensively, what kind of new chapter was opening up in the life of this beautiful young woman, whom she had known since Emma had been born, and whose love and friendship, she cherished above all others.

As Rose watched from the library window, as her exuberant, effervescent young niece ran down the steps and climbed into the waiting Rolls, she sighed audibly, and turned away.

'Good Lord, what on earth was that for my dear?' asked Charles, a slight frown creasing his brow. 'Surely you can't be worried about young Paul driving the Rolls?'

His wife gave a wan little smile. 'No

Charles, I wasn't thinking about the car,' she replied quietly. 'More about the passenger actually.'

'The passenger! Who, Emma? Why? You cannot possibly be casting aspersions upon my s — , upon Paul's integrity, are you?'

Rose realised she may have been a little too harsh in her judgment, and quickly tried to make amends. 'No my darling, not Paul. I was thinking of the beautiful, young provocative Emma, daughter of my late, beautiful provocative sister Charlotte, who on more than one occasion tried to ensnare you with her many womanly wiles! Though of course I must admit, quite unsuccessfully. So, let's hope the son is as strong as his father was, in a very similar situation!'

Charles was thwarted of any reply he may have made to those far reaching words, by the advent of Tom Laceby walking into the room. 'Did I just see that young Paul drive away with my daughter?' he asked, as he stood warming his hands before the fire.

Fortunately Tom had his back to the room, and didn't see the warning glances Charles and Rose exchanged, before he turned around.

'I don't think you have any need to worry about Emma,' began Charles, in a quiet voice. 'Paul is a well behaved, civilised young man, and they have only gone to collect his mother, if she will come here for Christmas.'

Tom laughed. 'I wasn't thinking so much about Emma, as Paul, you know she can be a little devil, when she feels like it. I hope he knows how to handle a young flirtatious female! Anyway, why just his mother? Doesn't he have a father?'

There was a pregnant pause, and Tom suddenly realised he may have touched a nerve, or a skeleton in someone's cupboard. However, before he could extricate himself from this obviously tense situation, Charles spoke.

'Did have,' he lied easily. 'Unfortunately, Paul lost his father whilst still a very young boy, and Rose, knowing Paul's mother, and being the angel she is, has kept in touch with them both, and this year has now invited them here for the Christmas festivities.'

As they drove along on that cold winter's afternoon, Emma stole a quick admiring glance at her stalwart companion. She loved his handsome profile, the firm strong brown hands upon the steering wheel, and the way he seemed to handle that big car with such consummate ease and confidence.

They both appeared quite happy and content to travel along in silence, just happy to be in each other's company. Finally however, Emma thought the time had come to try and find out more about this wonderful young stranger, to whom she had felt an instant affinity. Turning towards him, and having no idea she was about to probe a life long hurt, deep within his heart, she said lightly. 'I know we are going to collect your mother Paul, but what about your father? Where is he?'

For a long while Paul Hunt was silent, as he negotiated several twists and turns which were a nightmare to drivers on this particular stretch of road. Then realising Emma was still awaiting his reply, and endeavouring to keep one eye on the road, he partially turned to her. 'I'm sorry my dear, but I don't know. You see, I have never known a father! Right from being a very small child, I can never recollect having a father at any time during my life!'

Emma was immediately apologetic for reopening what was so obviously an old wound, and apparently so painful to this adorable young man. 'Oh! Paul. I'm so dreadfully sorry. I had no idea. Me and my big mouth. Anyway I promise, I shall never discuss it again.'

He reached over, and placed his hand over hers. 'That's quite all right Emma, I can forgive you anything!'

She thrilled to his touch, and then looking ahead, suddenly realised where they were. 'Where are you taking me Paul?' she asked, an excited tremor in her voice.

He laughed, the trauma of a moment ago forgotten. 'To our house of course, it's just there overlooking the park.'

She couldn't believe it, and laughed out aloud.

He stopped the Rolls outside his mother's house, turned and looked at her. 'What on earth are you laughing at darling?' a puzzled frown creasing his otherwise smooth brow.

Emma had ceased her hilarity as abruptly as it had begun. 'He had called her Darling'. 'You are never going to believe this Paul, not in a million years. Approximately ten houses further along this road, still overlooking the park, is where I live, with my father, and my companion Milly.'

He just sat transfixed, staring at her, incredulity written across his face. At length he found his voice. 'I say Emma, that's absolutely marvellous, incredible and highly unlikely, nevertheless wonderful. Are you sure you live along this road?' he sounded sceptical.

Again she laughed, a young lovely lilting, infectious kind of laugh, which all the more endeared this beautiful girl to Paul's affections. 'Yes dear Paul, of course I'm sure. I live in a house which mummy used to own.'

He was silent a moment longer, as he realised what little he knew of his delicious companion, but decided that would have to wait, before stepping out of the car, and walking round to open the door for Emma.

They walked down the path together, and Paul was just lifting his hand to ring the bell, when the door opened, and a very well preserved, middle aged woman stood there to bid them welcome. 'Hello Paul,' she greeted him, tilting her head for a kiss, her eyes alight with pleasure and curiosity, as she allowed them to flicker over his beautiful companion. 'Are you going to introduce me?'

He searched for Emma's hand, found it and brought her forward. 'Mother, please allow me to introduce Miss Emma Laceby. I probably shouldn't say this, but if Emma will have me, then this is the young lady, I shall eventually marry!'

Even as Emma remonstrated, his mother couldn't fail to see the happiness shining from her lovely eyes, and the adoring way she gazed up at Paul.

'Paul!' cried Emma, her voice filled with emotion. 'We only met today, you were quite right, you definitely shouldn't have said what you did.'

He appeared crestfallen. 'I'm sorry darling. I agree it was rather presumptuous of me, still I hope you're not angry with me.'

Her eyes softened. 'Angry? No I could never be angry with you. I'm sorry Mrs. Hunt, I know this seems totally preposterous, but I'm afraid I am falling desperately in love with your son!'

Dorothy Hunt held out her arms, and with tears pricking behind her eyelids, embraced this beautiful young girl her son had discovered, and brought home. He had left home that morning to visit Charles and Rose Cartwright at Mount Pleasant, and now here he was, only a few hours later with this lovely creature by his side, unable to take her eyes off him. Who on earth is she? Dorothy was sure she had seen her somewhere before!

As if able to read his mother's thoughts, Paul suddenly answered her unspoken question. 'Emma is Mrs. Cartwright's niece mother, apparently she lives in a house just up the road, overlooking the park, with her father and a companion. The house belonged to her late mother.'

Though Dorothy Hunt sat very still, her brain was in a turmoil. She took her mind back many years, through the mists of time, and saw once again that ravishing provocative sister of Rose Cartwright's. Charlotte! Yes, that was it. Her name was Charlotte. And Good Heavens! This angelic looking beauty, standing here, appearing so cool and confident, must be her daughter! And her Paul, had brought her home to this house!

Then Dorothy steadied herself, as another thought struck her. This couldn't be the baby she had seen with Charlotte, all those years ago. No, she must have had another child, and anyway, the other was a boy.

All these thoughts had skimmed through Dorothy Hunt's mind, in a matter of seconds, and now with none of them showing upon her countenance, she turned to her young visitor.

'I think I knew your mother,' she said quietly. 'I met her one day whilst walking with Paul in the park, and later we became quite close. Wasn't her name Charlotte?'

For a long moment Emma gazed at the older woman, wondering where this line of questioning was leading, though she didn't have very long to wait. 'Yes, her name was Charlotte, and you could easily have met her here in the park, for she lived quite near.'

Suddenly Dorothy Hunt picked up a magazine which had been lying upon the

366

table, and flicking through the pages, opened it and turned it round to face Emma, at the same time ejaculating a low triumphant 'Ah! I thought so, I knew I had seen you somewhere before young lady.'

Emma stared at the open page as though hypnotized, temporarily bereft of speech. For leaping out at her, was a picture of herself, holding aloft a silver cup with one hand, while holding the bridle of a horse with the other, and the heading read in large block capitals; THE YOUNG LADY EMMA BRACKLEY WINS AGAIN.

With an anguished cry, she turned away, and immediately Paul was by her side. 'What is it darling? What has upset you?'

His mother emitted a harsh laugh. 'Look Paul, look at this old copy of the County Scene, then you will see what you have brought home, and how you are being fooled by a fast little trollop who is no better than her mother was!'

The silence which followed that remark was pregnant with an almost tactile emotion, as Emma fought to control the latent explosive powers of temper and destruction, inherited from her late mother, and which, after all these years, were apparently still only simmering just beneath the surface.

At last, and in complete control, she

turned, and her head held high and proud, she faced her inquisitor, and smiling nonchalantly, though her eyes were like twin points of ice, she shook Dorothy Hunt to the core. 'Tell me Dorothy, may I call you Dorothy? Good, please tell me Dorothy, if you can. Who is Paul's father? Paul doesn't seem to know, so I wondered if perhaps you might?'

Paul's mother shrank back and almost fell, before lowering herself on to the nearest chair, her face devoid of all colour, finally fighting off the dizziness which threatened to engulf her. 'Get her out of here Paul!' she shrieked, 'and don't ever bring her back!'

Emma moved towards the door. 'Don't worry Dorothy,' she purred. 'He doesn't have to get me out, and there is definitely no chance of my ever coming back! Actually, your Paul and I, came here today with the intention of returning with you to Mount Pleasant for the Christmas Festivities, but now I suppose I shall just have to tell Aunt Rose that you are indisposed. What a pity. Ah well, A Happy Christmas, Mrs. Hunt! Do come along Paul.'

On the return journey, Paul was amazed by the way Emma chattered on incessantly, about Christmas and their future together, with no mention of the recent traumatic events at his mother's house. The weather was turning very cold, and the light was becoming rather dim as evening approached, consequently the flickering firelight from several of the downstairs windows of this lovely old house, made a welcome sight, as they came down the drive that Sunday night.

Though the following day was Christmas Eve, it was still Monday morning, and the men had to go to work, so Charles took James and Paul with him to the yard, leaving the other car at home, in case Rose required some last minute shopping.

However, they all returned just after three-o-clock, because most of the men had wanted to leave early for Christmas. Also James and Sophia were invited to a Christmas Eve Ball at Beverly, and needed to be all dressed and ready by five-o-clock.

Soon after the happy couple left, the weather, which had been deteriorating for the past two or three days, had now turned extremely cold, and the wind had veered to the north east, threatening snow from a leaden sky.

Some two hours after James and Sophia had left, Charles went to have a look outside, and he was appalled at what he saw. It was snowing hard, huge snow flakes, and the biting wind coming in off the north sea, was creating deep drifts, and he knew it would be impossible for his son to get back from Beverly for Christmas Day tomorrow!

Returning to the huge blazing log fire, and the warmth of this lovely room, Charles decided not to tell anyone of the desperate conditions outside, for he didn't want to worry Rose unduly, and anyway a thaw may set in, and it might have all gone by morning!

Such was not the case however, and when the populace stirred themselves on that Christmas morning, they awoke to a still silent world, completely enveloped in a thick, pure white blanket of virgin snow!

With a feeling of apprehension, Charles opened the door of his son's bedroom, only to find as he had dreaded, the bed had not been slept in. Padding silently downstairs to the hall, he lifted the telephone receiver and asked for the hotel number, where he knew the ball was to be held the previous evening. There was no reply, the line was completely dead!

On his way back upstairs, he knew he had to tell Rose, that James and Sophia had not returned home last night, and though he feared the worst, he realised he must endeavour to inspire some hope, and assure her that everything would be all right.

Everything wasn't all right though, for no one had seen the big Rolls since it left Mount Pleasant on that fateful Christmas Eve. Much more snow had fallen, and it had proved impossible for the telephone engineers to repair the lines. Whole communities were cut off, and apart from missing sheep and cattle, several deaths were later reported.

It was the end of January, four weeks after Christmas, before a farm worker inadvertently discovered the car. Apparently it had skidded off the treacherous snow bound road, down an embankment, turned completely over, and smashed into a tree! The two occupants were still inside, but the police and medical authorities were unable to prove, whether they had been killed outright in the accident, or rendered unconscious and later frozen to death, for it was still freezing hard.

★ ★ ★

This proved to be a terrible traumatic time for Charles and Rose, and it was only the wonderful love they had for each other, that enabled them to survive this sea of grief, which at times threatened to engulf them.

371

Epilogue

It was during late summer, while Emma was home on holiday from Switzerland, and she had just finished breakfast, when she noticed two or three different photographs had mysteriously appeared on the sideboard. Pushing back her chair, she walked over and began to examine them.

Suddenly Emma froze, as she stared at this photograph she held in her hand. For it was a picture of an angelic, chubby faced little boy, and Emma knew she had seen this photograph somewhere before, she also knew it wasn't in this house! It was then, like a shock wave it hit her as she remembered. She had seen, not this photograph, but one exactly like it, in the home of Dorothy Hunt, and that one was of her son Paul!

At that moment Rose came into the room. 'Good morning darling, have you finished breakfast? I see you are having a look at those old photographs I brought out last week. Yes that is rather a good one of Charles isn't it my dear?'

Emma could only nod dumbly, a myriad of jumbled thoughts cascading through her mind, though the one which was uppermost, was the way Dorothy Hunt had baulked at answering her, when she had asked her to name Paul's father!

Though Emma had only been home a few days, she was amazed at the change in her Uncle Charles, and she quickly realised the worry of not having an heir to inherit the shipyard, was the prime cause of why he appeared so gaunt and lethargic, for apparently he was beginning to lose interest in the yard, now he had no son to leave it to.

Turning to her aunt, and still holding the photograph, she said quietly. 'Aunt Rose, I'm terribly worried about Uncle Charles, and I think the trouble is, he thinks he has no son left to inherit the Yard, and the name of Cartwright.'

Rose looked upon her niece with a fond though rather puzzled expression. 'Sorry darling, what do you mean thinks? he knows he has no son.'

It was then that Emma, this beautiful daughter of Charlotte, the late wayward sister of Rose, had a wonderful inspirational idea, one which would carry the name of Earnshaw and Cartwright's Shipyard well into the current century, and possibly beyond!

'What about Paul, Aunt Rose? He is the son of Uncle Charles! Isn't he?'

Other books in the
Ulverscroft Large Print Series:

THE WORLD AT NIGHT

Alan Furst

Jean Casson, a well-dressed, well-bred Parisian film producer, spends his days in the finest cafes and bistros, his evenings at elegant dinner parties and nights in the apartments of numerous women friends — until his agreeable lifestyle is changed for ever by the German invasion. As he struggles to put his world back together and to come to terms with the uncomfortable realities of life under German occupation, he becomes caught up — reluctantly — in the early activities of what was to become the French Resistance, and is faced with the first of many impossible choices.

BLOOD PROOF

Bill Knox

Colin Thane of the elite Scottish Crime Squad is sent north from Glasgow to the Scottish Highlands after a vicious arson attack at Broch Distillery has left three men dead and eight million pounds worth of prime stock destroyed. Finn Rankin, who runs the distillery with the aid of his three daughters, is at first unhelpful, then events take a dramatic turn for the worse. To uncover the truth, Thane must head back to Glasgow and its underworld, with one more race back to the mountains needed before the terror can finally be ended.

ISLAND OF FLOWERS

Jean M. Long

'Swallowfield' had belonged to Bethany Tyler's family for generations, but now Aunt Sophie, who lived on Jersey, was claiming her share of the property. It seemed that the only way of raising the capital was to sell the house, but then, unexpectedly, Justin Rochel arrived in Sussex and things took on a new dimension. Bethany accompanied her father and sister to Jersey, where there were shocks in store for her. She was attracted to Justin, but could she trust him?

BIRD

Jane Adams

Marcie has come to the bedside of her dying grandfather to make her peace. For Jack Whitney was the man who raised her, who loved her as if she was his own daughter, and from whom she ran away when she was just sixteen . . . But Jack is haunted by the terrible vision of a body hanging from a tree and the ghostly image of 'Rebekkah', a woman he insists is standing beside him, a noose around her neck. Marcie vows to uncover the true story behind this woman — even if it points to her grandfather being a murderer . . .